DEATH AT BALSAM BAY

A TILLY LAFLEUR MYSTERY
BOOK 1

MAISIE GRAVES

TWISTED DAFFODIL PUBLISHING

Ebook ISBN: 978-1-7390699-4-0

Paperback ISBN: 978-1-7390699-5-7

Cover design by Getcovers (Getcovers.com)

First edition, 2025

Visit MaiseGraves.com for more information.

260401

For O—
The clues were cinnamon-sweet,
the mysteries steeped in Fog—
but the best part of author coffee nights
is always you.

LANGUAGE NOTE

This book was written in Canada, by a Canadian, about Canadians—so yes, the spelling is a little different. We do things like add "u" where others wouldn't, use "fibre" instead of "fiber," and don't blink twice at a "cheque."

Canadian English is a glorious mix of American, British, French-Canadian, and Indigenous influences. It's quirky, it's correct—and it's completely intentional.

So if something looks odd, just blame the maple syrup and carry on. We've got mysteries to solve.

- Maisie

My dad was happiest out on the water—paddle in hand, no set destination, just the rhythm of the lake and the quiet tug of the current. He used to say getting lost was part of the adventure. But this time he'd gone too far.

They found his canoe below Echo Lake Falls—damaged, empty, and caught up in driftwood like it had lost its way. After twenty years in search and rescue, I knew what that meant, but I came anyway.

As I turned off Route 312, the *Welcome to Balsam Bay* sign looked exactly as I remembered it—weathered cedar, gold lettering faded just enough to give it character, and those ridiculous carved birch leaves some local artisan had added for the town's anniversary when I was in high school. *Founded 1948 by Samuel Melvin, Prospector* was etched along the bottom, a reminder of the town's gold mining roots that most tourists probably missed as they snapped photos.

The population had gone up since I was last here, proudly listed at 3,647—though I suspected that included seasonal residents and possibly a few of the beavers from the north creek.

Callie sat beside me, headphones on, staring out the window. Her laptop was balanced on her knees, open to a draft titled *The Temporary Small Town Life Blog*. She'd been typing steadily since we left Victoria, documenting her temporary adjustment to life in the slow lane.

My daughter was used to cities with a coffee shop on every corner. To her, this felt like stepping off the grid.

"Almost there," I said.

She pulled off her headphones. "This town actually has a sign with the population on it? That's adorably retro."

The road into town circled around the eastern edge of Loon Lake. The first thing I noticed was the paved road. Before I left, everything outside of town was still gravel. There were also several new cottages along the water that I didn't recognize.

I guess they'd actually followed through on that long-term tourism plan. Back then, it was just a scatter of aging buildings visited mostly by hunters and fishermen passing through. By the size of the four-season cottages I saw along the lake now, it seemed good ol' Balsam Bay had found some deep pockets to keep it going.

"Is that a cottage, or a house?" Callie asked, pointing at one particularly ostentatious cabin with a three-car garage and private dock.

"Hard to tell for sure," I replied. "Might just be weekend warriors from the city looking for their slice of wilderness without actually having to rough it."

"Seems a bit much."

"Says the girl who packed three chargers, two cameras, and a backup ring light for a trip to her grandfather's general store in the middle of nowhere."

Callie smirked. "Documentation is an art, Mom. I'm curating the full experience for the blog."

"The blog that currently has, what, six subscribers?"

"Nine," she corrected, amused. "And they deserve quality content."

I couldn't help but smile. Her determination to find something worth documenting in Balsam Bay was endearing. When she graduated with her journalism degree a month ago, Callie had grand visions of travelling the world, capturing stories that needed telling. Now here she was, following me to northern Manitoba to take stock of her grandpa's store and deal with the aftermath of his disappearance. Not exactly the adventure she'd planned for her post-grad celebration.

On the last rise in the road before descending into town, I looked for the landmark that meant I was home. There it was. In the distance, the old mine shaft rose tall and proud, a relic that refused to be forgotten.

"You'll see it now," I told Callie.

I'm not sure who gasped louder, which surprised me, since Callie had no idea how much the sight below had changed.

At the top of the crest, we gazed down at a postcard-perfect little town tucked into the Canadian Shield. The old shoreline was now a proper beach with play structures. Downtown had expanded beyond Main Street, and new housing developments sprawled where forest once stood.

"Holy postcard, Batman," Callie mumbled, quickly pulling out her phone to snap a picture. "This is actually pretty."

"Don't sound so surprised," I replied, though I was equally taken aback by just how much Balsam Bay had leaned into its tourism transformation. Dad's letters over the years had mentioned changes, but seeing it in person was different.

I found Main Street despite all the changes. It wasn't difficult since the town had attractive metal street markers leading visitors to various landmarks around town.

"This is… not how I remember it," I said, taking in the fancy planters and decorative street lamps that definitely weren't part of my childhood.

Main Street used to be practical: a hardware store, a diner, the original miner's hotel at the end of the street. Now it screamed "tourist destination." The old diner had become *The Lumberjack's Daughter Coffee & Eatery* with a rustic-chic facade. A gallery displayed Indigenous artwork in the window. *Birch & Pine Outfitters* stood where the arcade used to be, with kayaks hanging from the front.

We rolled down Main Street, slower now. A group of tourists snapped photos in front of a carved wooden bear outside what used to be Sam Melvin's house—now the *Balsam Bay Heritage Museum*, complete with a brochure stand and welcome banner.

Kayakers were unloading gear near the public dock. Couples browsed clothing racks labeled *Wilderness Chic*, shopping for a curated version of the outdoors.

"Look at them," I murmured. "Paying premium prices to play rugged."

Callie didn't look over. "You sound a little bitter."

"I'm not bitter," I said—too quickly. "It's just strange, seeing it this way. When I was a kid, Balsam Bay was still trying to figure out who it was after the mine shut down."

"Well, looks like it figured it out," Callie said, nodding toward a glossy billboard that called the town *Manitoba's Backcountry Gem*.

I hadn't expected to feel nostalgic. Or guilty. The town I'd left behind had clearly moved on. I wondered how it would welcome me back.

My brother Jason—the responsible one who'd stayed in

Balsam Bay and joined the RCMP—had called me a couple of weeks ago with the news that Dad had gone missing after taking his canoe out on Echo Lake. I almost jumped on a plane right then, but Jason suggested I stay put until they had more information. They called off the official search five days later. Dad's damaged canoe had been found, but not his body.

Right away, I started packing to leave Victoria, which was complicated by not knowing how long I'd be gone. Callie insisted on coming. I tried to talk her out of it by mentioning post-grad parties and last-chance celebrations she'd be missing, but she wouldn't budge. Truthfully, I was relieved. It had been a long time since I'd been home, and I'd always told myself that whenever I finally made the trip back, Dad would be there, waiting with open arms. But now, that wasn't going to happen. And the more I thought about that, the more I realized how much I needed her with me.

We opted to drive for twenty-four hours instead of flying. Callie called it an adventure. I called it a test of endurance. She had never been on a cross-country road trip, and after a busy final year of university, it was a great opportunity for mother and daughter to spend some quality time together. It felt a little selfish, but with all the other emotions I was trying to work through, this one bothered me the least.

I slowed as we passed a town bulletin board plastered with colourful posters announcing upcoming events: *Balsam Bay Summer Festival*, *Paddle & Paint Weekend*, and *Naturalist-Led Hike Series*. A far cry from the community's annual fall pot luck and summer picnics we had when I was a kid.

We passed what had been Giesbrecht's Grocery, now an artisanal market called *Shield Harvest*, the library with its new reading garden, and the town hall, which had been fixed up to look extra historic. A few locals glanced at our car as we drove by, and I wondered how many would recognize me after all these years.

The competing yard signs caught my attention next: "Save Balsam Bay" in earthy green on one lawn. "Jobs Now!" in bold yellow on another. Some things never changed. Balsam Bay had always loved a good squabble, whether it was about the curling rink schedule or which road needed grading first.

"I'm guessing this is about the mine," I said.

"What mine?" Callie asked.

I pointed toward the distant mine shaft, now barely visible through the trees. "The old gold mine. It shut down before my time, but there's always been talk about reopening it."

"Why don't they?"

"Samuel Melvin—the guy who founded this place—he shut it down and left the rights to the town." I slowed as we passed more signs. "Some people think that was visionary. Others think it was stupid."

I turned the SUV onto Spruce Street, my hands remembering the route even after all these years away.

Callie, still struggling to get a signal on her phone, didn't notice my brief frown in the mirror. "Any chance the store has Wi-Fi?" she asked.

"I'll put that at the top of my priorities list," I replied dryly. "Right after figuring out what happened to your grandfather and deciding what to do about his store."

"I was just asking," she muttered, slipping the phone into her pocket.

"Sorry," I softened my tone. "Grandpa's on my mind, and coming back here and seeing all this is... a lot."

She nodded, understanding in her eyes. For all her youthful casualness, Callie had a perceptive streak that sometimes caught me off guard. She'd only met her grandfather a handful of times—brief visits when Dad had made the trip to Victoria, usually for her birthday or Christmas—but Callie had grown up on my stories about the store, the town, and the eccentric customers who'd been fixtures of my childhood.

"There it is," I said as McKay's General Store came into view at the end of the street, its large windows reflecting the early evening sun. The sign my father had carved still hung above the door, the stylized *M* with pine trees on either side as distinctive as I remembered. The wooden building was painted the same deep forest green it had always been, with crisp white trim that looked freshly done. Dad had maintained it meticulously, even as his joints had stiffened with age.

I put the car in park and turned off the engine. "Well," I said, forcing lightness into my voice, "we're here."

Callie looked from me to the store and back again. "You okay, Mom?"

I nodded, not trusting my voice for a moment. The reality of why we were here, what we'd have to do in the coming days, settled over me like a heavy blanket. Going through Dad's things. Meeting with his lawyer. Deciding the fate of the store that my father and mother started. And beneath it all, the question that had haunted me since Jason's initial call: What happened to Walter McKay?

I summoned up a smile that I hoped looked more confident than it felt.

"You bet," I said, trying to sound like I was ready for whatever waited inside. I reached out and squeezed my daughter's hand. "We're a team, right?"

Callie squeezed my hand back. "Of course we are."

"Good," I said. "Let's go figure all of this out together."

The bell above the door jingled as we entered. It smelled exactly right: coffee, disinfectant, and that strange blend of hardware and homemade fudge only a general store could pull off. For a second, I could almost see Dad behind the counter, a pen tucked behind one ear, reading glasses sliding down his nose. I heard his laugh—deep, sudden, the kind that startled tourists and made regulars smile. But Dad wasn't there, and the silence that followed felt like someone had cut the audio too soon.

Behind the counter stood Bertha Wise, the store's long-time employee. Her silver-streaked dark hair was pulled back in the same no-nonsense bun she'd worn since I was a teenager. She looked up; and for a moment, her expression flickered between surprise and something harder to read.

"Matilda." She used my full name, the one nobody but doctors' offices and Bertha ever used. "I was wondering if you'd show up at all."

"Hello, Bertha." I approached the counter, taking in the meticulously organized shelves and spotless countertop. "I came as soon as I could get things sorted in Victoria."

Bertha's gaze shifted to Callie, who was wandering the aisles with undisguised curiosity. "And this must be your daughter."

"Callie," I confirmed. "She just finished university. Taking some time to figure out what's next."

"Hmm." Bertha's hum contained volumes of unspoken commentary.

I straightened, scanning the store with the careful eye I'd developed during my years with search and rescue. Everything was neat and organized, but there were subtle signs of change: a new coffee corner with local pottery mugs, a shelf of home-made preserves with handwritten labels, and a bulletin board covered with community notices and photographs.

"When did Dad add the coffee station?" I asked, walking over to the small counter with its silver urn and stack of mugs.

"About five years ago. Partnered with the bakery. Gets fresh goods every morning." Bertha's expression softened. "It was his way of giving folks a reason to linger. Said a store ought to be more than just a place to buy things."

That sounded like my father. Walter McKay had always seen his store as the heart of Balsam Bay, not just a business.

Callie came around the corner from the hallway. "Whose posters are those in the back?" She asked.

Judging by Bertha's sigh, not hers. "Your grandfather's," she said with a tone of resignation.

"I didn't know he was into cricket."

"Walter loves cricket," Bertha said, surprising us. "He even put a couple of Australian TV channels on his cable plan so he could watch the games."

Callie nodded. "That would explain the Aussie World Cup posters, then."

There were so many things I'd missed by not being physically close to my father. "The house... is it—"

"Just as he left it," Bertha said quietly. "I've been airing it out this week. Changed the sheets yesterday."

A lump formed in my throat at this unexpected kindness. "Thank you."

The front door opened and a woman about my age bustled in, carrying a basket covered with a checkered cloth. Dark curls snuck out from beneath a flour-dusted bandana, and her apron bore the same logo I'd seen on the bakery sign as we passed.

"Tilly Lafleur! I thought that must be your car outside!" she exclaimed, setting the basket on the counter. "I'm Mandy Summers. You probably don't know me, but I've heard all about you."

I didn't know her, but her cheerful energy was a welcome interruption.

"Mandy owns the bakery across the street," Bertha explained. *The Lumberjack's Daughter*. You would know it as *Darlene's Diner*."

I nodded, and before I could say anything, Mandy pulled into a warm hug that smelled of vanilla and spice.

"I've heard so much about you from your father." She pulled back, her warm brown eyes crinkling at the corners. "I am so, so sorry about Walter. We're all just sick about it."

"Thank you," I managed, a little overwhelmed.

"And you must be Callie!" Mandy turned to my daughter, who had emerged from exploring the back aisles. "Your grandfather has your picture right by the register. He was so proud when you got into the University of Victoria."

Callie smiled, genuinely touched. "He sent me care packages every month. Always had the best snacks."

"Well, now I know who I need to impress," Mandy laughed, placing her basket on the counter. "A welcome home basket for you," Mandy said, pulling back the cloth to reveal an assortment of muffins and pastries. "Though I suppose 'welcome back' is more accurate. I even put in a few of Walter's Morning Glory Muffins," she said. "For tomorrow's breakfast. Made them fresh when I heard you were coming in."

"That's very kind," I said, the normalcy of the moment making my eyes sting unexpectedly.

Mandy seemed to sense my emotion. "Listen, you two must be exhausted from the drive. Why don't you get yourselves settled? I'm sure Bertha can hold down the fort."

"The store—" I began.

"—has been running just fine with me watching it," Bertha interjected. "A few more hours won't make a difference. We can talk about arrangements tomorrow."

I wanted to protest, to say that I needed to understand what had happened to my father right now, but exhaustion suddenly hit me like a physical weight. "Thanks. Maybe that would be for the best."

Bertha reached under the counter and produced a set of keys, sliding them across to me. "These are for you. The silver one is for the house, brass one's for the shop's front door, and the small one is for his office in the back."

"Come on, Mom," Callie said, taking the basket from Mandy. "Let's get going. You look like you need a cup of tea, one of those amazing-smelling pastries, and a good night's sleep, in that order."

As we headed toward the exit to get our things from the car, I glanced out the front window. A man was standing across the street, watching the store with unusual intensity. When he noticed me looking, he quickly turned and walked away. There was something furtive about the movement that set off my internal alarms.

"Who's that?" I asked, nodding toward the retreating figure.

Bertha and Mandy exchanged a glance.

"Gus, the mayor's son and gas station owner," Bertha said from behind us. "A Bugle by blood, but the family doesn't keep him in the Christmas photo, if you know what I mean."

Gus Bugle. That was a name I knew. "I went to school with him. Wouldn't have recognized him if you hadn't said his name, though. He seems... interested," I observed. "Has he been hanging around a lot?" I caught myself doing what I always did: watching for patterns, reading the edges of people.

"More than usual," Bertha admitted. "Especially since your father disappeared. He's the one who brought your father's truck back from the launch point, you know. Just showed up with it one day. Never said a word."

"Get some rest, Tilly," Mandy said, giving my arm a gentle squeeze. "Balsam Bay will still be here tomorrow, with all its quirks and questions."

Quirks and questions. That seemed about right, I thought, as Callie and I left, following the path that led from behind the store through the trees to my childhood home. And somewhere in those questions, I hoped to find out what had really happened to my father. Because Walter McKay might have loved canoeing, but he'd never been careless on the water a day in his life.

CHAPTER TWO

The ceiling in my old bedroom greeted me the next morning, unchanged, right down to the hairline crack above the window—the one shaped like a question mark. I used to lie there and wonder if it meant something. An omen, maybe. Now it just felt like a fitting welcome home.

For a moment, I could've sworn I'd slipped back in time. But then I shifted on the old coil mattress and the ache in my back reminded me how long it had been. I hadn't slept in this room since I was eighteen.

I found Callie already at the kitchen table, nursing a mug of coffee while scrolling through her phone.

"I never knew small-town shops opened so early," she said, not looking up. "There've been customers at the store since seven. It's practically uncivilized."

"You're up early yourself," I observed, heading for the coffeemaker. The sight of the ancient percolator made me smile. Dad had steadfastly refused to upgrade to an automatic machine while the old percolator was still doing its job. "Let me guess, you got tired of trying to find a Wi-Fi signal?"

"No luck in the house, and the connection from the store is spotty through the trees," she confirmed with a dramatic sigh. "But guess what? Mandy's bakery has a fast connection, and excellent coffee. I've already scoped it out."

I raised an eyebrow. "You went out? When?"

"About an hour ago. Don't look so surprised, Mom. I can function before nine when properly motivated by caffeine needs." She tilted her head. "Pretty sure the entire town knows we're here. I got stopped and interrogated three times before I even reached the bakery's front door."

"Interrogated?"

"Small-town version. 'Oh, you must be Walter's granddaughter!' followed by gentle probing about what our plans are," Callie mimicked, her voice taking on an exaggerated nosy-neighbour tone. "For the record, I kept it vague and commented on taking things one day at a time."

I smiled despite myself. "Good call."

I poured coffee into one of my father's mismatched mugs —this one advertising a fishing tackle company from 1987— and joined Callie at the table. The house was as I remembered it, with a few modernized touches. Dad had replaced the old refrigerator, added a small television in the corner, and there were more books crammed onto the shelves than before, but otherwise, it remained frozen in time.

"So what's the plan?" Callie asked, setting down her phone. "Are we actually at the store today playing shop-keepers?"

"Bertha's handling the store this morning," I said. "I thought we should talk to Jason first, get the official story. After that, I don't know."

I was hoping the official story would put my concerns about Dad's disappearance to rest, but I wasn't sure what I would do if it didn't.

"You don't think it was an accident, do you?" Callie said quietly, her perceptiveness catching me off guard.

I looked up sharply. "What makes you say that?"

"Because I know that face." She gestured toward me with her mug. "That's your 'something doesn't add up' face."

I took a deep breath. "Your grandfather was an experienced canoeist. He knew the river. He planned for problems three steps ahead. And yet... here we are."

"So we're actually here to investigate?" A gleam appeared in Callie's eyes.

"Slow your roll, Miss J-school grad. We're here to settle his affairs," I corrected firmly. "But if that involves getting clarity on what happened, then yes."

Callie sat back, looking thoughtful. "You know, I could start documenting everything. Not just for my blog, but as a record. I'm good at organizing information, and—"

The sound of heavy boots on the porch stairs interrupted her. Three sharp knocks followed.

"Tilly? Callie? Time to rise and shine." My brother's voice carried through the door.

"I will rise, but I draw the line at shine," I called back, making Callie snort.

Jason let himself in, filling the doorway with his broad-shouldered frame. At forty-two, my brother looked more like our father than ever: the same steady gaze, the same way of standing, like he was rooted to the spot. The RCMP uniform he wore added authority, but to me, he was still the little brother I'd pulled out of trouble countless times growing up.

"Uncle Jason!" Callie abandoned her coffee to give him a hug.

"Look at you, university graduate and everything." He hugged her back, his normally serious expression warming. "Your grandpa was so proud. Wouldn't stop talking about it."

A flicker of sadness crossed Callie's face. "I know. The last thing he sent me was the goofiest congratulations card with a singing moose on it."

That sounded just like Dad. My throat tightened as Jason turned to me, his expression shifting to something more complicated.

"Tilly." He gave me a brief, slightly awkward hug. "Glad you made it. Bertha said you got in yesterday."

"Just in time to crash," I confirmed. "But I'm ready to hear what happened now."

Jason nodded, his face settling into professional lines as he took a seat at the table, nodding at my offer of a coffee.

"The official report is straightforward," he began. "Dad told several people he was planning a solo trip. Joe Charles—you remember him? The dog musher?—said Dad left Des with him the day before he left."

"Des?" I interrupted.

"Dad's dog. He asked Joe to look after her." Jason's tone was matter-of-fact. "When he didn't come back after a few days, Joe called it in."

"And the search?"

"Teams combed both riverbanks from the falls. His canoe turned up two kilometres downstream, smashed up pretty badly. Looked like it had been through the wringer."

Callie had gone quiet, watching us both intently.

"Who found the canoe?" I asked. In SAR, I'd learned that the smallest detail could make the biggest difference.

"A geologist who's been staying in town. Sean Patrick. Said he was taking samples near the riverbank and spotted it caught on a fallen tree."

I made a mental note of the name. "And you're sure it's Dad's canoe?"

Jason's expression tightened. "Of course we're sure, Tilly.

Anyone around these parts would know that handmade canoe. The paddle was found another hundred metres downstream."

"But no—" Callie hesitated. "No body?"

Jason's face softened as he looked at his niece. "No. With the current this time of year, and the terrain... It's not uncommon."

I knew he was right. I'd been on enough searches to understand how easily the wilderness could hide a person—alive or dead. But something still nagged at me.

"What did you find with the canoe? His fishing gear? First aid kit? Food bag?"

Jason shook his head. "Nothing."

"You don't find that odd?"

"It could all be sitting at the bottom of the falls, for all we know."

"You said you found one paddle?" Jason nodded. "When have you ever known our father to get in a canoe without a backup paddle?"

I saw him hesitate. I knew he wouldn't be able to explain that, because it was just so unlike Dad.

"Look," Jason finally said, his voice softening. "I know this is hard. It's hard for all of us. Dad was..." He trailed off. "But the evidence points to an accident. An unfortunate, tragic accident."

I nodded, not wanting to push further yet. "What about arrangements? A memorial service?"

"Everyone was suggesting we wait a bit longer, given that —" Jason hesitated.

"Given that there's no body," I finished for him. "That's reasonable."

Jason looked vaguely relieved that I wasn't fighting him on this. "In the meantime, there's the question of the store. Obviously, everything goes to you and me, but we need to decide what to do with it."

"We just got here," I pointed out, the idea suddenly too painful to unpack. "Can't we take a little time to figure things out?"

"Of course," Jason said quickly. "It's just... There's been some interest. In buying the place."

I blinked in surprise. "Already? Dad's only been missing for two weeks."

Jason had the good grace to look uncomfortable. "There's a guy who's been after the property for months. Kansas McBride. He's been around a few years."

"And now he's circling like a vulture," I said flatly.

"He's been pretty persistent," Jason admitted. "Claims Dad was on the verge of selling to him."

"Was he?"

My brother shrugged. "Dad never mentioned it to me, but Kansas seems convinced."

"Well, he can stay convinced," I said firmly. "We're not making any decisions about the store until we've had time to properly go through everything."

"That's what I told him," Jason agreed. He drained the last of his coffee and pushed back from the table. "I'd better get to the station."

I followed him to the door. "Humour me. How's Dad's health been? Any chance he had an episode out on the lake, wandered off and left the canoe unsecured?"

"Healthy as a draft horse." He rubbed the back of his neck, eyes sliding to the floorboards. "But he was asking odd questions before he left—old mining permits, council minutes from the eighties. I figured it was just senior citizen restlessness, but—"

"But what?"

"I got the impression he thought something was off about how the mine closure was handled."

I crossed my arms. "And you didn't press him?"

"Tilly…"

"What?"

He exhaled the long-suffering sigh only a brother reserves for a sister who doesn't know when to quit. "I know how you get. Just try not to kick too many hornets' nests, okay? The town's already twitchy over all the mine talk, and with Dad missing…" He managed a thin smile. "Watch whose boots you step on."

"Same old story," I said. "Bugles trying to convince everyone the town should reopen what Sam Melvin deliberately closed."

"Well, technically, the town owns the rights," Jason clarified. "It has since Melvin died without heirs. The Bugles just have the political leverage to push council votes their way."

After he left, Callie raised her eyebrows at me. "Well, that was something."

"What was?"

"Uncle Jason sounded like he was trying to talk you out of solving the mystery before you even started." She picked up her mug, a small smile playing at her lips. "Almost like he knows you."

He did. They both did. I'd always had a habit of poking at things other people left alone. "Let's go see how Bertha's managing. Then maybe we can take a walk around town, get reacquainted with the place."

"And gather intel on this Kansas person?" Callie suggested innocently.

Despite everything, I found myself smiling. "Maybe that, too."

By the time we walked over to the store, it was bustling. Bertha moved like she owned the place—and honestly, after all these years, she'd earned the right. She rang up purchases with brisk efficiency, somehow managing to catch up on town gossip while keeping the line moving. She had it down to an art form.

A cluster of older men occupied the small coffee corner, engaged in what appeared to be a heated debate about fishing lures.

"Morning, Bertha," I said, sliding behind the counter with the ease of someone who'd spent her teenage years working the register. "Need a hand?"

She gave me an appraising look. "Can you still make change without the register telling you how?"

"Of course," I said, slightly offended.

"Then you can take over while I go check the delivery that just came in." She nodded toward the back room. "The coffee crowd won't need much attention. They're solving the world's problems, so it'll be at least an hour."

Callie wandered over to the community bulletin board, already snapping photos with her phone.

"You know," she called over, "this would make great content for the store's social media accounts."

"The store doesn't have social media," Bertha said, sounding scandalized.

"Yet," Callie replied with a grin.

I felt a pang of sadness. As I struggled with the question of what to do with Dad's store, Callie was innocently trying to modernize it. This store had been so important to Balsam Bay for so many years. Did I have the heart to sell it? The alternative meant managing the store from across the country. I didn't think I had it in me to do that, either. And I couldn't ask Jason to look after it. He had enough on his plate.

I brushed those complicated feelings away for now and settled into the familiar rhythm of the store: greeting customers, many of whom did double-takes when they realized Walter's daughter was back, ringing up purchases, and fielding carefully worded condolences. Everyone was kind, though I noticed a few exchanged glances when they thought I wasn't looking.

I could imagine what ran through their minds: surprise that I'd come back at all, memories of how quickly I'd bolted after high school, sadness over my father's accident, and maybe, quietly, the question of what would happen to the store now.

The bell rang out again. This time, it wasn't just the sound that caught my attention.

The man who stepped in had that weathered, capable look some men wore naturally—tall, sandy brown hair, striking blue eyes, dressed in worn jeans and a flannel shirt. He had steel-toed boots that had seen actual use, and a way of moving that told me he spent more time outdoors than inside. He paused just inside the door, letting his eyes adjust. Then he made a beeline for the rock display like it was an altar.

Walter never went in for tourist trinkets. These were real rocks, ones kids could touch, paired with hand-scrawled index cards about local geology. I'd helped him organize them when I was ten.

The man crouched, squinting at the cards like he was reading a sacred text.

I cleared my throat, not entirely sure why I felt the need to connect with him. Maybe it was the boots, or the farmer's tan I spied under the neck of his shirt. The kinship of a fellow outdoors person.

He pulled his eyes from the display and approached the counter. "Good morning," he said. His tone was rich, but with a slight rasp, like he didn't speak much unless he had something worth saying. "I was hoping to pick up a few supplies."

"Of course," I replied, noting the way his eyes lingered on my face with curiosity. "What do you need?"

"Just some basics. Batteries, propane for my camp stove, maybe some of those cinnamon rolls everyone talks about." He smiled, revealing laugh lines around his eyes. "I'm Sean, by the way. Sean Patrick."

The name registered immediately. The geologist who'd found my father's canoe.

"Tilly Lafleur," I said, extending my hand automatically. "Walter's daughter."

His hand was warm and callused as it shook mine. "I thought you might be. I'm very sorry about your father. It's a terrible loss for the community."

There was genuine sincerity in his voice, but something else, too. A careful assessment. He was reading me like I was a topographical map, trying not to make it obvious.

"I understand you're the one who found his canoe," I said, keeping my tone neutral.

Sean nodded, a shadow crossing his face. "I was collecting samples downstream from the falls. Spotted pieces of it caught in deadwood along the bank."

"You're a geologist?"

"That's right." He reached for a basket and began gathering items from his mental shopping list. "Working on a book about the geological formations in this region. Been here about three months."

"Find anything interesting?" I asked, watching how he moved: purposeful, efficient, someone used to carrying heavy packs over long distances.

He smiled. "Every rock tells a story if you know how to listen."

"How poetic," I remarked, aiming for lightness but feeling a smile tug at the corner of my mouth.

Sean's smile widened slightly. "Occupational hazard. You spend enough time alone with rocks, you get philosophical about them." He placed his selected items on the counter. "Your father mentioned you were in search and rescue. Out in British Columbia, wasn't it?"

The casual reference to my father made my chest tighten. "Victoria," I confirmed. "But I stepped back from that a while ago."

Sean nodded, not pressing further as I rang up his purchases. "Well, if you need anything, I'm staying at the old Willow Cabin out by the lake."

I wasn't sure what Sean Patrick thought I might need him for, but I thanked him for the offer.

Just as he finished paying, a couple entered the store. The man was stocky and balding, wearing an expensive-looking fishing vest and an air of impatient energy that didn't quite match the sleepy morning. The woman beside him was slim and polished, her blonde hair expertly highlighted. Her casual outfit probably cost more than most people in Balsam Bay made in a week.

"There she is!" the man exclaimed, striding toward the counter with his hand outstretched. "Walter's daughter. Finally! I'm Kansas McBride, and this is my wife, Frannie."

So this was Kansas. Jason hadn't mentioned how loud he was. Or that his presence filled a room like someone trying to prove he belonged in it.

I'd only just had a conversation with Bertha about him. Kansas wasn't from Kansas, despite what everyone assumed. He was Texan, apparently—though how he ended up in

Balsam Bay was anyone's guess. He'd been visiting for a few summers now, part of a rotating crew of corporate wannabe-adventurers who came up for guided fishing trips and wilderness experiences. But last year, he'd shown up with a new wife and a new plan. Announced he was staying permanently. Just like that. Within months, he'd joined the town council—somehow charming or buying his way into a seat, depending on who you asked.

"Tilly Lafleur," I said, shaking his hand with considerably less warmth than I had Sean's.

Frannie reached for me with a delicate hand. "Well, I told Kansas—when something like this happens, it really makes you appreciate how precious time is." She patted my arm like she was comforting a disappointing casserole.

"Thank you," I said, though it came out more reflex than response. There was something about her that didn't quite add up. Too smooth. Like she'd rehearsed this in the mirror over a mimosa.

Sean Patrick quietly gathered his purchases, nodded a goodbye to me, and slipped past the newcomers.

"Now, I know this is a difficult time," Kansas continued, barely pausing for breath, "but I wanted to touch base with you about the store. Your father and I had some preliminary discussions about me taking it over, and I just want to assure you that my offer still stands."

"Kansas," Frannie murmured, touching his arm. "Perhaps this isn't the moment."

He patted her hand absently. "Just getting the ball rolling, honey." Turning back to me, he continued, "I've got big plans for this place. Modernize it, expand the inventory, really bring it into the 21st century. Your father was warming to the idea."

"Was he?" I asked skeptically.

From the back room, I heard Bertha make a noise that suggested that point was up for debate.

"Absolutely," Kansas insisted. "Ask anyone. We were this close to shaking on it." He held up his thumb and forefinger with barely a space between them.

Somehow, I doubted that. My father loved this store just as it was: a community hub that sold a little bit of everything, not a slick retail operation.

"Well, as I told my brother, we're not making any decisions about the store right now," I said firmly.

Kansas's smile dimmed. "Of course, of course. Just wanted to put it out there. No rush." His tone suggested the opposite. "Here's my card. When you're ready to talk, just give me a call."

He placed a glossy business card on the counter, then steered Frannie toward the door without buying anything.

"Nice to meet you!" Frannie called over her shoulder, her smile looked pinned in place.

As the door closed behind them, Bertha emerged from the back room, arms crossed.

"That man," she said, her voice tight, "has been pestering your father for months. Got more pushy about it recently, too."

"Did Dad ever consider selling to him?" I asked.

"Walter," Bertha said, arranging cans with military precision, "would sooner have sold his kidney on the black market than sell this store to Kansas McBride."

I smiled, feeling a rush of vindication. "That's what I thought."

Callie wandered back over, her phone clutched in her hand. "So that was the famous Kansas? He's a lot. And she looks like she paid full price for 'rustic' without ever planning to leave the pavement."

Bertha made another sound that might have been a chuckle. Coming from her, it felt like a victory.

After a steady stream of shoppers—most seemingly more interested in getting a look at me than buying anything—the lunch hour lull finally arrived.

"I need some fresh air," I announced, feeling restless. "Bertha, would it be alright if I took off for a bit?"

"Suit yourself. Should be quiet now."

"Callie, want to come?"

"Actually," she said, looking sheepish, "I sort of told Mandy I'd help her set up an Instagram account for her bakery this afternoon. She's paying me in homemade soup and butter tarts."

I laughed. "Entrepreneurial already. I'll walk over with you, then I'll just wander around town, see what's changed."

Bertha's voice stopped us in our tracks. "Matilda, I hope you've outgrown that habit of sticking your nose where it doesn't belong."

I waved her off. "They actually encourage that in kids these days, Bertha. They call it intellectual curiosity." I gave Callie a wink.

Bertha sniffed but didn't argue. "The town's changed since you left. Mostly for the better. But it still has its knots, same as always." She turned back to the till, hands moving with the same precision I remembered. "If you're asking questions, ask them the right way. People here remember more than they admit."

I nodded slowly. "So—two ears, one mouth?" I asked, quoting the old line she used to throw at me in high school, when I had more opinions than patience.

Bertha gave a small smile. "Just so."

CHAPTER THREE

The bell over *The Lumberjack Daughter's* door let out a cheerful chime as we stepped into the warm, yeasty air of fresh baking and cinnamon. The smell ambushed me: Sunday mornings, Dad's newspaper crinkling, coffee bubbling, me sneaking an extra pastry for me and Jason while he pretended not to notice. For a second, I was back there—until the scent deepened, richer and more layered than anything from our old kitchen. This wasn't home. It was something else. But it still pulled at the same thread.

Mandy appeared from behind the counter in a cloud of flour and apricot glaze. "If it isn't my favourite new townies," she beamed. "Sit. I want you to taste a new maple cream cookie I've been working on."

We gladly obeyed. Mandy plunked down two mugs of coffee and a small plate of cookies in the middle of the table.

"So," she said, "how's the welcome home-slash-welcome back been?"

"Eye opening," I said, taking a bite of cookie. Rich, creamy, buttery... I'd have to start running more if I ate Mandy's treats every day.

Callie gave me a look. "Mom's acting like she's just here for the muffins, not the mystery."

"I am not," I said. "I'm observing."

"Oh?" Mandy said with interest. "And what observations are you hoping to make?"

I should have answered before Callie jumped in.

"Grandpa's accident doesn't make any sense. Mom wants to get to the bottom of it," Callie said.

Mandy smirked. "I knew I'd like you! Anyone with any sense could see that Walter's accident doesn't make sense." Mandy encouraged Callie to scootch over so she could join her on the bench. "Well, I can tell you a few things you might be interested in."

I raised an eyebrow.

"For starters," she said, taking a cookie for herself, "Gus has been trying to get the Canada Post contract from your dad for a few years now. If Walter's officially presumed dead..." She paused, a flicker of apology in her eyes. "He can petition to take it over."

"What's the contract about?" Callie asked.

I swallowed the last of my maple cream and stuck my hands under the table to stop myself from taking another. "Have you ever noticed that in some small towns there's no actual post office, just a sign outside someone's store?"

"Yeah," she said. "I've seen that. Never really thought about it, though."

"Your grandfather has had the Canada Post contract for Balsam Bay since I was in elementary school. Sounds like Gus has his eye on it."

Callie washed her cookie down with a slurp of coffee.

"Must be worth something, then. There's good money to be had, I'm assuming?"

"Yes, and no. Dad pays a hefty franchise fee to keep the contract, but it brings people into the store. That regular traffic helps business."

Callie took another cookie. "So Gus thinks it would boost his gas station traffic."

"Exactly," Mandy said. "And he's been hanging around the store since Walter went missing—almost like he's waiting to hear something official so he can call Canada Post the minute they declare him gone."

I leaned back and let that sit for a moment.

"Wouldn't that pit Gus up against Kansas?" Callie asked. "If Kansas bought the store, wouldn't he be the one to continue the post office contract?"

Mandy shrugged. "You'd think, but those two were friendlier than you'd expect. Unlikely pair—Gus with his quiet routine, Kansas with his flashy everything—but they'd grab a beer now and then. Maybe more alike under the surface than either would admit."

Another fair point. I suddenly knew two people who would benefit from Dad being gone.

I left the bakery while Callie went over the social media plan she'd quickly thrown together for Mandy. I needed some sun and a breeze, so I wished them well, with Callie promising to text me when she was done.

I was walking past *Fo(u)r Furry Feet* pet shop when I spotted the back of Sean Patrick's head.

Following at a discreet distance, I tried to look as if I was casually window shopping. I watched Sean turn onto Birch Avenue, cross the street, and head for the building on the corner. His orange backpack bounced as he hopped the few stairs into the *Balsam Bay History Museum*.

The building had originally been Samuel Melvin's residence. As town founder, he built quite a grand house for the area, although no one minded much, since Sam regularly held parties and gatherings, inviting everyone in town. Sam lived there alone until his passing, then left the house—in addition to his mineral rights for the mine—in his will to the town. Residents voted to turn it into a museum in his honour. I'd only ever known it as the town museum, and I knew it well.

It was quiet inside, save for a ticking clock somewhere nearby. A welcome table stood in the foyer with a young man seated behind it, manning the donations box. No admission fee, here. I dropped a five into the box, then headed to the first door on my left.

I wandered through the parlour, the study, then the kitchen. Everything was the same since I'd last visited. I ran my hand over Sam Melvin's grand oak desk that had seen little use. Apparently, Samuel was the hands-on type. Most of his meetings happened on-site at the mine—or during his downtime. He liked to fish and hunt and had no trouble convincing people to talk business in the bush.

The kitchen was one of my favourite places in the house. The yellow walls were as bright and sunny as the June light coming through the windows. According to the laminated pages on the counter, Samuel had a housekeeper during the day who did most of Sam's cooking, even storing meals in the fridge for the weekends during her days off. I wasn't much of a cook, but I imagined I would have enjoyed preparing meals in such a cozy space.

I'd always felt at home in this house. The ghost of my mother's presence probably had a lot to do with that. I could see her handiwork scattered about the building, in the handwritten labels, the arrangement of furniture, and her choice of photos on the walls.

As I turned down the hallway to the main floor bedrooms, I heard a soft noise coming from the dining room. I backtracked and paused at the doorway's edge.

The double pocket doors stood open, framing the room like a stage. Two ladies sat together at one end of a long table, quietly discussing one of several books in front of them. Sean sat at the other end, his backpack open beside him, some of its contents spilling out onto the tabletop. His head was lowered as he concentrated on papers in front of him. The buffet and hutch that I remembered, still sat along the far wall displaying pieces of Sam Melvin's good china, but two of the other walls were lined with shelving. The short wall was filled with books, while the long wall displayed various objects.

I walked in, keeping my gaze on the long wall. Pieces of old mining equipment and prospector items were arranged on the shelves, with tags identifying each one, along with a write-up of what each item was used for. There were also a few antiques from the 50s and later—donations from families in town, I realized, recognizing almost every one of the surnames attached to the items.

I snuck a glance at Sean. He had a pencil in his hand and was busy sketching something from a book in front of him. Since the ladies were engaged in their own conversation, I saw no harm in starting up one of my own.

I pulled out a chair near Sean. I looked over at a small pile of rocks in front of his backpack, and seeing my opportunity, picked up one of the smaller ones. Sean raised his head and watched me study it. "Interesting grain," I said offhandedly.

He looked mildly amused. "You a collector?"

"Not a serious one, but I have a small collection from trips I've been on. Mostly sentimental." I returned his rock to the pile.

His smile was genuine, and disarming, if I was being

honest with myself. Judging by the laugh lines near his eyes and mouth, he was at least as old as I was, yet he moved with the lanky ease of a man twenty years his junior.

"This must be from around here," I said, gesturing to the rock I had selected.

"You're right. About fifty kilometres north."

I didn't want to come across as if I was interrogating him, but I was genuinely interested in learning more about Mr. Sean Patrick. "Where are you from?"

Sean closed his journal. "Edmonton, originally. Haven't called it home for a long time since I've been working on different projects around the globe, but that's where I was born."

"So Balsam Bay was on your travel wish list?"

He chuckled. "I'd never actually heard of Balsam Bay before I got here a few months ago."

My attention was drawn to the sudden silence at the end of the table. The ladies were staring at us, lips tight and brows furrowed. I leaned into Sean. "I think we might be making too much noise."

A small smile tugged at his lips as he nodded. He pulled his backpack toward him and started putting his belongings away. "Why don't we take this conversation outside, then?"

Heat flushed up my chest, then straight to my face like I was sixteen again.

When was the last time I blushed?

As soon as we stepped through the front doors of the museum, we both burst into laughter, the tension from our awkward encounter peeling away in the sunlight.

"That felt like being scolded by a pair of librarians," Sean said, grinning.

"Oh? Have a history of library misconduct?" I teased, matching his stride.

"Not since high school," he said, adjusting the strap on his backpack. "You grew up here. Ever get kicked out of the museum before?"

"Once or twice," I admitted, a flicker of memory catching me off guard. "My mom was the original curator."

"That explains your rock collection," he said, giving me a look that landed softer than I expected. "She must've passed on her knack for guarding beautiful things."

I felt my cheeks warm. "I never thought about it like that... but maybe."

We wandered with no actual destination in mind. My feet seemed to know where they were going before I did—toward the lake, of course. The air was warm, with just a hint of the heat to come. Sean stayed close as we reached the water's edge, the two of us falling into a comfortable quiet.

"Walter said your daughter's a journalism major?" he asked eventually, his voice gentle in the stillness.

"Graduate, actually. As of a month ago."

Sean's eyebrows lifted. "Well, congratulations. You and your husband must be very proud."

I watched a pair of ducks skimming across the lake. "We are. Though we've been divorced for some time."

He stepped a little closer. "Oh! Sorry to hear that." The small smile on his face suggested he wasn't very sorry at all.

Right on cue, my phone buzzed—Callie. Saved by the kid.

"Sorry, that's my daughter. I should get going."

"Of course." Sean walked with me back toward the main path near the wooden bear carving, and stopped where we'd part ways. "Well, Tilly Lafleur. It's been a pleasure."

"So you're staying in town a while?" The words were out before I could pull them back.

He smiled again. Had I noticed that dimple before? I was pretty sure it hadn't made an appearance earlier.

"I might have to head to Winnipeg for a few meetings, but I've rented the cabin for the rest of the summer."

"Oh. Great," I said, aiming for casual. "Good to know." I glanced at my phone again, though it hadn't buzzed a second time. "I should go. Callie'll worry."

He turned away from town, opposite the way I was headed, then paused. "I'd love to see your rock collection some time."

That dimple again. Yep, definitely hadn't noticed it before.

"I'd like that," I said. Then, before my brain could catch up to my mouth, I added, "You can always find me at the store."

"I know," he said, half-laughing. "See you around."

I rolled my eyes at my foolishness—smooth as a teenager writing her crush's name in cursive. I wasn't sure what to make of Sean Patrick just yet, but I knew I definitely wanted to see him again.

I was still watching him walk away when another voice cut through the warm hush of the lakeside.

"Well, look who's back in town," came a voice I hadn't heard in years. "Tilly Lafleur, down by the lake just like old times."

Gus Bugle. He'd filled out since high school, but I'd know that crooked half-smile anywhere. Same curly hair, just thinner now. He still met your eyes before glancing away, especially when things got uncomfortable. Thirteen years in the same tiny school meant you knew people in a way that stuck, even if you never ran in the same circles.

"I'm sorry about your dad," Gus said, his tone softening. "Walter was a good man. Not a lot of that going around anymore."

"Thanks," I said, watching as he shoved a hand into his front pocket—an old habit from when he used to get called to the board in math class. His right hand hung by his side, a bandage wrapped around it, preventing him from shoving it in the other pocket. "I saw you outside the store yesterday. Something you needed?"

He didn't flinch like I expected, just gave a little shrug. "Been checking in on Bertha. Your dad asked me to keep an eye on her before he left on his trip. Make sure she wasn't working herself into the ground."

"No one mentioned that."

"Wasn't a big deal," Gus said, meeting my gaze for half a second. "Just neighbours looking out for each other."

The way he said neighbours made me pause. Like there was more packed into the word than he wanted to explain.

"Sounds like you two were on good terms."

He gave a small shrug, eyes dropping. "Walter had a knack for seeing people for who they really were. Not just their last name. Not who they were connected to. Just... them."

Coming from Gus—the mayor's son, a Bugle through and through—that was saying something. And it sounded like Dad. He always looked past the packaging.

"Speaking of last names," I said, watching his face, "I hear the Mayor's pushing to reopen the mine."

Something flickered in his jaw. "My dad thinks it'll save the town. Yours thought it'd finish it off."

"And you?" I asked.

"I think carburetors and timing belts make more sense than town politics." He gave a half-smile. "The garage keeps me busy enough."

The answer was smooth. Too smooth. Like something he'd said often enough to wear down the edges.

"Anyway," he went on, "just wanted to say hello, and..." He

gestured vaguely in the air. "You know. Sorry about everything."

He turned to go, then hesitated. "If that old truck of your dad's gives you trouble, bring it by. No charge."

"Thanks, Gus."

He nodded, walked a few steps, then stopped again. "Your dad was honest, Tilly. This town's gotten too big and seems to have forgotten what that means. Don't forget that about him."

Before I could answer, he was off again, hand in his pocket, shoulders hunched like he was bracing for a wind that hadn't come yet.

I watched him disappear around the curve of the path, his last words still echoing. A warning? A confession? I wasn't sure, but something about Gus's words stuck.

The Gus I remembered had been quiet but direct. This version felt like he was trying to say something without really saying it.

And what did he owe my father that made him offer free repairs?

My phone buzzed again—Callie, this time with actual impatience. I texted back *on my way* and turned toward the bakery, my brain turning over the afternoon's events, looking for a thread that connected them.

First Sean and his charming curiosity. Then Gus, with his cryptic comments and unnecessary generosity. Both of them connected to Dad. Both with stories they hadn't finished telling.

I picked up Callie outside the bakery, and we headed back to the store to finish out the day. Over dinner that night in Walter's snug house, I found myself staring at the empty chair at the head of the table.

Why did you go over those falls, Dad? Did you miscalculate the speed of the current? Did you have a heart attack? Hit your head and become disoriented? Those would be reasonable explanations, and I'd willingly accept any of them if not for two things: no body, and no supplies were recovered. It didn't make sense.

Two days back in Balsam Bay, and I had more questions than answers.

CHAPTER FOUR

Callie was already at the little table by the front window, fingers flying across the keyboard. Steam curled from her mug while the morning light caught the bold stickers on her laptop: snark, travel, and one that just said, "I brake for conspiracy theories."

"You're up early again," I said.

"Reframing the blog," Callie said, typing with focused precision. "It needs a stronger hook if I want to build real traction."

I glanced over. "Didn't you already have a hook?"

She turned the laptop toward me, showing off the sleek new banner she'd designed: *Temporary Town Life: Dispatches from a City Girl Stuck in Small-Town.* Below it, the tagline read: *Unpacking small-town charm, whispered rumours, and the stories people tell without meaning to.*

I lifted an eyebrow. "Impressive. Should I be worried?"

Callie gave a small, confident smile. "Relax. It's light observation, not an exposé. But it's useful. People don't hold back when they think you're just there for the vibes. I posted one entry about our walk through town yesterday, and the comments already hint at which buildings are falling apart and who wants them 'revitalized.'"

I settled into a chair. "So this is your way of gathering intel while I figure out what happened to Grandpa?"

"Not exactly," she said thoughtfully. "It's a way to understand the community. Gossip, trends, unguarded comments—it's all data. And let's be honest, Mom—people are talking. This way, they get to talk, and I get to listen."

Bertha arrived at the store at her usual time (precisely 6:39 a.m.) and glided through the store like clockwork: efficient, silent, already halfway through the next task. She paused only briefly to acknowledge Callie's presence with a polite nod before disappearing into the stockroom.

"She seems annoyed," Callie murmured.

"She's feeling the loss of Dad, too. Everyone grieves in their own way."

Bertha returned, dropped a box of peanut butter on the counter, and put her hands on her hips as she glared at us. Or rather, me.

"Everything okay?" I asked.

"I saw that look in your eye when you were talking to Sean Patrick in the store yesterday."

I laughed, ignoring the butterflies I'd felt when I was around him. "Bertha, I haven't had 'that look' in my eye since well before my divorce."

Her expression didn't change as she stared at me, waiting for what I could only assume was my acknowledgment that she saw something in me I didn't. Or, more plainly, that I was lying to myself as well as to her.

"I heard you two looked quite cozy in the museum and down by the lake."

Callie turned to me and raised an eyebrow. I could have done without the smirk on her face.

"I don't know what you're talking about," I said, busying myself by straightening the line of cans I'd just straightened.

"Sean Patrick may seem like an easy-going guy, but I've seen him fly off the handle. I'm telling you, Matilda, be careful."

While Bertha had occasionally given me mother-like advice as a teenager—probably feeling badly about my lack of maternal influence—this was as close as she'd ever come to meddling in my private life.

"What do you mean?" I asked.

"Well, there's nothing wrong with him, exactly. It's just..." Bertha paused, clearly wrestling with whether to continue. "Your father had a feeling about him."

"What kind of feeling?"

"The kind where he was sure he'd seen Sean somewhere before, but couldn't place where. At first, anyway. This was a couple of weeks before Walter left on his canoe trip. Your dad was behind the counter and I was in and out of the storeroom putting away a delivery. I heard Sean tell Walter that he was leaving the next day to do some research further north. He and Walter started talking about different paddling routes and such, then suddenly, Walter lets out a *whoop*! Said he finally figured out how he knows Sean."

Bertha paused. I didn't know if she just wanted to interject a little drama into her story or if she was waiting for me to say something, so I nodded. "Okay. So how did he know him?"

"Your dad said he saw Sean on TV. The kid denied it up and down, but Walter was positive he saw him on one of his Australian TV shows. "Walter thought it was hilarious. Sean, not so much—he turned beet red, looked like he might launch himself over the counter. I half expected Walter to end up with a black eye, and a broken screen door."

"What did Dad do?"

"He was oblivious, the old fool. He acknowledged he'd embarrassed the heck out of Sean, but he couldn't stop laughing. I thought I was going to have to butt in and diffuse things before Walter ended up flat on the floor. Sean left, but he was spitting nails as he went. Almost pulled the screen door off its hinges."

Callie looked like she'd just been given the juiciest gossip she'd heard in weeks. "Did Grandpa say anything about the TV show he saw Sean on?"

"Not much. Something about a reality show. They made Sean the patsy for whatever went down. Apparently, it became a hot topic down under."

I glanced at Callie, who was already making notes on her phone. "And nothing happened after that?"

"Nope. I was just glad the kid was on his way out of town. Hoped he stayed away a good long time, or at least long enough to calm down about Walter. No luck there. He turned up a few weeks later, having found Walter's canoe smashed under the falls."

I tried to picture Sean—the quietly competent, rock-obsessed geologist—bumbling through some overproduced, sand-blasted reality TV show. It didn't quite line up. Sean seemed more like the type to talk to trees than producers. But life's weird. People surprise you.

This was serious. I needed to talk with Sean, and not for the reasons I'd been looking forward to seeing him again.

The door jangled, and a chorus of squeaky soles and enthusiastic chatter drifted in—like a fitness class had taken a wrong turn and ended up at the general store. I glanced up to see a trio of women in sun visors and brightly coloured sneakers, toting matching canvas bags and radiating a certain brand of cheerful authority that made me sit up a little straighter.

"She said to him, plain as day, 'If you think I'm paying for stale croissants again, you've got another thing coming!'" a voice rang out before its owner even crossed the threshold.

They moved as one, like a well-rehearsed performance. Their water bottles jangled softly in their bags, every step a confident claim to the space. These weren't just longtime residents. They were women who ran the town—socially, at least.

I froze with a jar of peanut butter in hand.

Callie glanced up from her phone, a sly grin already spreading across her face. "Brace yourself," she whispered.

If Callie already knew these ladies, they must have been part of the friendly interrogation she received yesterday morning.

Bertha, standing at the till tallying a delivery invoice, muttered just loud enough to be heard, "Friday already."

The first woman, tall and slender with a thick silver braid, spotted me and beamed. "You must be Tilly. We're so sorry about Walter, dear. Devastated." She squeezed my hand without waiting for permission. "I'm Enid. This is Nora, and Trish."

Nora, round and rosy-cheeked, waved a napkin-wrapped pastry. "We brought scones. Mandy made extras, and we figured grief is best handled with carbs."

"Also," Trish added, adjusting her visor, "we have questions. But friendly ones! Think of us as... a community welcome committee, with follow-up."

I blinked. "Thank you... I think."

"Oh, she's got Walter's humour," Nora said with a fond smile. "You're going to fit right in."

The three made themselves at home around the small

coffee corner near the window. Nora flipped the "Local Events" newsletter to the crossword, Enid began reorganizing the sugar packets, and Trish pulled out a battered notebook and clicked a pen like she was about to interview the Prime Minister.

I raised an eyebrow at Callie, who just smiled and mouthed, "You're welcome."

"I suppose you knew my dad well?" I asked, still standing awkwardly with the jar.

"Not in the biblical sense, dear," Enid said, utterly deadpan, "though it did cross our minds."

Nora elbowed her. "Oh, stop it. We adored Walter. We walk here every Monday, Wednesday, and Friday, like clockwork. Always end our route here, just to harass him. He pretended he didn't like it, but he made sure the coffee was fresh and the good cookies were out when we arrived."

"He said we scared off customers," Trish added. "But then he started putting extra chairs around the table."

"We were his fan club," Nora said proudly. "Now we're yours. If you'll have us."

I sat down slowly, setting the jar in my lap. "That's... incredibly kind. And a little intense."

"We don't do halfway," Enid said. "We're retired. We have time, no filters, and a very active group chat."

"About?" I asked, already knowing the answer.

"Walter," Trish said, voice lowering. "We don't believe for a second he just fell into the river. He was careful. Experienced. And he was always on the tourists about being safety conscious on the water."

"He's been running the water safety course at the community centre for years!" Enid added.

"But he looked tired just before he left," Nora added, almost reluctantly. "Worried."

Callie moved to join them, phone in hand. "What kind of worried?"

"He didn't laugh at our jokes," Enid said, which made all three nod gravely.

"That's dire," Bertha said, not looking up from her receipts.

"We're not here to pry," Trish said, flipping to a fresh page in her notebook. "Just to help. If you want it."

I looked from their eager faces to Callie's raised eyebrows, then finally to Bertha, who gave the smallest of nods.

"Well," I said, leaning in, "why don't you tell me everything you've heard?"

Nora passed the scones. "Oh, sweetie. You're going to need two of these."

***

"I'm trying to imagine Grandpa around those ladies, and I… just can't," Callie said with a laugh, fiddling with the air vents for the third time since we'd left the driveway.

"Oh, I can see Dad enjoying the banter," I said. "In small doses. I'm sure he revelled in the attention they gave him."

Walter's fan club had dished up plenty of juicy town gossip, and more than a few details I'd quietly filed away for later.

And of course, they weren't the first to ask about Dad's dog —the same one Jason had mentioned so casually. Walter had never brought her up to Callie or me. Then again, there were plenty of little things that slipped through the cracks when you lived far apart for so long. So now Callie and I were officially on the hunt for Des.

"Did you notice how Bertha practically pushed us out of the store?" I said, glancing at Callie. "She must've asked me three times if I remembered how to get to Joe's."

"She must have a soft spot for Des," Callie said, grinning.

I smiled. "She says it's the regulars who miss Des. I think Bertha just hates admitting she got attached."

"That seems uncharacteristically sentimental for Bertha."

"People can surprise you."

"Are you sure we're going the right way?" Callie asked, checking her phone for what seemed like the twentieth time. "We haven't seen a house in at least ten kilometres."

"That's because Joe doesn't live in a house, exactly," I replied, guiding the SUV along the winding dirt road. "At least, he didn't when I was growing up. He had what Dad called a 'homestead'—part cabin, part workshop, all character."

The road curved around a stand of tall pines and suddenly opened into a large clearing. Off to the side, we spied a sturdy log cabin with a wide porch, a large outbuilding that served as Joe's workshop, and several well-maintained dog kennels.

"Okay, I admit it," Callie said, taking in the view. "This is pretty cool."

As I parked, the cabin door opened, and a tall figure emerged onto the porch. Joe Charles looked just as I remembered him: long dark hair now streaked with silver, the same weathered face with deep lines around his eyes, and the quiet, watchful presence that had always made me feel like he knew more than he let on.

"Tilly," he called, his voice carrying across the yard. "Thought that might be you coming up the drive."

I stepped out of the SUV, oddly nervous. "Hi, Joe. It's been a long time."

"Too long." He descended the porch steps with an easy grace that defied his age. "And this must be Callie."

"Nice to meet you, Mr. Charles," Callie said, extending her hand.

"Just Joe," he replied, shaking it warmly. "Nobody calls me

Mr. Charles except the bank, and I try to avoid them when possible." His smile reached his deep brown eyes. "Come on in. I've got coffee on, and Des has been waiting to meet you."

The inside of the cabin was a cozy jumble of practical and personal: handcrafted furniture built to last generations, shelves lined with well-worn books, and a wood stove that would enjoy a break for the next few months.

"You've done some renovations," I observed, noting the updated kitchen and large windows that hadn't been there thirty years ago.

"Somewhere around sixty, even stubborn men like me start to value insulation and indoor plumbing," Joe replied, gesturing for us to sit at a sturdy wooden table while he poured coffee into ceramic mugs. "Walter helped with some of it. He had a good eye for these things."

At the mention of my father, there was a soft whine from another room. Joe glanced toward the hallway. "She knows that name. Been watching the door whenever I say it."

While Joe busied himself with our coffee, I found myself scanning the room for photos or mementos of my father. There, on a bookshelf, stood a framed picture of Dad and Joe standing proudly beside what looked like a newly built shed, tools still in hand.

"That was two summers ago," Joe said, noticing my gaze. "We spent a weekend putting that smokehouse together. Your father insisted on doing things the old way. No power tools."

"That sounds like Dad," I said, smiling. "He always said you couldn't truly know wood if you didn't work it by hand."

After a moment of comfortable silence, Joe turned toward the hallway. "Des? Come on out, girl. Meet your people."

A blur of gold and black bounded into the room and skidded into a sit beside Joe's leg, making him chuckle. Des looked like someone had tried to paint a shepherd and a lab on the same canvas: bright eyes, an easy grin, and a tail with opinions. With tongue lolling, tail wagging, Des gave us both a once-over—curious, calm, and way too clever.

"Hello, Des," I said softly, holding out my hand palm-down at the level of my thigh.

Des approached slowly, her gaze never leaving my face. There was something in those eyes—a depth of understanding that reminded me, painfully, of my former K9 partner, Lucy. I'd sworn off working with another dog, and search and rescue altogether. Couldn't bear that kind of connection again. But Des wasn't asking for anything. She just sniffed my hand gently—simply checking me out.

"She's beautiful," Callie murmured.

"And smart as they come," Joe added with obvious pride. "Your father did a great job with her, especially considering she was a rescue."

"Rescue?" I asked, my fingers automatically finding the soft spot behind Des's ear.

"Would have been about a year ago. My friend at the band office arranged for a rescue organization to come help with the stray dog situation," Joe explained. "Walter and I got talking about it, and he mentioned he'd been thinking of getting a dog for some companionship. Asked me to keep my eye out for something special, if I was going to be up that way."

"And you chose Des," Callie said, reaching out to let Des sniff her hand as well.

Joe smiled. "She chose us, really. Had that look in her eye— like she was sizing us up rather than the other way around. Walter fell for her right away."

Des had settled on the floor between us, close enough that I could easily reach her.

"How old is she?" Callie asked.

"Just coming up on four, we figure," Joe replied. "Young

enough to have plenty of energy, old enough to have some sense about her."

"Did Dad bring her here often?"

"They'd visit about once a week. Walter liked to help with projects around the place, and Des enjoyed running with the other dogs." Joe's expression grew more serious. "The day before he left, he asked if Des could stay with me for a while. Said he needed some time to himself."

I looked up sharply. "Did he say why?"

Joe's eyes met mine, steady and knowing. "Not exactly. Just that he might be gone longer than usual. When I asked when he'd be back, he said it depended on how things played out."

"That's an odd thing to say before a canoe trip. Did he seem worried?" I asked, choosing my words carefully.

Joe considered this. "Not worried. Resolved. Like a man who's made up his mind to do something difficult but necessary."

Des's ears pricked up, and she lifted her head to look at Joe. It was almost as if she understood what we were discussing.

"Bertha mentioned Dad seemed preoccupied with the old mine," I ventured. "Did he talk to you about that?"

"Some," Joe acknowledged. "Walter had concerns about the reopening proposals. Your father believed this place should be more than just a resource to be stripped."

"Was that Sam Melvin's vision?" Callie asked.

Joe nodded. "He wanted a place where people could make a good life without destroying what made it worth living in. That's why he willed the mineral rights to the town when he died—wanted them to be stewards, not just owners."

"But the Bugles are pushing to reopen it anyway," I said.

Joe nodded grimly. "Political power trumps all, apparently. There's always been a Bugle as mayor, and they've never forgotten that mine. Your father was one of the few people willing to stand against them publicly."

Des had inched closer to me during this conversation, and without thinking, I found my hand resting lightly on her back. Her fur was softer than it looked, and warm.

I wasn't surprised that Dad was willing to speak out. It sounded as if everyone knew Dad's opinion on the matter.

"If you're interested, the council's holding its first town hall on the issue Sunday evening." Joe said. "Maybe you'd like to find out what your dad felt so strongly about."

That sounded like an excellent idea. "Will you be there?"

"I think most everyone in Balsam Bay will be there," Joe said.

Well, that settled it, then. Across from me, Callie tapped something on her phone—likely adding the event to her calendar.

I ran my fingers through Des's soft fur, drawing idle circles along her back. "Bertha says the store's been quiet without her," I said, eyes still on the dog. "Apparently, the morning regulars keep asking about her."

"She belongs there," Joe said simply. "Walter knew it, and I think you do, too."

I hesitated. Taking on a dog—especially one that had belonged to my father—felt like a commitment I wasn't sure I was ready to make. But looking at Des, I felt something shift inside me.

"We'll take her back with us today," I decided. "Just a short-term visit. See how it goes."

Joe nodded, as if he'd expected nothing less. "I've got her bag ready. Walter always packed her stuff when they came over: food, brush, favourite toy."

He returned with a well-worn canvas bag, with "DES" embroidered on the side in neat stitching.

"Aw, isn't that cute?" Callie read the name with a questioning look. "I expected the name 'Des' to have a 'z'."

Joe smiled. "It's short for Desdemona. Walter picked the name himself."

I took the bag carefully, a lump rising in my throat. "Dad made this?"

Joe smiled softly. "Said he wanted Des to know she had a permanent home."

If I'd harboured even a sliver of doubt about how much my father cared for this dog, it vanished now. "Thank you, Joe. For everything."

"Your father was a good man, Tilly," Joe said, his voice quiet but firm. "One of the best I've known. Whatever you're looking for, I hope you find it. And I'm always here if you need."

As we drove back toward town, Des watched the passing landscape through the window, occasionally making a soft sound that wasn't quite a whine.

"I think she misses Grandpa," Callie observed from the passenger seat.

"Yes," I agreed, glancing in the rearview mirror at Des's attentive profile. "I think she does."

That makes two of us, puppy.

CHAPTER FIVE

Two nights later, the Balsam Bay community centre had been set up for the evening's town hall. Rows of metal folding chairs faced a table where Mayor John Bugle sat flanked by several town councillors, their expressions carefully neutral. A projector hummed quietly, casting the town logo—the outlines of a balsam fir on a craggy outcrop with a few waves and a circle to represent the sun—onto a pull-down screen that had definitely seen better days.

I slipped into a seat near the back just as the meeting was called to order. Callie settled beside me, thumbs at the ready to jot down anything interesting.

"Full house," she murmured.

She wasn't wrong. Nearly every adult in Balsam Bay seemed to have turned out. Mandy caught my eye from a few rows ahead and gave a small wave. I spotted Bertha sitting ramrod straight in the front row, notebook in hand. Even Gus lurked near the exit, nervously twisting his usual ball cap in his hands.

I let my eyes sweep further. Kansas sat stiffly a few rows

from the front, arms crossed, jaw tight, his usual bluster noticeably absent. Frannie, perfectly coiffed, perched beside him with a polished smile, scanning the room as if taking inventory. She touched his arm lightly once, but he didn't seem to notice.

Mayor Bugle tapped the microphone, producing a squeal that made everyone wince.

"Evening, folks," he said, his voice carrying the quiet authority of someone used to being heard. "Thanks for coming out tonight. As I'm sure everyone's heard by now, your town council has been discussing options for economic revitalization in Balsam Bay. Today's meeting is to share some exciting possibilities with you all."

Exciting wasn't the word I'd have chosen. The mine had been the talk of the town for months—more shouted than whispered, judging by the lawn signs and bakery gossip. Everyone already knew what was on the table. This meeting wasn't about breaking news. It was about selling it.

The mayor yielded the floor to a man I didn't know: tall, lean, and distinctly out of place in his tailored blazer. Too polished for Balsam Bay, with salt-and-pepper hair and wire-frame glasses that screamed "I'm an intellectual, trust me."

"For those who haven't met me yet, I'm Devon Fontaine." He smiled, but without warmth. "I've got a little place on the north side of Echo Lake that I've been enjoying seasonally for almost ten years. Last year, I started spending more time up here, and apparently Mayor Bugle noticed—" he caught the mayor's eye who gave him an *aw, shucks* look—"and after a few months of twisting my arm, I took him up on his offer of joining town council," he said, looking to Mayor Bugle for confirmation. I noticed Kansas shift uncomfortably in his chair. "My day job is regional executive with Northern Prairie Lumber Company."

Plenty of folks in Balsam Bay still hadn't forgotten the clearcutting mess near Spruce Ridge. Northern Prairie's name didn't sit easy with everyone—especially not the ones who could still see the stumps from their kitchen windows.

A murmur rippled through the crowd. Devon waited for it to subside, his confidence unwavering.

"The Samuel Melvin Mine has been dormant for decades, but recent geological surveys suggest there's significant untapped potential. We're proposing the town exercise its rights to reopen operations using modern techniques that would bring jobs and prosperity back to Balsam Bay."

I shifted in my seat, noting how carefully he phrased it. Not "our rights" but "the town's rights" — a telling distinction that most people probably missed.

Random comments hurled from the crowd: "Here, here! About time!"

Next came a glossy presentation—job creation projections, economic forecasts, and carefully selected photos of gleaming mining operations. Each slide slicker than the one before.

"They've certainly spent money on the presentation," Callie whispered. "That animation package isn't cheap. Think he made it himself, or hired someone to make him look good?"

I scanned the room, taking in the reactions. Tourism was clearly thriving in Balsam Bay—but judging by some expressions, not everyone felt they were sharing in the success. A few faces lit up at the mention of new jobs, especially among those hit hard by the sawmill's cutbacks. Others sat stiffly, arms crossed like personal shields against the sales pitch.

Then a hand shot up from the middle rows.

"Yes, Mrs. Walchuk?" the mayor acknowledged.

"What about the environmental impact? Samuel Melvin closed that mine because he believed in caring for the land. He left the mineral rights to the town so future generations could protect what made this place worth living in."

Devon stepped forward smoothly. "Great question. Mining technology has advanced tremendously since Mr. Melvin's day. The town council, with Mayor Bugle's leadership, would ensure that modern methods minimize—"

"But we're talking about transitioning to an open pit mine, aren't we?" another voice interrupted. "That's what those geological surveys you just showed us recommend. That would kill our tourism."

Devon's smile didn't quite hold. "There are various options being considered. Open pit extraction is one possibility, but I assure you, any development would include comprehensive environmental safeguards."

"This is great!" someone else called out. "We've got enough shops selling candles and homemade jam. If this town's going to survive, we need something solid. We're going to need more industry to create more jobs."

A woman stood up, red-faced. "Who said we wanted it to grow? Things are fine the way they are. You want more industry?" She made a sweeping gesture with her arm and pointed to the back exit. "Move to the city."

The discussion continued, but with each question, Devon's answers grew more polished, yet less specific. All frosting, no cake. I noticed Sean Patrick near the side wall, watching with an intensity that suggested more than casual interest. When our eyes met, he gave a slight nod before returning his attention to Devon.

Gus slipped out before the presentation ended, phone pressed to his ear. Something about his shifty movements raised the fine hairs on my neck. Not exactly subtle, that one.

When the meeting began to wrap up, Mayor Bugle made

his way toward me, threading through the thinning crowd with practiced ease. His expression was all solemn concern, but the calculation behind his eyes wasn't doing a great job of hiding.

"Tilly, good to see you. I wanted to express my condolences personally," he said, lowering his voice. "Such a tragedy about Walter. Perhaps we've reached the right time for a memorial service? The town would like to pay its respects properly."

I stiffened. "I'm still processing everything, John."

"Of course, of course. But a service might provide closure... for you and the community," he persisted. "Walter was beloved here. We should honour his memory."

Something in his tone made my stomach tighten. The push for a memorial felt less like concern and more like a desire to officially close the chapter on my father.

"I'll let you know when Jason and I are ready," I replied, keeping my voice steady while fighting the urge to ask him why he was in such a rush to bury my father.

He nodded, squeezing my shoulder. "Take your time. And if there's anything I can do to help with the store or... anything else you might need to settle, please don't hesitate to ask."

As he walked away, Devon approached, extending his hand. "Ms. Lafleur, I presume? I wanted to introduce myself properly."

His handshake was firm, his smile practiced. "I knew your father, though not well. He had strong opinions about land use in Balsam Bay."

"That sounds like him," I said neutrally.

Devon chuckled. "He certainly made council meetings interesting. A principled man. Rare these days." He glanced around before continuing in a lower voice. "I understand you've taken over the store. If you ever decide it's not for you, there are plenty of interested parties. I'd be happy to make introductions."

I couldn't figure out why everyone cared so much about the future of a dusty general store. It wasn't Fort Knox.

Before I could respond, movement at my side caught my attention. Kansas and Frannie were making their way past, murmuring polite apologies as they squeezed between the chairs. Kansas brushed a little too close to Devon, and for the briefest second, the two men locked eyes, something sharp and unsaid passing between them. Devon's smile stayed fixed, but his jaw tightened ever so slightly. Kansas gave a clipped nod before steering Frannie toward the exit, his hand firm at her back.

Callie appeared at my elbow. "Mom, we should head back. Des might be getting anxious with no one around."

I excused myself, grateful for the interruption. As we neared the exit, Sean fell into step beside us.

"Quite the sales pitch," he commented. "Devon's good. Makes open pit mining sound like planting a community garden."

"You know something about mining?" I asked.

"I've spent a lot of time around mining companies. If you ever want another perspective, I'm around."

"I'll think about it," I said, surprised by the offer—and by how easily he met my gaze. But I still couldn't shake the image of him looking angry enough to hit my father.

Outside, the evening air was crisp and clear after the stuffy meeting room. Callie kept a quick pace to get us back home, but something made me pause and look back.

Through the community centre windows, I could see Devon and Mayor Bugle in close conversation, their expressions far less genial than they had been minutes before. The mayor gestured sharply, and Devon's response, though I couldn't hear it, carried unmistakable tension.

Whatever partnership existed between them, it wasn't as smooth as their public performance suggested.

Dad's house felt eerily quiet when we returned, despite Des's enthusiastic greeting. She circled us with wiggling excitement, her tail swishing like a metronome on caffeine.

"At least someone's happy to see us," Callie said, kneeling to ruffle Des's ears. The dog leaned into her touch, eyes half-closing in contentment.

I hung my jacket on the hook by the door, my mind still replaying fragments of the town hall meeting. "Devon Fontaine certainly came prepared."

"Prepared with a truckload of corporate nonsense," Callie snorted. She yanked open the fridge. "Think anyone actually believed that an open pit mine would be good for tourism? 'Come see our giant hole in the ground! Take pictures of our dirt piles!'"

"Some did," I admitted, filling the kettle. "Sounds like there are more than a few people here struggling to make ends meet. Jobs sound appealing when you're worried about paying bills."

Des padded over, pressing her nose against my leg. I reached down automatically to give her a quick pat, more for my comfort than hers. Joe's suggestion that I take her had triggered all my old hesitations, but knowing this was Des's home, watching us with those expectant eyes—I felt I was doing the right thing.

"The mayor was eager to have Grandpa's memorial," I said, changing the subject as I threw tea bags into the pot. "Almost pushy about it."

Callie closed the fridge and leaned in. "He's just ticking boxes, right? 'Express condolences, tick. Get memorial over with, tick. Move on to mining profits, tick.'"

"Maybe," I said, unconvinced. "Or maybe they're in a hurry to declare Dad officially gone."

"Because of the store?"

I shook my head. "I'm not sure. Something doesn't add up."

Des suddenly trotted to the hallway leading to Dad's study, looking back at me with hopeful eyes. When neither Callie nor I moved, she gave a soft whine.

"I think she's trying to tell us something," Callie said. "Either that or she's found where Grandpa hid the dog treats."

I followed Des into the study, a room I'd been avoiding since we arrived. Dad's presence lingered here most strongly—his reading glasses still perched on a stack of books, a half-filled coffee mug alongside them. Papers were arranged in neat piles across the desk, typical of his methodical nature.

Des nudged a lower desk drawer with her nose.

"What is it, girl?" I murmured, kneeling beside her. The drawer was locked.

Callie appeared in the doorway. "What's she found?"

"A locked drawer," I replied, running my fingers along the edge. "I don't suppose you've come across any keys?"

Callie shook her head. "I'm still trying to figure out where the light switches are."

A memory surfaced: me and Dad in this very room years ago, him showing me where he kept important things. "Wait," I said, standing to examine the row of books on the shelf above the desk. I pulled out a weathered copy of *Never Cry Wolf* and carefully opened it. Inside, a section had been cut out, creating a small cavity where a single key rested.

"No way," Callie whispered. "That's straight out of a movie.

Next, you'll tell me there's a secret passage behind the bookcase."

"Dad always said the best hiding place is something personal that others wouldn't think to check," I said, taking the key. It fit the drawer perfectly.

Inside lay several nondescript folders, a small notebook, and some loose papers, all covered with Dad's meticulous handwriting. Resting on top of the papers was a beat-up rubber ball—faded, scuffed, and chewed on one side. Des's ears perked, and she nudged it once with her nose before sitting beside me.

"Think he left that for her?" Callie asked quietly.

"I think he left it so she'd find this."

Des flopped beside me with a sigh, the rubber ball tucked neatly between her front paws, as I opened a folder. Inside were newspaper clippings, photocopies of old documents, and handwritten notes about Samuel Melvin and the town's founding.

"What is all this?" Callie asked, leaning in over my shoulder.

"Research," I said, scanning the notes. "Dad was digging into something about the town, but it's not clear what. These look like bits and pieces."

The kettle beeped from the kitchen, letting us know it had come to the boil.

"I'll get it," Callie offered, and Des followed her out.

I spread the papers across the desk, trying to find a pattern. Dad's notes were methodical but disconnected, like puzzle pieces without the picture on the box. One page was marked "missing from archives" and another said "check mineral rights transfer." There were references to old town council meetings, but no clear thread to tie them all together.

Whatever he'd been investigating, it had been serious

enough to make him cautious. But without the rest, I couldn't see what had made him so wary.

I gathered the papers, slipping them back into the drawer, and went to the kitchen. Callie poured our tea and placed the pot on the trivet, sliding a red-and-white striped cozy over it to keep it warm.

"It looks like Dad was trying to piece something together," I said as she added milk to our mugs. "But either he didn't finish, or part of it's missing."

"Why would he hide it?" she asked, setting my cup in front of me.

"Maybe he found something he wasn't supposed to." I took a sip as Callie scrolled through her phone.

"So how's the new blog doing?" I asked.

Her eyes lit up. "Better than I thought! It's been shared a few times—one of them must've had a big following. It's over 250 subscribers, and the site's had more than three times that in visits since it went live."

I wasn't sure I fully grasped what that meant, but her excitement made it sound like good news.

"I posted a few shots from the town hall. It's already got a few dozen comments. Look."

She turned her phone toward me. Most of the comments echoed what we'd already heard from the crowd.

"What's that flashing circle at the top?" I asked, pointing.

"Oh—hang on, I got a DM." A few taps later, her expression shifted. "Mom... is that...?"

I stood and leaned over her shoulder. The photo had been taken at night. It showed a large, dark SUV idling at the bottom of the store's driveway. The brake lights glowed red, exhaust puffing faintly in the cool air. A man stood on the passenger side, duffel bag in hand, caught mid-motion before climbing in.

I leaned closer, heart thudding.

"What are you trying to see?" Callie asked.

"His face."

She zoomed in—and there he was.

"That's Grandpa," she whispered.

I nodded. "Where did this come from?"

"Through the blog. No name, no message. Just a random string of letters for the email address."

I studied the image again, noting the angle. "It's taken from down the street. Probably near Mandy's bakery."

"Look at the timestamp," Callie said softly.

May 23. 1:07 a.m. Just hours before Dad's supposed canoe trip.

"Why would he be getting into someone's car that late?" she asked.

A chill crept over me. "I'm starting to think he never went on that canoe trip at all." Des took her usual spot beside me, wordless and warm.

"But we don't know that," Callie said, frowning at the image. "He could've come back later and left then."

"Look closer," I said. "What's missing from the driveway?"

She squinted. "His truck. It's gone."

"Exactly. And he's holding a packed bag. He doesn't look like he's heading out for a paddle."

Callie stared at the screen. "He looks... worried."

I took a breath, letting the pieces settle in my mind. His canoe recovered without supplies, the push for a memorial, the pressure around the store—it all pointed to something bigger.

"The RCMP missed something," I said, standing. The weight of uncertainty gave way to clarity. "Dad's not just missing. Something spooked him, and he left fast."

"We need to tell Uncle Jason."

I shook my head. "Not yet."

"Why not?"

"Because he's RCMP and family. His colleagues will think he's chasing ghosts if he pushes this with no proof. We need something solid."

"But this is—"

"Close," I said. "But not enough. Even you said it—he could've come back."

Des stood, alert beside me. For the first time since arriving in Balsam Bay, I felt a steady sense of purpose—the same instinct that had carried me through countless search and rescue operations.

"So then, what do we do?" Callie asked.

"We find the truth."

She emailed me the photo. I studied it again, and the unease that had been building finally solidified into something sharper.

"I think Dad found something," I said slowly. "Something that made the wrong people nervous."

"Like what?"

"I'm not sure yet. But if it ties back to the mine... it might explain why he hid his notes."

Callie was quiet for a moment. "And you think that's what made him leave?"

"Maybe." I glanced at the image again. "If Dad is still alive, he's counting on us to figure this out."

I didn't say the other possibility out loud. I couldn't.

"Then we make sure whoever's responsible doesn't get away with it," Callie said, her voice firm.

Des gave a quiet woof, as if in agreement. In the quiet of Dad's study, we stood shoulder to shoulder. Not just grieving anymore. Ready.

A search and rescue mission of a different kind.

Since Jason first told me about the canoe, I'd been drifting. But now, I had direction. Dad wasn't careless. He was deliberate. Thoughtful. Prepared.

If he'd vanished, there was a reason.

And I was going to find it—whatever it took.

CHAPTER SIX

I slept badly, tossing through dreams full of shadowy SUVs and glimpses of Dad's face staring in through windows. At some point during the night, Des climbed up onto the bed and curled at my feet. She didn't ask permission, just climbed up like she'd always belonged there. Every time I jerked awake from another dream, she shifted a little closer, like she could feel the unrest in my head.

By the time the sky began to lighten, I'd made up my mind. The photo had changed everything—but it didn't offer answers, just new questions. Maybe Dad had gone paddling after all and something went wrong—he could've slipped on wet rock, capsized near the falls, or misjudged the current. It happens, even to experienced paddlers. Or maybe someone had gone after him during the trip. Hurt him. Hid what they'd done.

But now, a third possibility had crept in—one I couldn't shake. Maybe he never made it to the lake. Maybe someone forced him to leave, and the canoe was just for show. Getting into that SUV didn't mean he was safe. Maybe that's where the real danger began.

I didn't know what had happened that night, but I knew where I had to start looking.

That photo was our first real lead, and Sean Patrick made the most sense to start with. He'd found the canoe, and there was that argument with Dad that Bertha had mentioned. I couldn't ignore the fact that he was the first person to find evidence of the accident.

By the time I came downstairs, I had a plan. Des followed close behind, tail wagging like she approved of the mission.

Callie was on the porch, wrapped in one of Walter's flannel shirts with her coffee and laptop. Funny how fast a routine can sneak up on you. A few days in, and this already felt like the way mornings had always been.

"No word from our anonymous tipster," she said without looking up. "But I did fall down a geology rabbit hole."

"Anything else useful?" I caught the way she stared at the blog stats a little longer than necessary. Like she was watching numbers when what she really wanted was answers.

"Not really. I found a couple of geology articles under Sean Patrick's name—some fieldwork in Australia and South America. Nothing shady, at least on the surface."

She paused, thumb flicking across her screen. "But here's the weird part—I can't find a single mention of that reality show Bertha talked about. No cast lists, no clips, no snarky blogs. And believe me, the internet never forgets... unless someone gives it a reason to."

I raised an eyebrow. "You think it was deliberate?"

"If it wasn't," she said, "it's the first reality show in history that didn't leave a digital footprint."

She took a long sip of coffee. "So—what's the plan for

today? Chasing down leads? Charming the locals? Wearing down Bertha with relentless optimism?"

"I'm going to talk to Sean," I said. "Directly. No games."

Callie raised an eyebrow. "You think that'll work?"

"Probably not. But at least I'll get to see how he reacts when I push."

"I could come as backup. Pretend to be engrossed in my phone while secretly recording everything…"

I smiled. "Tempting, but I think this needs to be one-on-one. Besides, someone needs to help Bertha with the store."

"Fine," Callie sighed. "But if you're not back in two hours, I'm sending a search party. Or at least Des."

"Speaking of—" I looked around. "Where is she?"

At the sound of her name, Des padded out from the kitchen and nosed her way onto the porch, tail giving a hopeful little swish.

"I think she's hungry," Callie said, setting her mug down.

"Yeah, good call." I retrieved the canvas bag Joe gave us, and found the kibble and scoop. "Here you go, girl."

Des waited politely until I set the bowl down, then ate like she was trying to impress a panel of judges. The routine tugged at something familiar—muscle memory from my days with Lucy. It didn't hit the same raw nerve it used to. Not quite.

"If Bertha asks where I am, just tell her I've gone to talk to Jason about Dad's affairs."

Callie's head snapped up. "Why can't you tell her?"

"Because she'll ask seventeen follow-up questions, and I'd rather avoid an inquisition this morning."

"Nope," Callie said, standing. "I am not doing your dirty work. You want to fib to Bertha Wise, you go right ahead. I am not getting caught in the middle."

I stared at her, hands on my hips. "It's not even a real lie."

"She's the closest thing we have to a human polygraph. I'm

not getting grilled over a half-truth. You're on your own, Mom."

I sighed, already dreading it. "Fine. I'll go."

"Good luck," Callie called after me, way too cheerfully. "Take Des. She can act as moral support, or a distraction. Maybe both."

I stepped into the store, Des at my side. Bertha was behind the counter, sorting a stack of receipts with terrifying efficiency. She glanced up and narrowed her eyes.

"You don't look like you're ready to work."

"Good morning to you, too," I said. "I'm heading out to talk to someone."

Her brow arched. "This wouldn't be related to a certain geologist, would it?"

I blinked. "How—"

"I know you, Matilda," she said simply. "And this town doesn't do secrets very well."

Fair point.

"I just need a few hours," I said. "Callie's working on the blog, then she'll be in to give you a hand."

"Give me a hand—?" Bertha shook her head like she couldn't believe what she'd just heard. "I've already restocked the jam display, wrangled the credit card machine back into working order, and smacked the coffee machine—twice. I think I can manage."

I shrugged. "I can tell her not to come. She'd probably love more time to work on her blog—"

"You'll do no such thing. I was simply pointing out that I can manage on my own. It would be good for her to get away from those screens for a while."

I turned to leave, but Bertha's voice stopped me.

"Before you go..."

I paused, turning back to find her watching me with that

sharp, unblinking look that always made me feel like a kid caught sneaking cookies.

"Anyone with any sense could see that Walter's accident doesn't make sense."

I raised an eyebrow.

"Your father had been digging deeper into old town records lately," Bertha said, not looking up as she straightened some papers behind the register. "More than usual, I mean. Always asking if I remembered specific council meetings from years ago, or who voted which way on particular land transfers."

"That sounds pretty detailed, even for Dad."

"It was. Walter always cared about town business, but this was different. More... focused. Like he was trying to prove something specific."

I let that sink in. "And you didn't think to mention this before?"

Bertha gave me a look. "Last time I saw you, it was the morning after your high school graduation. You walked in here with your bags packed, so eager to race off to that summer job up north before university started, you barely said goodbye. You couldn't wait to leave, and you never looked back. Not once. We haven't seen you in this store again until now, all these years later. How was I supposed to know who was walking through that door after twenty-odd years?"

I stared at the floor. I couldn't look her in the eye. She wasn't wrong, and I wasn't proud of it. "You know how hard it was for me after mom died," I countered.

"I did what I could, didn't I?" She asked it once, but the weight of it hung between us.

"You did," I said quietly.

"You were an obstinate, headstrong teenager. Up in everyone's business, always questioning things, always playing devil's advocate."

Bertha paused. When she resumed, her tone was gentler. Her volume soft. "And while most of the time I couldn't stand your cheekiness, I could see that it was simply your way of making sense of the world. You've always had a big heart, Matilda. And regardless of your bluster, all you were ever trying to do was get down to the roots of things and make them better. And I loved the bones of you because of it."

I finally struck up the courage to look at her then, and the tears I saw glistening in her eyes almost did me in.

"I'm sorry," I said. And I meant it.

Bertha nodded. "I'm glad you're here now." She went back to organizing her receipts. It took me a moment to compose myself.

I took a step toward the door, causing Des to pop up from her rest position. "I won't be long," I told Bertha. "I'll take over from you when I get back so you can have the afternoon off."

Bertha raised an eyebrow. "We'll see." Then she added, "Don't let a dimple fool you, Matilda. Plenty of charm in this town's been used for worse."

The Willow Cabin looked just like I remembered: one room, sturdy, with a little covered porch tucked in among the trees at the quieter end of Loon Lake. Back in high school, it had a bit of a reputation as the go-to party spot when the owners were out of town. I was never cool enough to show up—not when my idea of a good time involved solo hikes and survival manuals instead of music and cheap beer. Most people didn't quite know what to do with a girl who preferred the backcountry to a bonfire.

Sean's truck was parked off to the side. A decent mid-range model with shiny-new *Friendly Manitoba* plates. Nothing flashy, nothing beat-up. Looked like a vehicle you could trust to get you through a logging road without falling apart.

Des trotted beside me, relaxed but alert, like she was on the job. We reached the porch just as I heard running water inside, then footsteps. I knocked.

"Just a sec!" Sean's voice called out.

The water shut off. A few beats later, the door opened.

Sean stood there in jeans and a faded UBC T-shirt, hair still damp, like he'd just rinsed off the sleep. His eyes widened, then dropped to Des like she might explain my presence.

"Tilly," he said. "And Walter's dog. Morning."

"Hope I'm not catching you at a bad time," I said, glancing past him at the breakfast dishes still on the table.

"Not at all. Just getting going." He rubbed the back of his neck and gestured vaguely at his damp hair. "Coffee?"

"Sure," I said. And despite everything—despite why I was here—I meant it.

"Come in. Sorry about the mess." He stepped back to let us in.

It wasn't messy, really. The bed was made, the little kitchenette looked wiped down, and most of the clutter was of the professional variety: papers, books, a few chunks of rock scattered across the table. His laptop was shut. A neat line of hiking boots sat under the window. If anything, the space had the quiet hum of someone who worked alone and liked it that way.

Sean moved to the coffeepot, and I took in the place while Des sat politely near the door, observing.

"Sugar? Milk?" he asked, cracking the fridge.

"Milk, please."

"She's well-trained," he said, nodding toward Des as he handed me a mug.

"Seems Dad put a lot of time into her."

We stood there in that odd pause that happens sometimes,

where both people are waiting for the other to speak. I sat down at the table. Sean shuffled a few pages into a folder, not quite hiding it, but definitely not showcasing it, either.

"Working on something interesting?" I asked.

"Just notes from the field," he said, sliding the folder aside. "Nothing groundbreaking."

I took a sip of coffee, then decided to just go for it.

"I wanted to ask you about my dad."

His face shifted—slightly more careful. "I didn't really know him well. We only talked a handful of times."

"Including the time he recognized you from somewhere? I heard you weren't pleased about that."

Sean's cup froze halfway to his lips. A muscle in his jaw tightened briefly before he set the mug down with deliberate care.

"Ah," he said. "Bertha told you about that, I suppose."

"Was Dad right? Were you on a show?"

Sean sighed, running a hand through his damp hair. "It's not something I advertise. But yes, about six years ago, I took part in a reality competition show called *Survival of the Smartest*. Think *Survivor* with more snakes and academic posturing."

"That doesn't sound so embarrassing."

"It wouldn't have been, except I was edited to look like a complete fool." His expression darkened. "They took footage out of context, spliced comments to make me seem arrogant and clueless. I became the season's villain, then the laughing-stock when I failed a simple challenge."

The bitterness in his voice had the ring of truth. Still, I pressed on.

"And that's why you reacted so strongly when Dad recognized you?"

"You have to understand, the experience almost ruined

me," Sean said, a hint of defensiveness creeping in. "I couldn't land a project after that. Everyone in the industry recognized me as 'that guy from that show.' Your father found it hilarious, kept trying to remember specific embarrassing moments while I stood there."

I could picture it: Dad's innocent amusement colliding with Sean's raw humiliation. A perfect recipe for tension.

"Is that why you argued with him?"

Sean frowned. "We didn't argue. I left abruptly—rudely, I admit—but there was no argument."

"That's not how Bertha described it."

"Bertha wasn't there for the whole interaction." Sean set his mug down with a little too much force, causing coffee to slosh over the rim. "Look, I was embarrassed and reacted poorly. I apologized to Walter the next time I saw him, and he was gracious about it. End of story."

I watched him closely, trying to read beyond his words. His discomfort felt genuine, but there was something else there. Something he wasn't saying.

"Funny thing," I said, keeping my tone casual. "Callie tried to look up the show. Couldn't find a thing—no clips, no cast list, not even a snarky forum thread."

Des shifted, just a little. Not a growl, not even a warning—just the subtle, alert posture that meant she was listening harder than I was.

Sean blinked. "Really?"

"Seems odd," I said, studying him. "The internet usually clings to that kind of embarrassment like a burr on hiking pants."

He gave a short laugh, but it didn't reach his eyes. "Well, maybe I finally caught a break."

Des hadn't moved, but I noticed she was watching him intently, head tilted. Not tense, just... tuned in.

"So," I said, "you just happened to find my dad's canoe while doing fieldwork?"

His face softened. "Yeah. I just wish it hadn't been under those circumstances."

I kept my expression neutral. "Were you out there looking for something specific?"

"Just rock formations. The river cut through some exposed layers I wanted to check out."

"Do you think it was an accident?" I asked.

Sean looked me straight in the eye. "Isn't that what everyone thinks?"

I didn't answer that.

"My dad was an experienced paddler," I said instead. "He wouldn't have gone near enough to those falls for it to be an issue."

"I believe that," Sean said. "He struck me as the type who triple-checks everything."

We sat in silence for a beat. The wall clock ticked. Des exhaled a soft dog sigh.

"I get that you're trying to make sense of what happened," Sean said. "But I'm not sure I'm much help. I barely knew him."

"Did you and Dad ever talk about the mine?"

His gaze flickered, almost imperceptibly. "He asked me once if I knew anything about the original geology reports. Stuff from when it first opened. I told him I didn't."

"Didn't that strike you as a little odd?"

"Not really. With all the talk of reopening it, I figured he was just curious."

"But he wasn't just curious, was he?"

Sean didn't answer right away. He ran a finger along the rim of his mug, considering his next words.

"He seemed... concerned. About the town council rushing things through. Asked if I'd seen any of the environmental impact studies." Sean's eyes met mine. "I told him I wasn't involved in that part of the process."

"What process?"

Sean's mouth tightened. "Figure of speech. I meant I'm here for the geology, not politics."

"Yet you're attending town meetings about the mine. Sitting in on presentations."

"Professional interest," he countered quickly. "Wouldn't you?"

I leaned in a little. "How well do you know the Bugles?"

Sean's answer came a little too fast. "Barely at all. The mayor welcomed me when I got here, that's it."

Des stood up suddenly, ears perked. A second later, I heard the crunch of tires on gravel outside.

Sean went to the window. "Expecting someone?"

"I was going to ask you the same thing."

A pickup pulled in beside his. The driver stayed in the cab. No company logo. Just a dusty brown truck with tinted windows.

"Delivery," Sean said quickly. "Field equipment."

But he didn't go out to meet them. Didn't even open the door. Just stood there, hands on his hips like he was waiting for me to leave first.

I checked my watch. "I should get going. Bertha's probably plotting my downfall as we speak."

Sean didn't argue.

Outside, it was full-on summer. Warm air, birdsong, sun glinting off the lake like nothing was wrong in the world.

Sean stood on the porch, hands on his hips. "Walter was well-liked. I hope you get the answers you're looking for."

His tone was soft, but the words felt pre-packed—like something he'd decided to say before I even walked through the door.

"I hope so, too," I said.

Des and I turned down the path. I glanced back just once, in time to see the delivery driver step out of the truck. Tall guy, ball cap low over his eyes. Something about the whole setup made me pause. Probably nothing, even so, my gut prickled.

"What do you think, Des?" I muttered. "Is he hiding something?"

Des didn't answer, just gave me that look of hers. Watchful. Knowing.

I stared down the trail as we walked.

I wanted to believe he was just a guy with a past and a rock hammer, but that delivery driver was sketchy. And Sean didn't want me to see what was in that folder of his.

And Des? Des was still watching the cabin long after we'd left it behind.

Back in town, everything had snapped to life. Brooms out, bakery line curling past the door. Someone had a radio playing classic country nearby, the kind of song that made you hum along without realizing.

"Tilly!" Mandy called from her bakery stoop. "Got a sec?"

I crossed over, Des at my side.

"Morning. How's it going?"

"Booming. Your daughter's a social media miracle worker. Maple butter tarts are flying off the shelves."

I grinned. "Callie does have a knack."

Mandy smiled, but her expression softened as she lingered. "She mentioned you were trying to piece together what your dad was up to before the accident."

My breath hitched just slightly. "Yeah. Trying."

Mandy shifted, lowering her voice. "I don't know if this

helps, but... your dad was in here a lot those last few weeks. Always at the same table, papers spread out, scribbling notes. He didn't chat much. Just... focused."

"Focused how?"

"Not upset or anything. Just focused. Like he was racing the clock to solve something."

A knot tightened in my chest. That sounded like Dad—chasing a finish line only he could see.

"Thanks, Mandy."

She handed me a warm paper bag. "Croissants. One's for you, one's for her." She nodded at Des.

Des perked up, clearly understanding her name and the scent of baked goods.

As we headed back to the store, my phone buzzed with a text from Callie: *Bertha is NOT happy. Says you're gallivanting while she's 'the only one keeping your father's store running.' Her words, not mine. Also, Kansas called. Again. Wants to meet about a 'generous offer' for the store.*

I groaned. Of course he did.

But now things were starting to line up. Dad had been looking for something—something hidden. And someone had made sure it stayed that way.

Des nudged my hand.

"Yeah, I know," I said softly. "We're getting closer."

The store came into view, green facade and all. Through the window, I saw Bertha holding court, giving directions to a stock boy with one hand and the till with the other.

The bell announced me as I pushed open the door.

"I'm back, Bertha."

She didn't even look up. "Didn't think you'd be gone this long."

"Sorry, I ran into Mandy on my way back."

Bertha's sharp gaze flicked to the paper bag in my hand.

"Mm-hm. Delivery's come. Boxes are in the back. You get the high shelves."

I smiled. "Sounds good."

As I turned to go, she added, "And Matilda?"

I glanced back. "Yeah?"

"Don't drop a box on your head. I can't spare time for hospital runs today."

A laugh bubbled up before I could stop it. "Noted."

I grabbed a box and headed for the shelves, still smiling. It felt good to be useful again.

CHAPTER SEVEN

The *Balsam Bay Gas & Service* looked like it had fallen asleep in the sun. A fly buzzed lazily near the office window, and somewhere behind the garage, classic rock played on—low, familiar, and probably from an era before it had earned the word 'classic.' The scent of gasoline, hot asphalt, and motor oil hung in the air, mingling with the sticky-sweet scent of sun-faded evergreen air fresheners someone had wedged in the window frame years ago.

The lot itself was empty, no customers at the pumps, no cars lined up for service. It was the kind of stillness that made me understand why Gus wanted that Canada Post contract so badly. Regular mail traffic might be the only steady heartbeat this place ever saw in the off-season, when cottagers weren't constantly needing their boat motors fixed or their ATVs tuned up.

I'd only meant to walk to the bank machine at the drugstore, but when I saw Gus hunched over the hood of a pickup, I veered across the road without letting myself think too much about it.

"Hey, Gus," I called out as I stepped over a patch of oil-stained gravel that had probably been absorbing spills since before I was born.

He looked up, startled, and gave a squint that might've passed for a smile in a place with less harsh sunlight. "Tilly. Didn't hear you coming."

"Still have ninja reflexes," I said. "Even in hiking boots."

He gave a soft grunt of amusement and wiped his hands on a rag that was doing a terrible job of staying clean.

"Mind if I grab a root beer?" I asked, nodding toward the convenience room. "This heat's brutal." My shirt was already sticking to the small of my back, and it wasn't even noon yet.

"Go ahead. Cooler's stocked." He pointed with a wrench.

I pushed open the glass door, greeted by a blast of air conditioning like a cold washcloth. I pulled open the humming cooler, the glass fogging instantly from the humidity I'd brought in with me. The root beers were right where they always were, third shelf from the top. I grabbed two, letting the heavy door swing shut with a satisfying thunk.

When I returned to the garage bay, Gus had his head buried deeper under the hood, muttering something that sounded like a mix of prayers and curses. I twisted the caps off both bottles, the metal edges digging into my palm as they gave way with twin hisses.

"Peace offering," I said, holding one out.

Gus emerged from the engine compartment, a smudge of grease on his forehead that made him look like he'd been marked for something ominous. He looked surprised at the second bottle, but took it with a nod of thanks.

"So, what's the diagnosis?" I asked, leaning against the truck's fender and peering into the engine bay. My dad had taught me the basics when I was a teenager—enough to get myself out of a jam on the back roads if I needed to. Which, more than once, I had.

Gus took a long swig of his root beer, his Adam's apple bobbing as he swallowed. "Flooded engine. Again. Third time this month. Keeps holding the gas pedal down when he starts it, then wonders why it sputters out."

"Let me guess. Gary Swain?"

"How'd you know?" He raised an eyebrow, the grease mark shifting with the movement.

"Dad used to call him the 'Rain Man of bad driving habits.'" I smiled at the memory, the taste of root beer suddenly sweeter. "Once watched him stall three times, pulling out of the store lot. Dad said Gary was the only man he knew who could flood an engine in a drought."

That earned me a genuine chuckle from Gus, a low, rusty sound like a seldom-used door hinge. "Your dad had a way with words. Never met a man who could insult you so well you'd thank him for it."

I set my bottle down on the workbench and reached into the engine bay, pointing to the air filter that was specked with tiny black dots of old oil. "Mind if I take a look? Dad showed me a trick once for these old engines when they get temperamental."

Gus hesitated, then stepped back with a sweeping gesture. "Be my guest. Just don't tell Gary I let someone else touch his precious truck. Man thinks vehicles have feelings."

I rolled up my sleeves and leaned in, the familiar smell of oil and metal triggering a cascade of memories: Dad's patient hands guiding mine as I held a wrench for the first time; the row of tools arranged on the garage wall at home, each with its own shadow painted behind it; the sound of his off-key whistling as he worked. I removed the air filter casing, inspecting it with more confidence than I truly felt.

"When Bertha mentioned you brought Dad's truck back from the launch point that day, it reminded me of all the times he'd show me what was under its hood," I said, keeping my voice casual even as I watched Gus's face for any reaction.

Gus glanced at me, but didn't miss a beat. "Yeah. Jason called me to move it once the site was cleared." He bent to adjust something near the fan belt. "Your dad kept that thing running like a Swiss watch. Never seen a man so religious about maintenance schedules."

I nodded, filing away the fact that he hadn't even paused when I mentioned Bertha. No flicker of surprise. Almost like he'd been waiting for that one.

"Here," Gus said, handing me a wrench, his fingers grease-stained against the metal. "Try loosening this. Quarter turn, no more."

I took it, feeling the weight settle comfortably in my palm, and bent to adjust the distributor cap the way Dad had taught me. The metal was hot from sitting in the sun, and I had to be careful not to burn my fingers. "You saw him that week, right? Before he went missing?"

Gus reached past me to adjust something else, his hands moving with practiced efficiency, each motion economical like he'd done it a thousand times before. "Came by for a clamp for his canoe rack," he said after a moment. "Wanted everything 'shipshape,' he said."

"That sounds like him," I said, stepping back to wipe sweat from my forehead with the back of my arm, careful not to smear any grease on my face. "Always ready for anything."

Gus grabbed a rag and cleaned some grime off a spark plug, his movements precise. "Joked that I'd have to be Bertha's on-call handyman while he was on his trip."

I smiled, despite myself, and reached for a socket wrench hanging on the nearby pegboard. The metal was cool from being in the shade. "Did Kansas ever help you out here?" I asked, gesturing around the garage with the tool. "Seems like the type who'd want to get his hands dirty once in a while. For the authentic small-town experience." What I really wanted to know was how friendly the two of them had been. Mandy had mentioned they'd caught a beer together now and then—but how far did that friendship go?

Gus snorted, the sound somewhere between amusement and derision, and handed me a socket that fit perfectly over the bolt I was eyeing. "Once. Thought WD-40 was magic in a can. Sprayed it on everything, including himself. Got grease in his eyebrows, ruined a hundred-dollar shirt. Whined about it for a week."

"Hold this?" I passed him back a part we'd removed, our hands briefly meeting in the exchange, his rough skin a stark contrast to mine. I noticed a thin scar running along the palm of his hand, pink and puffy in the light. "Hard to picture you and him hanging out."

"We don't much anymore." Gus tightened something I couldn't see, muscles in his forearm flexing with the effort. There was a tattoo peeking out from under his rolled-up sleeve —some kind of geometric pattern, faded from years in the sun. "He got ideas. Big ones. Didn't want to be seen with a guy with dirt under his fingernails."

I picked up a bottle of engine cleaner from the workbench, studying the label with its warnings about skin contact and flammability. "So when he started chasing the store, that didn't cause problems? With your Canada Post contract hopes, I mean."

Gus's movements slowed, but he didn't stop working. A bead of sweat trickled down his temple, leaving a clean trail through the dust on his skin. "No. That was all settled. If he got the store, I'd get the contract."

"Huh." I set the bottle down and reached for my root beer, taking a long drink. The sweetness cut through the bitterness in my mouth that had nothing to do with the beverage. "No conflict? No awkward overlap?"

"Nothing like that," he replied, his voice even as he reattached a hose with a soft click. The radio switched tracks, the volume nudging up just enough to feel like it was covering something.

With the engine reassembled, I stepped back, drinking the last of my root beer as Gus closed the hood with a solid thunk that seemed to echo across the empty lot.

"Try turning it over," he said, nodding to the driver's seat, which was visible through the open window, the leather cracked from years of sun exposure.

I slid behind the wheel, feeling the worn leather against my back, the seat hot even through my jeans. I turned the key, and the engine coughed once, twice, then roared to life with a satisfying rumble that vibrated up through the floorboards and into my bones.

"Not bad for a city girl," Gus said when I climbed out, the smallest hint of approval in his voice.

"Dad would be proud." I smiled, then glanced at my watch. "I should get going. Heard Frannie's been fussing over her tomato plants. Promised I'd share some of Bertha's canning tips with her."

Gus looked at me sharply, his eyes narrowing. "They'd be at the cabin."

"I figured." I kept my face neutral, though my pulse picked up at the confirmation.

He wiped his hands again, slower this time, like he was stalling. "Tilly..." He hesitated, then gave a small shake of his head, like whatever was on his mind was better left unsaid.

I gave him a long look, trying to read between the lines. "If there's something I should know, now's the time."

But Gus just offered a tired, thin-lipped smile that didn't reach his eyes, the corners crinkling with something that looked like regret. "See you around."

It was only a ten-minute walk to the McBrides' cabin, but the sun made it feel longer. The lake glittered through the trees in short, teasing flashes, and a group of dragonflies tangled above a patch of lupines near the path. I didn't have any canning secrets with me—that had been a convenient excuse—but Gus's quick tip-off and that strange, unfinished warning had nudged my curiosity into overdrive.

I was twenty yards from the cabin when I heard them. Not shouting exactly, but Kansas's voice carried, the words indistinct but the tone unmistakable: insistent, frustrated. Then Frannie's response, crisp and clipped. By the time I reached the edge of their property, silence had fallen.

The cabin itself was charming—all weathered cedar and wide windows—but what caught my eye was the enormous outdoor kitchen that dominated the back deck, visible from the side path. Kansas was there, fussing with dials on a stainless steel monster of a grill, while Frannie stood with arms crossed, her wide-brimmed straw hat throwing her face into shadow.

"Well, I hope you kept the receipts—" I heard Frannie say before Kansas spotted me and his face transformed, irritation melting into a practiced smile.

"Look who's here!" he called, waving a metal spatula like a conductor's baton. "The keeper of commerce herself!"

Frannie pivoted, her posture shifting from rigid to welcoming so quickly it was almost comical. "Tilly! What perfect timing." She hurried down to meet me, brushing at invisible dirt on her pristine linen skirt. "We're just about to have lemonade."

"Lucky me," I said, climbing the steps. "Wasn't sure if you'd be home, but Gus mentioned you two were around."

She hesitated just a beat before recovering with a gracious smile. "We're trying to soak in as much lake time as we can." Her eyes flicked briefly to Kansas. "This place is the best thing he's invested in all year."

Kansas's jaw tightened before his showman's smile reasserted itself. "Come see what I've been setting up," he boomed, gesturing me toward the deck. "State-of-the art. Imported from Germany."

Odd, I thought, as I followed them up. This house had been a rental forever, owned by an older couple in Brandon. The McBrides were acting like it was their place.

Kansas guided me to what could only be described as an outdoor chef's paradise—gleaming steel appliances, granite countertops, a pizza oven, and the centrepiece grill that looked like it could launch into orbit.

"Impressive," I said.

"Not for me, mind you," Kansas said, flipping open cooler lids to reveal marinating steaks that probably cost more than my weekly grocery budget. "Frannie here is the cook in our family. Isn't that right, darling?"

Frannie's smile tightened at the corners. "I've been trying to perfect my grilling technique." She turned to me, brightening artificially. "Let me get that lemonade. The heat is just dreadful today."

While Frannie disappeared inside, Kansas ran his hand lovingly over the grill's hood. "German engineering," he purred.

"Must have set you back."

"The best things in life aren't free, Tilly." He winked. "Speaking of which—"

"Kansas!" Frannie called from inside. "Your phone!"

He frowned, hesitating.

"It's Devon," she added, voice tight.

Kansas's expression shifted. "Excuse me. Business call." He patted the grill once more. "Make yourself comfortable."

Alone, I took stock. Everything was pristine, barely used. Price tags had been removed, but a folder labelled "Warranties" sat on a side table—alongside what looked like a financing statement, half-tucked beneath it. The corner peeked out, showing a bold due date circled in red. I glanced at the receipt: just shy of thirty thousand dollars.

Frannie emerged with a tray holding three glasses of lemonade, and caught me looking. "Kansas loves his toys," she said, setting the tray down. "And he always says I deserve the best."

I accepted a glass. "Must be nice." Before I could press further, Kansas strode back out, phone still in hand.

"Sorry about that. Devon's always calling with some crisis or another." He slipped the phone into his pocket. "Where were we?"

"I was admiring your outdoor kitchen," I said. "Quite the investment for a rental."

Kansas's laugh came a beat too late. "Well, funny story. We actually bought the place." He glanced at Frannie. "Well, finalizing next week. It took many months of wearing them down, but the Hendersons finally accepted our offer."

Frannie's fingers tightened around her glass, and her smile faltered just slightly. "Kansas didn't mention the paperwork had gone through," she said lightly, but her tone had a hairline crack.

"Congratulations," I said, noting Frannie's surprise. "Buying property is a big step."

"Speaking of property—" Kansas leaned against the counter, casual but calculating. "Let's talk about your father's store."

"Kansas," Frannie murmured, a warning.

"What? Just making conversation." He turned back to me. "I've got some new ideas," Kansas said, too quickly. "Mixed-use development. Store on the bottom, condos above. It's practically guaranteed income—pre-sales alone could carry the whole thing."

He wasn't looking at me when he said it. He was looking past me, like trying to sell the idea to someone else. Or maybe to himself.

I sipped my lemonade. Tart and sugary. "I'm not here about the store, actually."

"No?" Kansas tilted his head, looking faintly disappointed.

"I'm here about my father."

The shift in atmosphere was subtle but immediate. Kansas suddenly became very interested in adjusting the grill temperature. Frannie set her glass down with a sharp clink.

"Such a shame about Walter," Frannie said, voice softening with practiced sympathy. "Have there been any... developments?"

"That's what I'm trying to determine," I said, keeping my tone light. "I'm curious where you both were early that morning. The day Walter left for his canoe trip."

Kansas's spatula paused mid-flip. "Early morning? I was probably still in bed. Why?"

"I'm just trying to piece together his last movements," I said, watching their reactions carefully. "Someone must have seen him before he left."

Kansas resumed his cooking with forced nonchalance. "I

was definitely asleep. Haven't been an early riser since my twenties."

"I was up," Frannie offered, swirling her lemonade. "I've been battling terrible insomnia this past year." She glanced at Kansas. "Remember? I made that early grocery run."

Kansas's brow furrowed momentarily before smoothing out. "Right, right. You brought back those pastries from the bakery."

She turned back to me. "I only remember because I ran into your dad the day before, and he mentioned he was heading out early the next day. I was jealous—I hadn't slept at all, and there he was planning a paddling trip at dawn."

"The thing is," I continued, "Walter was methodical. Careful. Not the type to make amateur mistakes on the water."

Kansas looked up sharply. "What are you suggesting, Tilly?"

"I'm not suggesting anything," I said evenly. "Just that someone or something might have intercepted him before he even reached his canoe that morning."

The sizzle of meat on metal filled the silence. Kansas's jaw worked as he flipped another steak.

"Are you asking if I had something to do with Walter's disappearance?" he finally asked, voice tight. "Because I've been nothing but supportive of your father, even when we disagreed."

"No accusations," I said calmly. "Just covering ground. Maybe it wasn't about confrontation. Maybe it was about opportunity, like someone with a vehicle pulling up at just the right time with the right kind of offer Walter couldn't refuse."

The steaks hissed as Kansas flipped them with unnecessary force. "I don't like what you're implying, Tilly."

My mind flicked, uninvited, to the anonymous photo Callie had received: Walter stepping into a black SUV. No proof, no explanation, just a whisper that something about his last hours didn't line up.

"Do either of you drive a black SUV?" I asked, as casually as I could.

Kansas's hand froze mid-flip. Frannie stepped forward, placing herself between us.

"Certainly not Kansas," she said, her tone light but eyes sharp. "He's absurdly attached to that old truck of his."

Kansas regained his composure. "While you only drive in luxury, isn't that right, my dear?"

Something flickered across Frannie's face—annoyance, maybe concern—before she smoothed it away. "If you're wondering about black SUVs," she said, her hand gliding once, deliberately, down the front of her skirt, "you might try Devon. He's the one who breezes into town like he's scouting a movie set."

Kansas shot her a narrow look but kept his mouth shut, focusing instead on the steaks.

"Devon Fontaine?" I asked, tilting my head.

"Speaking of Devon—" Frannie started, but Kansas cut her off.

"Devon's an opportunist," he said, pressing a steak with his spatula, harder than necessary. Juices sputtered angrily on the grill. "He's tight with the Bugles. And he's got business partners in Winnipeg and Ontario who don't like slow money."

"Kansas," Frannie said, her voice taking on a warning edge.

He ignored her. "Tilly, I can't imagine how hard this is for you, but I'm starting to feel like you're looking to lay blame somewhere. I just want to let you know that as much as I think your father's store would be better off in my hands, I would never do anything to harm him."

The steaks were beginning to char. Frannie reached over to adjust the heat, but Kansas waved her off.

"In fact," he continued, "I've started speaking out, same as your father. Not many of us were willing to stick our necks out, but I've changed my mind about the mine."

I frowned. "Sorry, I don't follow."

"You want to talk about people with motives, Tilly, you should ask Devon. That guy's got his eye on the entire province. He wants to pave paradise and put up a lumberyard." Kansas chuckled at his own joke, but there was an edge to it. "He doesn't care about the mine itself, he just wants his logging permits approved faster. And backing the Bugles' push to reopen the mine gets him the political support he needs."

Frannie's phone chimed. She glanced at it, shoulders tensing. "That's the bank," she murmured to Kansas, who gave an almost imperceptible shake of his head.

"I think we've all had enough theories for one afternoon," Frannie said, her voice light but her posture rigid.

"It's not speculation if it's true," Kansas said, but he didn't press it.

Smoke began rising from the grill in earnest. The steaks were ruined.

Kansas swore under his breath. "Stupid German engineering," he muttered, shutting off the gas with a sharp twist. He took a long swig of lemonade, as if to wash away the bitter taste of failure.

I finished my glass and set it down carefully. "Thanks for the chat."

"You're leaving? But we haven't eaten," Frannie protested, her hospitality reflexes kicking in despite the tension.

"Another time," I said, already moving toward the steps.

Kansas followed, wiping his hands on a pristine apron that had clearly never seen a speck of food before today. "Just remember: progress waits for no one. Your dad understood that, even if he didn't say it outright."

Frannie trailed behind with a pleasant smile fixed in place, but as I reached the bottom step, she murmured, "Do let me know if you'd like a proper tour of the cabin sometime. And bring your appetite! There's that kitchen garden out back I'm quite proud of."

I smiled back. "Sounds lovely. I'll bring some of Bertha's canning tips next time."

I turned to go, then stopped. "Just one last thing, Kansas. Did you and Gus ever have any trouble between you?"

"Gus Bugle?" he asked, as if there might be another.

"Yeah. About the store. I heard he wanted the Canada Post contract. Figured if you bought the place, he'd lose his shot."

Kansas laughed under his breath. "No drama there. Gus and I already talked. If I got the store, the contract was his. That was the deal. I don't need to play postmaster, and he didn't want to run a full shop."

Frannie's phone chimed again. This time, Kansas's jaw tightened visibly.

I tilted my head. "So no friction?"

He shook his head. "If Gus had a problem with me, I'd know."

Out in the heat again, I tucked that entire exchange into a corner of my mind marked for further examination. Frannie was too smooth. Kansas was too eager. And despite all his talk about investment and progress, something about his financial situation didn't add up. The outdoor kitchen was a statement piece, but for whom? And neither one of them looked me straight in the eye when it counted.

As I walked away, I heard their voices rise again, Kansas's defensive, Frannie's cutting. Perfect house. Perfect setup. But the truth felt just out of reach.

CHAPTER EIGHT

I didn't expect to see Devon Fontaine at the bakery.

He didn't strike me as a butter tart kind of guy. Too slick. Too straight-backed and curated, like he was posing for an updated headshot in a quarterly shareholder report. But there he was at the counter, sleeves rolled just enough to look approachable, chatting with Sheila behind the till like it was a daily routine.

From the way she blinked at him and nodded too many times, I figured it wasn't.

The morning rush was in full swing: Walter's fan club occupied their usual table by the window, Mayor Bugle was holding court with two town councillors near the pastry case, and several tourists clustered around the specials board, pointing at Mandy's hand-lettered descriptions of maple cream scones.

"One pistachio, one chocolate," Devon said, pointing to the croissants. He turned when I walked in. "Tilly Lafleur," he said, like we were old friends catching up at a charity brunch. "I was hoping to run into you."

That made one of us.

I gave a polite nod and made a beeline for the sourdough shelf. Two round loaves left. I grabbed one while he followed at a careful distance. I could feel it—the way some people walk like they've been trained not to loom, but still manage to loom, anyway.

"Do you have a minute?" he asked, his tone dropping to something more confidential as we moved away from the counter.

We hovered near the pastry case until Sheila called out that my coffee was ready. I stepped up to grab it, hoping he'd take the cue and wander off. He didn't.

"I know you've been talking to people," he said, voice lower now. "About Walter. About what might've happened."

"That's not exactly a secret."

The bell above the door jangled as the mayor excused himself from his table and headed outside, pausing just long enough to catch Devon's eye in what looked like a pre-arranged signal. Devon gave a small nod before returning his attention to me.

"Great to see the store doing so well under your management," he said, suddenly louder, as if wanting to be overheard by the visor squad, who had gone suspiciously quiet. "Your father would be proud."

I took a slow sip of coffee, trying to reconcile this public performance with his hushed concerns of moments before. "Thanks."

He moved toward an empty table, gesturing for me to join him. As we sat, his phone buzzed. He glanced at it, then placed it face-down. "Sorry about that. Where were we?"

"You were about to tell me why my questions about my father make you nervous," I said, keeping my voice just low enough that the nearest tourists couldn't hear.

Devon's smile tightened faintly. "Not worried. Just... concerned you're putting pressure on yourself that may not lead anywhere useful."

Useful. That was a word with teeth.

The chatter patrol chose that moment to approach our table, Enid leading the charge with determined cheerfulness.

"Devon! Just the man we wanted to see about the summer festival sponsorship," she announced, effectively derailing our conversation.

Devon's transformation was seamless—from intense private discussion to community benefactor in the span of a heartbeat. "Ladies! I was just telling Tilly how much I'm looking forward to it."

As Devon fielded their questions about donation levels and signage placement, I caught something in his eyes—a calculated awareness that this interruption had saved him from my line of questioning. He played along enthusiastically, all while maintaining eye contact with me over Trish's shoulder, silently communicating that our conversation wasn't over.

When the trio finally retreated, satisfied with whatever promises they'd extracted, Devon leaned in again.

"I'd be happy to continue our discussion later," he said, sliding a business card across the table. "Perhaps somewhere more private."

The way he emphasized "private" carried a weight I couldn't quite interpret—invitation, warning—or both.

"I think they should be nervous," I said, pocketing his card.

"Who?"

"Whoever's trying to bury what happened to my father."

Devon's smile remained fixed, but something flickered in his eyes. Recalculation? He glanced around the bakery, noted who might be listening, then pitched his voice for my ears only.

"Are you accusing me of something, Tilly?" he asked lightly, like we were flirting at a dinner party.

I smiled, thin and flat. "Not yet."

He laughed again. "Fair enough."

Before he could respond, Mayor Bugle reappeared in the doorway, making a subtle gesture that drew Devon's attention immediately.

"Unfortunately, duty calls," Devon said, rising smoothly. "But my offer stands. When you're ready to have a real conversation about what's happening in Balsam Bay, you know where to find me."

As he made his way to the door, I noticed how the other patrons tracked his movement: some with admiration, others with wariness. Devon moved through the space like someone who had calculated the precise impression he wanted to leave on each person present.

He paused at the threshold, glancing back. "For what it's worth, I don't think you're wrong to ask questions. Just... maybe be careful how loudly you ask them."

"And maybe be careful who you try to silence."

He gave a low whistle. "Touché."

Then he was gone, striding away with Mayor Bugle like a man who'd just successfully planted a seed.

I sat there for a moment, the bustle of bakery business going on around me, and pulled out my phone. *Can you do a deep dive on Fontaine's company? Northern Prairie Lumber. Anything sketchy: fines, shell companies, lawsuits.*

Callie took less than a minute. *Check your inbox. Not a good look.*

I opened the document and scrolled through the kind of corporate grime that looks tidy until you turn on the lights. Environmental citations. Quiet settlements. Land rezoning done through third-party numbered companies and flipped for profit. One case from Swan River was particularly bad. Runoff from logging operations had contaminated part of the local creek. No formal charges, but the locals had protested for weeks. Nothing proven. Nothing clean.

I stood up, the sourdough in my tote suddenly feeling heavier than it should.

"Hey, Sheila?" I called toward the counter. "Would you mind holding this for me for a bit?"

She looked up from the espresso machine and nodded. "No problem. Everything okay?"

"Going to take a walk. Just need to clear my head."

I slipped my phone back into my pocket as I headed for the door, the chill in my chest lingering longer than it should have.

Just because something looks clean doesn't mean it is.

I took advantage of my morning off, walking a loop around the lake to shake off my run-in with Devon. By the time the coffee in my hand had gone lukewarm, I had decided I needed the comfort of a friendly face. Mandy's was becoming the kind of place for me where you could catch up without having to explain yourself first.

Inside, the lunch crowd was thinning, but the place still buzzed with low conversation and the scent of baked apples. The espresso machine hissed behind the counter, and someone was laughing in the back.

Mandy glanced up and caught my eye. She raised a brow and nodded at the coffee in my hand. "Coming for a refill?"

"Looking for something savoury to balance it out," I said, perching on one of the counter's bar stools. "And maybe a little quiet."

"You've got the wrong place for that," she said, but her

smile was soft. "How's Callie holding up?" Mandy asked, as she put an egg and cheese pastry on a plate and slid it toward me. "She's putting on a brave front, but you can tell she's running on fumes."

I nodded, unsure of what to say. Callie had always been strong-willed—but even strong-willed daughters miss their grandfathers.

"You know... " I said with a shrug.

Mandy nodded like she understood what I'd left unsaid and poured me a fresh cup of coffee.

"You look like you've been cornered."

"I was. Devon Fontaine. Right here, a while ago."

Mandy winced. "Let me guess. Polished, polite, and full of purpose?"

"He offered help. Twice."

"You going to take it?"

"I'm not going to not consider what angle he's working."

Mandy passed me the creamer. "You know he's got a reputation, right?"

"Who, Devon?"

Mandy nodded. "I assume you know he's filthy rich."

"So I've gathered."

"He grew up in northern Manitoba, moved to Quebec, made a name for himself in the lumber industry there, then moved back to Manitoba after his wife died. He bought that mansion of a cottage on Loon Lake about ten years ago."

"I didn't know he was a widow. I just assumed he was divorced."

Mandy rubbed at a nonexistent spot on the counter, ending with a flourish. "And that's where things get interesting."

"Oh, do tell!" I said, leaning in closer.

"Now remember, the rumour mill in small towns is at once the best way to find things out, and shouldn't be trusted."

"Says the woman dishing out the gossip."

Mandy blushed. "I just want to be clear this doesn't come from first-hand information or anything." She glanced around to see if anyone was listening in, then leaned a little closer, anyway. "The rumour is his wife didn't die of natural causes." She tilted her chin down, giving me a knowing look from beneath her lashes.

"What the heck does that mean?"

"A lumber rep from Ontario was here for a guys' weekend a few years back. He heard that Devon Fontaine lived here. Over beers one night, he told his friends that the behind-the-scenes talk out east is that Devon killed his wife."

I gave Mandy a skeptical glance. "That sounds like pure rumour."

She lifted a shoulder. "Maybe. But here's what people whisper—she was the clean-living type. Ran a wellness studio, brewed her own kombucha, all organic everything. Then one batch turned up laced with wildcrafted foxglove—the deadly kind. The official story was it was a tragic mix-up, but some folks think Devon knew just enough about her hobby to turn it into an opportunity."

I frowned. "That's awful."

Mandy's mouth tightened. "Yeah. And Devon? Didn't seem all that broken up about it. The studio was on the market within the week, and they were in Winnipeg before anyone even had a chance to drop off a casserole."

"I'm not particularly fond of the guy," I said, "but do you think that lumber rep might've just wanted to knock down his competition?"

"Maybe. But where there's smoke..."

I didn't know why Devon would want his wife dead—but if

he was capable of that, who's to say he couldn't make an old man disappear, too?

"You know," she said, quieter now, "you've got people talking."

"Figured as much."

"It's not everyone. Just murmurs." She leaned in on her elbows. "Some folks think you're stirring things up. Asking too many questions. Especially with Jason involved."

"They think I'm stepping on RCMP toes."

"They think you're stepping on your *brother's* toes. That's different."

I rubbed the back of my neck. "That's not what I'm trying to do."

"I know," she said. "And he probably does, too. But this town doesn't love a stirrer. Especially when the dust hasn't settled on your father's case, yet."

I nodded, trying to absorb her words without letting them settle like a weight in my chest.

Before I could say more, Enid, Nora, and Trish waltzed in.

"Speaking of gossip," Mandy muttered. She gave me a look and slipped into the kitchen, leaving me alone in the path of the incoming breeze.

"Tilly!" Enid beamed as she claimed the chair beside me. "Just the woman we were hoping to run into."

"Of course you were," I said, but it was too late. The ladies had settled in.

"We thought you might need a rescue earlier," Nora said, lowering herself onto the stool beside Enid. "That Devon fellow looked like he had you cornered."

"We thought we could give him a reason to wrap it up," Trish added, not quite sheepish.

I smiled, genuinely grateful. "It gave me a second to breathe, so thanks for that."

"Our pleasure," Enid said, giving Nora an encouraging pat on the shoulder. "Go on, tell her."

"We were out the other night," Nora said. "At *The Rusty Lantern*."

"Karaoke night," Trish added. "We never miss it."

"They call us the Balsam Belles," Enid said proudly.

"They don't," Nora muttered.

"Well they should! Anyway," Enid went on, "we had a perfect view of the back corner booth. Guess who we saw?"

I raised an eyebrow.

"Gus Bugle. With Kansas and Frannie," Trish said, as if announcing a royal sighting.

"They were tucked away, trying not to be noticed," Nora added, "but Gus isn't subtle when he's had a few."

"Which he had," Enid confirmed. "He was telling them something. A story, or a secret—it was hard to tell—but it got their attention. Kansas looked like he'd been slapped."

"Kansas got angry," Trish said. "He raised his voice. Gus leaned in like he was trying to hush him, but then he said something, loud enough for everyone nearby to hear."

"And that's when we heard it," Nora said, eyes wide. "Gus stuttered like a man trying to one-up someone's story. He told Frannie that Kansas was broke. Lost all his U.S. businesses. Barely a dime left to his name."

"Frannie went pale," Enid added. "You could see it. She had no idea."

"She stormed out," Trish finished. "Kansas on her heels. Gus stayed behind, but he looked like the ground had opened up beneath him. Like maybe he'd just realized what he'd done."

I sat back and let the pieces fall into place.

Gus spilling the truth. Kansas reacting. Frannie blindsided. The timeline made my skin itch.

Mandy emerged from the kitchen with a plate of lemon squares. "Ladies, my treat." She placed the plate in the middle of the group, leaning close enough to whisper in Tilly's ear as she did so. "Listening to these gossips won't help the wagging tongues," Mandy said. She straightened and gave me a wink as she left. A cautionary tale, but she didn't sound entirely serious.

The door opened, and as if summoned, Kansas walked in.

He looked tired and tightly wound, like a man whose morning hadn't gone to plan. His eyes found me fast.

"I need to talk to you," he said, loud enough that half the café turned their heads.

The walking club ladies froze, then scattered with a grace that only comes from years of eavesdropping. Kansas waited until they were gone before he spoke again.

"I gave Walter the paperwork weeks ago," he said, voice lower now, eyes darting toward the windows. "He had everything he needed to sign. We had an agreement—and I need to move forward."

"You seem awfully eager for a man without the means to pay for it."

His face turned a violent shade of red. "That's none of your business." He stepped forward, just a fraction. "You think you know everything," he said, low. "But you don't know what the actual truth is."

"So enlighten me."

But he turned before I got the last word out.

The café fell quiet. Mandy hustled over, wearing a look of concern. "You okay? I've never seen him like that before."

I looked over to the three ladies who stayed tightly grouped by the cream-and-sugar station, quietly discussing the show they just watched. Enid looked over at me and tilted her head as if to say, "See? We told you so."

"I think Gus and Kansas know something about my father, and they were in on it together," I said to Mandy. "And I think Frannie just found out."

Mandy nodded, but there was caution in her eyes. "And what are you going to do with that thought?"

I picked up my coffee again. "What Walter would've done." I answered. "Keep going."

CHAPTER NINE

I was halfway through my first cup of the day when Des nudged my knee with her nose.

"I know," I murmured. "Too early for people."

She wagged once and settled beside me on the porch, her head resting on my foot while I scribbled notes into my notebook.

Callie had managed to sweet-talk Bertha into letting her open the store this morning in exchange for getting the afternoon off. Half the town drops in for the morning rush with coffee and complaints, so Bertha was quick to say yes.

Callie said it was for the blog. I suspected it was the gossip she liked. For someone who rolled her eyes at rural life, she sure perked up whenever someone came in ranting about last night's raccoon incident, or debating whether Mandy's scones had changed since last summer.

I was glad she had something to focus on. Everyone has their own way of grieving, but if I was being honest with myself, I was a little worried about Callie. She'd been quiet after I told her about Dad's canoe being found near the falls—

concerned, yes, but she hadn't said much beyond that. Maybe she was still processing. Or maybe, like me, she was waiting to see if this was really as tragic as it seemed... or if there was more to the story.

Parenting didn't get any easier when they became adults, I thought. You just worried about bigger things.

A soft *boof* from Des pulled me out of my thoughts. Jason's truck eased into view at the end of the drive.

He stepped out looking like he hadn't slept more than a few hours, his shoulders squared in that I'm-not-tired posture I'd seen since we were kids. Des trotted down to greet him, and he gave her the kind of absentminded ear scratch he probably didn't even realize he reserved for dogs and toddlers.

"You're up early," he said, climbing the porch steps.

"Says the man who just rolled in from the station."

"It's been a few days, so I thought I'd check in before the day gets away from me."

That was Jason-speak for I couldn't sleep, so I made myself useful. I gave him a sideways look. "Any updates?"

"Nothing that makes sense." He rubbed the back of his neck. "Still waiting on some lab stuff, but no sign of foul play. Officially, it's still 'missing, presumed drowned.'"

"And unofficially?"

He let out a slow breath. "Unofficially, I think Walter was too stubborn to go that quietly."

That pulled a smile out of me. "You and me both."

I circled the top of my mug with a finger, unsure how to bring up the topic that needed to be aired. If the town whispers were saying I didn't think my brother was a good cop, not only could it drive a wedge between us as siblings, it could reflect badly on his career, and the local detachment as a whole.

In the end, it came out in a rush. "I just want to clear up something that's apparently making its way around town. I don't think the RCMP is doing a bad job, and I'm not trying to step on anyone's toes. Since the day you phoned to tell me Dad was missing, I knew in my heart this had to be more than just an accident. And the longer I'm here, the more sure of that I become."

I glanced at my brother. He sat in a brightly coloured metal chair, staring at the ground. I knew he was taking in every word, even though his face was a mask.

"What I'm trying to say is, I don't want you to be mad at me. The only thing I'm trying to prove here is what happened to Dad—nothing more."

We sat there for a moment, listening to the birds and the occasional plunk of water dripping from the eaves. Des flopped down at my feet again, her chin resting on her paws.

Jason stared at the ground. Then finally, "Look, Tilly... off the record? I get it. I can't say this out loud, and I definitely can't put it in a report, but you're not the only one who's wondering if the official story fits."

I said nothing. I knew better than to interrupt when Jason was wrestling with a truth.

"The detachment's already stretched. They ruled it accidental early on, and now I've got brass breathing down my neck to wrap it up neatly. Which means if something doesn't line up..." He shrugged. "It won't be the RCMP looking into it. Not officially."

"So you want me to keep going?"

"No," he said firmly. "I want you to stay out of it. But I know you won't."

"Not if it means figuring out what really happened."

He let out a sigh and gave a tiny shake of his head. "Just... promise me you'll keep it quiet. Stay under the radar. If you start kicking up dust in the wrong places, it's not just your safety I'll be worried about."

"I'll be careful," I said.

"That's what you said before you set Dad's woodshed on fire trying to smoke out a wasp nest."

"That was an accident."

"Exactly."

He stood and gave my shoulder a squeeze. "Call me if anything weird happens."

"Define weird."

"You'll know."

He turned to go, then paused. "Town social's this weekend. You planning on showing up?"

"Do people still dance to 'Boot Scootin' Boogie'?" I asked.

"Some things never change," Jason said with a half-smile. "Mandy mentioned they're looking for more contestants for the annual Perogy Palooza."

"They still do that?" I asked, memories drifting back of mothers and grandmothers competing with treasured family recipes while everyone pretended not to care who won.

"Bigger than ever. Sounds like a good place to observe people when they're relaxed."

I nodded slowly. "I'll think about it."

He didn't wait for a goodbye, just headed back to his truck with that long, steady stride that always made it look like he had some place urgent to be.

When the sound of his engine faded down the lane, I leaned back against the swing cushions and stared out at the tree line. The breeze was cool but hinted at the heat coming later. Somewhere in the distance, a woodpecker started up, its rhythmic tapping cutting clean through the morning quiet.

I reached for my notebook. Time to line things up.

I flipped to a blank page and wrote a single word at the top: *Suspects*.

Des gave a small sigh at my feet, like she was already unimpressed with my list. Her chin rested on the porch boards, eyes half-lidded but watchful. I tapped my pen against the margin and started with the one who'd been lingering at the edge of my thoughts more often than I liked to admit.

Sean, I wrote at the top of the page.

He was easy to talk to. Thoughtful. Maybe a little too polished around the edges, but not in a way that set off alarm bells. Still, I couldn't shake that moment at Willow Cabin—how his body language shifted when I brought up Walter. And that disagreement between them? I hadn't forgotten.

But... no. I didn't get danger from him. Secrets, maybe. Regret. But not malice. If anything, Sean struck me as someone trying to prove himself, not hide something sinister.

I moved on.

Gus Bugle.

His name came out heavier on the page.

There'd always been something about Gus that didn't quite match the Bugle name. He wasn't polished like his cousins or sharp-tongued like his father. As a kid, he'd hovered at the edges of things, awkward and overlooked, but eager enough to fall in line when pushed. He didn't seem dangerous. But guilt? Yeah. I could believe he was carrying some of that.

He had motive. Even if the Canada Post contract was supposedly "settled," he still stood to gain from Dad disappearing—which made it harder to believe it was just coincidence. And that bar conversation with Kansas was still echoing.

But if he was hiding something, why tell Kansas? Why make a scene in public? Unless he wasn't hiding it—unless he wanted someone to stop him from shouldering it alone.

Or maybe he was drunk and just slipped. Or maybe it wasn't a slip at all.

I looked at Des. She was watching me now, ears slightly lifted. "Yeah," I said. "That one's messy."

I put a small question mark beside his name and moved on.

Devon.

Motive? Check. Walter had been in his way. Backing the mine reopening would grease the wheels for his logging permits. And if Devon was behind something ugly, he'd keep it neat. Clean hands, spotless blazer, airtight alibi.

I boxed his name. Not off the list, just... contained.

Then I hesitated.

Frannie.

I wasn't sure what to make of her. Smooth. Controlled. Polished in a way that didn't quite feel lived-in. She played the perfect hostess, but there was always something measured behind her smile. Not guilt. Not fear. Just... calculation.

I wrote her name lightly, then added: *odd vibe?* And promptly scratched it out. Sloppy note-taking irritated me.

That left the name I'd been circling for days. The one that kept worming its way into every theory, every question, every gut feeling.

Kansas.

I wrote it slowly. Let the ink soak in. Then I circled it. Once. Twice. Hard enough that the pen dragged the paper fibres up a little.

He had motive: wanted the store. He had opportunity: he was in town. And he was hiding something—his finances, if nothing else. The outdoor kitchen was better equipped than most restaurants, and from the look on Frannie's face, she hadn't signed off on it.

Kansas was all ego and ambition—charm turned up high, even when no one asked for it. And he was getting twitchy.

If I was being honest, I didn't just suspect Kansas. I felt him in this. Like the tension in the air before a summer storm breaks loose.

Des let out a soft *whuff*, like she agreed.

I closed the notebook and set it aside. "If Kansas didn't do it..." I murmured, "then why is he acting like he did?"

I took one last sip of my coffee—cold, now—and let my eyes drift over the trees. Light crept toward gold, wind rustling the spruce. Somewhere down the street, another dog barked, sharp and short, before falling quiet again.

The day was waking up. And I was running out of excuses not to confront Kansas McBride.

It had been a busy couple of days at the store, and I was grateful to finally have a few hours to myself Friday evening. I laced up my runners and headed out for a run. The sun was still lingering above the trees, casting a golden haze over the lake trail. Wild roses lined the edges, their scent drifting on the breeze, and Des trotted ahead with her usual mix of enthusiasm and selective hearing. The mosquitoes hadn't yet organized into a proper swarm—a small miracle.

By the time we looped back toward town, the streets had settled into that quiet, in-between hour when dinner's done but dusk hasn't quite arrived. I spotted Sean outside the Pig & Paddle, balancing a foil-wrapped bundle in one hand and a cherry soda in the other.

"Evening," he called as we approached. "You training for something I should know about?"

"Just outrunning the week," I said, brushing sweat off my forehead. "Barbecue night?"

"Finally," Sean said, lifting the bag slightly. "Thought I'd never get my order. I had the misfortune of walking in right after Kansas placed a feast-sized order for his poker crew."

"Hungry guys."

"Yeah. He invited me over to Len's, but…" Sean shrugged. "Not really my scene."

"Poker?"

"Oh, poker's fine. But I'm pretty sure it's less 'poker night' and more 'Kansas monologues with snacks.'"

I snorted. "He does love a captive audience."

I wished Sean a good evening, then glanced at my watch and sighed. I'd promised Callie I'd pick up a few things before heading home. She was making dinner and asked if I'd check the store for bread since the bakery was already closed.

The store lights were still on when I arrived, though it was past regular closing time. I pushed through the unlocked door. Parker, the high school stock boy, glanced up from behind the counter where he was sorting through packages.

"Hey, Tilly," he called. "Almost done, then I'll lock up."

"Bertha let you close?" I asked, spying one last loaf on the shelf.

"Her sister needed her for something." He shrugged, then turned his attention back to a box with bright yellow labels. I caught the words DRY ICE and PERISHABLE as I passed.

I took the last of the bread and brought it to the counter. Parker was on the phone.

"Yes, Mrs. McBride, it just came in. Okay, see you in a few minutes."

He hung up and rang me through. "Sorry about that."

"No problem," I said, handing him the payment. "Don't stay too late, Parker."

"Just waiting on this pickup, then I'm out," he assured me.

I took the path to the house. The porch light clicked on automatically, even though the sky still held a stubborn streak of summer blue. I'd stayed out longer than I meant to, letting the quiet do its work.

Callie was in the kitchen, frying something in the cast iron and humming a song I didn't recognize. There were tomatoes on the cutting board, a half-wrapped block of feta on the counter, and Des had already relocated to her post by the fridge.

"Thought you were avoiding carbs," I said, handing over the loaf.

"I'm making garlic bread for you," she said without turning. "Which is my passive-aggressive way of telling you to eat more."

I smiled despite myself, then wandered over to help. "What's the occasion?"

"No occasion. Just seemed like a pasta night."

I reached for a zucchini and started chopping. "I've been thinking about Gus."

"That's never a good sign."

"He told Kansas something."

She looked up now, curiosity flickering behind her eyes. "When?"

"At the bar. Gus was drinking, Kansas was listening, and the next morning Kansas was acting... off. Jumpy. Watchful, even."

Callie set the wooden spoon down and leaned her hip against the counter. "You think Gus confessed something?"

"I don't know. Maybe not outright. "But he said something serious enough that Kansas was clearly spooked by it—like it was weighing on him, but he didn't know what to do with it."

Callie frowned. "You mean that line he gave you about you not knowing the actual truth?"

"Exactly."

She nodded, slower now. "That *was* weird."

"Kansas wanted the store," I continued, going through my mental checklist. "Dad wouldn't sell. Bertha said they argued about it. Frannie's been evasive every time I bring it up. And Dad had something Gus wanted: he was next in line for that Canada Post contract."

"So you think, what? Kansas killed him? Or Gus did, and Kansas found out?"

"I don't know yet. But if Kansas knows something, I need to get it out of him. Sooner rather than later."

Callie picked up her spoon again. "Sean seems too sweet to be involved in anything. Frannie's odd, but she's not exactly cutthroat. And Gus... he's like a nervous chipmunk in a ball cap."

"He's also a Bugle," I said, softer now. "And the Bugles play the long game. If he got in over his head, he might not know how to get out."

Callie stirred the sauce. "If you're right about Kansas, he's rattled. People don't stay rattled forever. They either break, or they do something worse."

I opened the cupboard and pulled down two plates, letting the silence settle around us like steam from the pot. Then Callie reached into her back pocket and slapped something folded onto the counter with a thunk.

"Saw this front and centre on the bulletin board at the store," she said, pointing to the glossy flyer.

"What is this?" I picked it up. Bright colours, stars and music notes dancing around cheerful fonts.

"Some kind of community thing," Callie said. "Mandy says the whole town shows up. Thought you'd want to see it before you come up with an excuse not to go."

"Oh, it's the Balsam Bay Summer Social." I read the flyer aloud: "A community dance and fundraising silent auction under the stars... music, food, door prizes, and don't forget to enter the 33rd annual Perogy Palooza."

Callie looked vaguely alarmed. "Wait. Dance? I thought it was just like a picnic or something."

"Nope." I folded the flyer in half. "It's a Manitoba thing. You rent a hall, sell tickets, play loud music, maybe auction off a few donated items. People drink, dance, and gossip about whomever they're not standing with."

"Huh," Callie said. "So high school—with perogies."

I chuckled. "Exactly."

Des, hearing about snacks, thumped her tail against the floor.

"Oh, I almost forgot," Callie added. "Guess who Mandy said was asking about entering the perogy contest when I stopped by the bakery today? Frannie McBride."

I raised an eyebrow. "Frannie? The woman who wears cashmere to get the mail?"

"That's what I thought!" Callie said. "Apparently she came in all enthusiastic about participating. Mandy said she seemed really determined to enter. Said she was going to make something special.'"

"That's... unexpected," I said, tucking the flyer into the corner of the fridge magnet. "But Kansas did say she was the cook in the family. Maybe he's pushing her to get more involved in town events?"

"Or maybe she just really likes perogies," Callie shrugged.

"I suppose it wouldn't hurt to mingle," I said. "If Kansas is going to crack, it won't be on a front porch with a cup of tea. It'll be with a drink in his hand and too many people around to keep his mask on."

Later, after the dishes were done and Callie had disappeared into a phone call with one of her friends from uni, I called Des and stepped outside.

We took the long way around the house, past the lilacs and out toward the gravel path that curved toward the old trail-head. The air smelled like pine and heat-stilled lake water, and the quiet didn't feel empty. It felt like the woods were holding a secret.

"I feel like I'm one step ahead for once," I murmured to Des.

She looked up, wagged once, and trotted a little closer.

Still, the prickle at the back of my neck stayed with me. Not fear. Not exactly.

Just that stillness, like the moment before a branch snaps.

CHAPTER TEN

"No milk?" I stared into the fridge, blinking. "Seriously?"

The coffee was already percolating—loud and smug—and I wasn't in the mood to drink it black.

"You drank the last of it, didn't you?" I called to Callie, who was curled on the couch with her phone and a smug little smirk that confirmed everything.

"I left some!" she said innocently. "It just might not be visible to the human eye."

Des let out a sigh worthy of an Oscar.

"Quick milk run," I told her, grabbing my keys. "I'll be back in ten."

I grabbed my shoes, the store keys, and a five-dollar bill from the jar near the breadbox.

The morning was cool enough that my breath made little clouds as I walked the short path to the general store. Birds called from the trees, and somewhere nearby, someone was splitting wood. The steady rhythm of axe strikes carrying through the still air.

Bertha wasn't due for another half hour, so I let myself in. I headed for the dairy case and grabbed a carton of milk before stopping at the register.

Bertha was a stickler about inventory, so instead of writing an IOU and leaving it on the counter, I rang up the purchase. As I pushed the till shut after making change, I spotted a single envelope in the locked basket that held the after-hours mail drop.

Curious, I unlocked the basket and took out the envelope. Plain white. Handwritten, with just my name: *Tilly*.

My chest tightened.

I slipped my thumb under the flap and opened the envelope. The note inside was short. My pulse kicked up a notch.

Tilly,

I have important information about your father. If you're willing to discuss selling me the store, I'll tell you everything I know. This is just between us.
—Kansas

My fingers curled around the note. Kansas knew something about Walter. Something he thought was valuable enough that I'd trade the store.

I folded the note, slipped it into my pocket, and locked up behind me, my thoughts crowding each other. What did Kansas know? And why now?

Back at the cabin, Callie was out on the porch, legs tucked under her as she sat in one of the red Muskoka chairs. She looked up as I climbed the steps.

"No milk?" she asked, catching sight of my empty hands.

I sank into the chair beside her and pulled out the note. "Didn't get that far. Found this instead."

She took it, eyes scanning quickly. Her brows knit together. "Where'd you get this?"

"Post office drop box. Must've left it late last night."

Callie leaned back, her expression unreadable. "Well... this changes things. If it's real."

"That's the question, isn't it?" I said. "Either he actually knows something about Dad, and thinks it's worth trading for the store keys, or he's throwing bait and hoping I'll bite."

"You think he'd lie just to get the store?"

"Maybe," I said. "Or maybe he's hoping to get me alone."

Callie straightened in her chair. "You don't think... what if he did something to Grandpa? What if this is how he covers his tracks?"

"It crossed my mind," I admitted. "If he's guilty, this could be a trap."

"Then don't go. Call Jason. Let him deal with it."

"I'm not walking into anything blind." I reached down to rub behind Des's ears after she nosed open the screen door and padded out to join us. "But I am going to talk to him."

Callie gave me a look. "Seriously?"

"Tonight. At the social."

"That's the worst possible place to confront someone—"

"It's the safest," I said. "Public, crowded, noisy. We can find a quiet corner, and if anything goes sideways, there'll be a dozen witnesses between the potato salad and the raffle table. He won't risk anything in a room full of neighbours."

Callie hesitated, then exhaled. "You scare me when you sound so reasonable about this."

I gave Des one last scratch and stood. "Better to face it than let him control the story."

A sharp knock at the door cut through the morning quiet. Bertha's silhouette stood beyond the screen, upright and unmistakable. She held something in her hands.

"Matilda? You left milk on the counter." Her voice carried clearly across the porch. "At least I'm assuming it's you, unless someone broke in, rang up a sale for a carton of milk, left it on the counter and locked up again."

"Sorry, Bertha. Got distracted."

"Clearly." Bertha pushed open the screen door and stepped onto the porch, holding out the milk and a plastic container. "I had a loaf of bread I needed to use up, so I made extra French toast."

"Thank you," I said, touched by the uncharacteristic gesture.

She quickly read our tense expressions. "Well," she said, her tone softer, "looks like you're too busy to make breakfast, anyway."

She glanced at the note in Callie's hand, but didn't ask. Instead, she straightened her shoulders and added, "I need that container back by Wednesday. Not a day later. The quilting bee ladies are expecting their custard squares."

"Wednesday," I agreed, fighting a smile. Trust Bertha to find normalcy in the middle of chaos.

Bertha nodded, satisfied, and turned to go. At the steps, she paused, as if wanting to say more, and then she was gone.

"So what now?" Callie asked.

"Now we eat." I set the container on the table and went to grab maple syrup from the fridge.

By the time we arrived at the community centre, the parking lot was full and the music had already started—more bass than melody, but it had a beat you could move to. Strings of lights stretched from the hall's roofline to the old flagpole, flickering in the dusk like they were trying to distract from the mosquitoes.

Inside, it was loud. Music thumped from rented speakers,

and the air smelled of floor wax and body heat. Tables lined the walls with prize baskets. I could see a lottery tree, a BBQ and smoker, remote car starter, and an adventure package with a paddle board and kayak. Snack tables were near the back, and the bar line curled past folding tables stacked with pop bottles and plastic cups.

Callie paused just inside the door, scanning the crowd. 'This is… something.'

'It's a social,' I said. 'Drinks, raffles, rye bread, and loud music. Classic Manitoba.'

She raised an eyebrow. 'I was picturing a church potluck, not whatever this is.'

I grinned. 'You're not in Victoria anymore.'

Des trotted beside us, nose twitching with interest. She got a few smiles, a quiet 'Good girl' or two, but most were more focused on drinks and gossip.

The walking club found me before I made it ten feet inside the door.

'Well, look what the lake washed up,' Enid said, pressing a cup of white wine into my hand.

'We were just talking about you,' Nora added, waving her 50/50 tickets like a fan.

"About how good I look in denim, I hope."

That got a snort from Trish.

"About how you've been sticking your nose into things again—"

"Not that there's anything wrong with that," Enid said with a smirk.

Nora looked at Enid like she was a runaway chicken. "And how we think you're right."

I blinked. "About what?"

They leaned in, as if we were swapping spy secrets instead of gossip over a plate of pickles and cheddar cubes.

"Walter," Enid said simply. "You already know we never believed the canoe story. It was too... tidy."

"And Kansas," Trish added. "He's been wound tighter than a clothesline in a windstorm."

Nora gave me a once-over. "You're not going to confront him here, are you?"

"Wouldn't dream of it," I lied.

They gave me matching looks that said they didn't believe me for a second, then melted back into the crowd.

I was still smiling when I spotted Sean near the raffle table, squinting at a prize basket filled with camping gear.

"See something you like?" I asked, stepping beside him.

He startled slightly, then grinned. "More like figuring out what half this stuff is. I've never seen a foam can cooler with a nightlight. Or a hammock bath tub."

"You've clearly never been to a Manitoba social."

"I can't believe you didn't warn me," he said in mock accusation. "There are cheese cubes and deli meat trays on ice next to a karaoke machine."

"It's a cultural rite of passage."

We stood there a beat longer than necessary, his elbow brushing mine. His smile softened at the edges.

"You look like someone who's not here for the door prize," he said.

"I'm not. But Callie made me promise not to interrogate anyone before the first dance."

"Good thing this doesn't count as interrogating," he said.

"It doesn't," I agreed, "unless you've got something you want to confess."

He laughed, low and warm, then got called over by someone at the drinks table.

I watched him go, then turned back toward the crowd, and saw Gus. He stood near the wall, half in shadow, beer in hand.

Alone. His eyes kept flicking toward Kansas, who was working the room with a little too much charm. Gus didn't look jealous. He looked… worried.

Devon was easier to spot, mostly because he dressed like a man trying hard not to look like he was going to a business meeting. He was mid-conversation with Mayor Bugle, both of them laughing at something that didn't look all that funny.

Bertha passed me with a plate piled high with ripple chips. "Don't make that face," she said without breaking stride. "I haven't eaten."

Mandy followed a few paces behind, cheeks flushed from dancing. "Is it me," she said breathlessly, "or is everyone a little… extra tonight?"

"It's the heat," I said.

"The crowd's just prickling with tension," she countered before sighing. "Well, time to get to work."

"Work? It's a social, you don't have to work."

"I volunteered. I know, I know, I'm a glutton for punishment. But I've been serving food to this town for a while, now. Someone's gotta keep everyone in line during the palooza."

I didn't disagree.

I watched Kansas moving from group to group, louder than usual, laughing too hard at jokes no one else was telling. Like he wanted to prove he was fine, or prove something else entirely. He was also drinking faster than usual, judging by the number of times Frannie was sent to the bar for refills.

I was working up the nerve to close the distance when Callie reappeared at my side, holding a small gift basket in her arms.

"Look what I won," she said. "Artisanal jam. I'm basically a local now."

"Careful," I said. "Next thing you know, they'll be asking you to run for town council."

She grinned and handed me one of the jars. "Smell this. It's like strawberries went to finishing school."

Before I could respond, a warm voice chimed in behind me.

"Well, if it isn't little Tilly McKay. Though I suppose you're not so little anymore. And no longer a McKay."

I turned, already smiling. "Mabel Whitfield. You haven't changed a bit," I said, seeing past the stoop in her shoulders and the years on her face, to the woman who used to hand me mystery novels with a wink.

"Oh, lie to me, dear," she said, patting her silver chignon like a model. "It's good for the joints."

She wore a coral blouse with pearls and clutched a raffle envelope like it was a designer handbag. Mabel had been the town's librarian and unofficial keeper of local lore for as long as I could remember.

A gaggle of boys hustled past, and Mabel's eyebrows shot up.

"Richard? What on earth is in your hands?"

The boy and his two friends looked to be about twelve years old, and each carried paper plates piled high with perogies, generous dollops of fresh sour cream on top.

Richard looked caught. "Hey, Grandma." He blushed. "Sorry, I know we weren't supposed to stay. We're leaving right now, I promise."

The other boys dug into their plates like they were racing a clock. Richard didn't touch his.

"You were supposed to drop off those food trays from your mother and head straight home. What are you doing with plates of food? I think between the three of you, you must have half of the palooza entries."

"Sorry," he mumbled, clearly sheepish. "We've never seen so many kinds of perogies before! We just wanted to try a few. No one seemed to mind."

"Those are for the contest. Your mother stocked the house with snacks for you and your friends. Shame on you, Richard." Her words were firm, but her tone held only mild reproach.

Richard glanced at his friends' nearly empty plates, then back at his own, still full. "We're sorry. We're leaving now." He leaned over to toss his mostly untouched food into a nearby trash bin.

"Stop! For heaven's sake, Richard, you've already taken the food. No use wasting it."

But he didn't pause. The plate hit the bottom of the bin with a thunk. "Sorry. I shouldn't have taken it. It tasted funny, anyway. See you later, Grams."

He turned and followed his friends out the door.

Mabel shook her head, a smile tugging at her mouth. "Boys," she said. "Bottomless pits." She gave another small shake of her head before turning back to me. "Anyway," she said, slipping back into the moment, "I was telling Agnes you're back in town," she added, referring to her younger sister. "She still talks about your mother, you know."

A little knot tightened in my chest. Mom and Agnes became fast friends soon after Mom moved to Balsam Bay. "Hard to believe it's been over thirty years," I said.

"She left her mark. The museum hasn't felt the same since she was in charge. She made our history come alive." Mabel touched my arm gently. "You've got your mother's eyes, you know." Her eyes twinkled as she looked at me, then Callie. "If you ever want to poke around the archives, you know where to find me."

And with that, she disappeared into the crowd, as elegantly as a woman in orthopedic shoes could.

Callie turned to me, her voice a little quieter. "I didn't know Grandma curated the museum."

"She started it, really," I said. "Collected old mining tools and stories from all over the region. She wanted to make sure the town remembered where it came from."

Callie was quiet for a beat. "Mandy said she died in a hiking accident." She said it quietly, almost apologetically. I was the one who needed to apologize, though, for keeping stories about my mother so close to my chest for so long.

I nodded slowly. "She was out alone. Knew the woods like the back of her hand, but... she must have misjudged her step. They found her a couple of days later, at the bottom of a ravine."

Callie winced. "That's awful."

"It was," I said. "Still is, some days."

The weight of it settled between us for a moment, heavy but not unwelcome—like we'd set something down between us that had been carried alone for too long.

Callie looped her arm through mine, grounding me with a gentle squeeze. "We should go to the museum sometime," she said. "I'd like to see it. Learn more about her."

That earned a small smile from me. For a moment, the air felt easy again. But even as I thought about it, the old doubt stirred. The thing that never fully settled.

Then across the room, Kansas laughed too loudly at something, and the spell broke.

When his eyes found mine, the mask cracked. It wasn't guilt. Or fear. It was desperation, raw and unresolved.

And in that instant, I felt it. Now was the time to talk.

He looked away first, then angled through the crowd with a plate in hand—stacked high with perogies, a swirl of sour cream threatening to slide off one edge. I followed, keeping enough distance not to arouse others' suspicion. He slipped out the back exit near the kitchen, past the recycling bins and into the narrow patch of grass behind the community centre.

When I stepped outside, the sound of the social dimmed

behind me. Mosquitoes hovered in the warm night air, and the scent of fried dough clung to my clothes.

Kansas was already tucking into his dish. He gave me a weary half-smile.

"I figured you'd come find me," he said.

"You left a note," I said, nodding toward the plate. "Didn't realize we were doing this over supper."

He shrugged. "Couldn't wait for the contest."

I folded my arms. "You said you had something to tell me. About my father."

He picked at a perogy with his plastic fork, suddenly fidgety. "Yeah. I—" He paused, blinking hard.

My instincts flared. "Kansas?"

He dropped the fork. "Something's... not right."

Then everything happened at once. His hands went to his throat, eyes wide, breath coming in sharp gasps. The plate hit the ground, scattering perogies across the grass.

"Kansas," I said sharply, stepping forward. "What's the matter?"

His hands shook as he lowered them to his pants pockets, searching for something. He was trying to answer, but couldn't form words. His lips were already starting to swell.

I grabbed his arm, guiding him to the ground as gently as I could. "I think you're having an allergic reaction," I said, trying to keep my voice calm. "Do you have an EpiPen?"

He nodded his head, barely.

I checked his pockets. Nothing. I cursed under my breath. "Stay with me, okay? Help is coming."

I shouted for someone—anyone—to call an ambulance, then leaned in again, watching his breathing. It was getting worse—rasping gasps, eyelids fluttering.

"Oh no!" someone yelled from the building. "He's having a heart attack!" A commotion started as people went to get help.

I turned back, one hand on his chest. "Hold on," I murmured, mostly to myself.

But as I watched, I knew. The signs were all there—textbook anaphylaxis, and no epinephrine in sight. The progression was fast. Too fast.

Frannie burst through the door behind me a moment later. Her eyes locked on Kansas, and she let out a high, keening cry. "No, no! What happened?"

"He's in anaphylaxis," I snapped, not bothering to cushion the blow. "Does he have allergies? Does he carry an EpiPen?"

She stared at me, frozen. "I—I've never seen him like this before."

Kansas made one last effort to sit up, then went limp.

I was still holding his wrist when his pulse stopped.

"Let me take over." It was Mrs. Kowalski: a retired nurse, hair tucked into a loose bun, sleeves already rolled. I shifted to let her in, backing up as Henry Klassen, a former paramedic, crouched beside her. No hesitation. The pair started working in practiced rhythm.

I looked back toward Kansas, his body half-obscured now by the people trying to help. Frannie still performing, her sobs louder than the crowd's hush.

Bertha was suddenly there, pressing her hand to my back. "What happened? Everyone's saying Kansas had a heart attack."

I shook my head. "Anaphylaxis. No one had an EpiPen."

Mandy appeared at the door, face pale. "The ambulance is on the way."

"Too late," I said.

Frannie had sunk to the ground, her hands over her mouth. Her shoulders shook, but when she looked up, her eyes remained dry, the skin around them unmarked by tears despite the theatrical sobs.

I glanced down at the scattered food, the smears of sour cream on grass. Something about this wasn't right. I could feel it like a splinter under the skin.

A soft rustle near my side caught my attention. Des, ears slightly back, edged forward with cautious steps. She lowered her nose, sniffing first at the fallen perogies, then hesitating near Kansas's outstretched hand. There was no excitement or agitation in her movements, just a wary, puzzled tension, as if something about the scent didn't fit. I placed a light hand on her collar, feeling her tremble faintly beneath my fingers. She gave one last hesitant sniff, then backed away, slipping behind my legs.

And deep down, I already knew—this wasn't an accident.

Jason arrived faster than I expected, eyes scanning the crowd. When someone gestured toward me, he gave a nod.

"The caller said you were the first responder?" he said once he reached me. "Walk me through it," he said.

"We came out here to talk. He was working his way through a plate of perogies. All of a sudden, he started choking. Everything swelled up."

"He choked? The caller said he was having a heart attack."

"I don't think so," I said quietly. "It looked like anaphylaxis."

Behind us, through the doorway, the music started up again. Someone must have bumped the wrong button on the DJ board, and a too-happy beat flooded the air for half a second before it was silenced again.

"Mom." I turned. Callie was weaving through the crowd. "You okay?"

"Yeah," I said. "I think so."

Callie stepped in beside me, not touching—anchoring. Her presence slowed something tight and fluttering in my chest I hadn't realized was racing.

"What happened?" she asked softly. "I just heard someone yell."

"He just... stopped." I swallowed. "It was fast. I think it was anaphylaxis. I didn't have my aid bag."

She didn't say anything. She didn't need to. She knew what it meant for me to stand at the edge of an emergency empty-handed.

The ambulance arrived forty-eight minutes later.

No sirens. Just the distant crunch of gravel, a soft hiss of brakes, and two paramedics stepping out with the kind of quiet purpose that only ever meant one thing. Calm, respectful. Too late to rush.

The crowd parted. Even the building seemed to understand: this wasn't a party anymore.

Kansas was lifted gently onto the stretcher, his body covered. Frannie followed a few steps behind, her arms wrapped around herself like she was bracing against a storm that hadn't hit yet.

Bertha walked with her, murmuring something low and steady. No one else moved.

Once the ambulance pulled away, people drifted back toward the hall in subdued clumps. The silence stretched, thick and uncertain. It was the kind that didn't end—not really. Just settled in behind your ribs and waited.

Callie and I made our way toward the doors, Des following in step, her entire posture low and alert. She hadn't made a sound during any of it. Just watched.

We passed the auction table. Lights unplugged. Raffle baskets slumped like forgotten party guests. That's when I heard it.

"First her dad, now this…"

Not loud. Not cruel. Just a whisper between two women standing too close to the punch bowl, like it was a fact they'd decided on.

I didn't stop walking. But the words hooked deep, anyway.

Callie noticed. "Mom?"

I didn't look at her. "Sounds like someone's keeping score."

"People talk when they don't know what else to do," she said gently.

"Yeah. And I'm ending up on the wrong side of it."

She didn't argue. Just stayed close, steady as her namesake.

"Let's go home," she said.

The sky had gone ink-black by the time we arrived. Crickets sang like nothing had happened. The kind of summer night that tried its best to be ordinary, even when it wasn't.

I grabbed Des's leash. "I just need a walk," I told Callie.

She didn't argue. Just nodded and let the screen door close behind me.

We took the path behind the house, the one that followed the tree line down toward the lake. Des padded beside me, quiet and sure, her body loose but alert. Always alert.

My head was buzzing, but underneath that was something else. Not fear. Not exactly.

Kansas was dead.

I'd come to the social convinced he was the key. That if I pressed him, he'd crack. He knew something about Walter. Knew something Gus had said. He was panicked, unravelled, and I thought if I pushed just a little harder, the whole story would spill out.

But I was wrong.

He'd never get the chance to talk. And whatever he was about to say—or do—was buried with him now.

A twig snapped somewhere off the path. Des flicked an ear but didn't stop walking.

I used to think I was following one thread. Find Walter, find the truth. A straight line, even if the road was messy.

But Kansas's death changed the shape of everything.

This wasn't just about a disappearance anymore. Or a canoe. Or one man with too many secrets.

Someone must have killed to protect something. And I'd been walking in circles, too focused on Walter to see the bigger picture.

I glanced at Des. "We've been looking in the wrong direction, girl."

She gave a soft *chuff*, as if she agreed.

I looked up at the stars. Still shining. Still distant. Like they didn't care either way.

But I did, and I wasn't going to stop now.

CHAPTER ELEVEN

I stared at my list, Kansas's name crossed out in thick black ink. A mug of cold coffee sat at my elbow, but I couldn't be bothered to brew another pot. I'd been up since dawn, My mind wouldn't let up after the events at the social. Every time I closed my eyes, I saw Kansas's face—his lips turning that unnatural shade of blue, gasping for air as he collapsed before we could even begin our conversation about my father.

And I'd failed him. Failed to take his note seriously. Failed to realize that he might have been in danger, too—not just playing games to get the store. The note had been clear: he had information about my father. Real information. And I'd dismissed it as another scheme.

Des nudged my hand, like she knew I was unravelling. I scratched behind her ears absentmindedly.

"I've been looking the wrong way, girl," I murmured. "Kansas wasn't the answer—he was another victim."

The thought had hit me just before sunrise. Kansas wanted the store, sure. But what if that wasn't the point? What if he'd found something he shouldn't have? Something that got him killed?

Because it wasn't a heart attack. I'd seen enough medical emergencies during my SAR days to recognize the signs. It looked more like anaphylaxis or poisoning. And from the hushed conversation I'd overheard between the paramedics, they suspected the same.

The pieces were lining up now. The argument at *The Rusty Lantern* between Gus, Frannie, and Kansas. The cryptic note in the store mailbox after that. Whatever Gus said that night had triggered something. I didn't know if Gus was guilty or just a reluctant participant, but I couldn't avoid it anymore.

"I have to talk to him," I said.

But first—I needed real coffee.

I swung by Mandy's on the way. The closed sign was still up, and the lights were off except for a low glow behind the counter. I tested the door—it pushed open easily, unlocked more out of habit than intent, it seemed.

The second I stepped inside, my tension loosened by half.

Mandy glanced up from behind the counter. Her eyes softened. "Tilly. You look like you've barely slept. Sit down. I'll bring you something."

I slid into a chair by the window. I seemed to be the only person in the shop besides Mandy, a hush still hanging over the town after Kansas's death. Glancing outside, I realized only the pharmacy down the street looked open.

She brought me a cup of coffee and set it down gently. "On the house," she said. "Rough night?"

I wrapped both hands around the mug, trying to soak in the warmth. Down the street, a dusty brown pickup pulled up in front of the pharmacy. My pulse kicked as I recognized the driver—the tall man in the ball cap I'd seen at Sean's place.

"Mandy," I asked, sharper than I meant to, "who's that?"

She followed my gaze, a bit puzzled. "That's Jake. One of the local Prairie Wind drivers. Handles the express orders."

Relief flickered, though the tension didn't fully leave my chest. Just a delivery guy. My nerves were seeing threats in every corner.

Mandy sat across from me, her expression kind but tired. "We're all still reeling. You, too. You don't have to chase answers today."

"I feel like I do," I said. "If I don't, something else will slip through the cracks."

"It's Sunday. Most of the stores are closed, and the rest are mourning."

"Not the gas station," I said, certain.

"Sign's been dark since I got in. Gus isn't open."

"Maybe he's just opening late today. After all, you're at work," I said hopefully.

Mandy gave me a wry smile. "I only came in to take care of Audrey. Besides, the coffee's better here than at my house."

I frowned, trying to place the name. "I don't think I've met Audrey. Is she your new baker?"

"No, Audrey II is my sourdough starter," she said with a wink.

My smile widened. "Right. You have to feed those every day."

"Twice a day," Mandy said. "Just call me Seymour."

I laughed, despite everything.

"It's good to see you relax a bit." She reached over and gave my shoulder a gentle squeeze. "Give it a day, Tilly. Let the town catch its breath. You can figure it out tomorrow. You're no good to anyone running on fumes." I looked down at my empty mug. The idea of going back to the house, sitting with Callie and Des, not thinking for a few hours—it didn't sound like giving up. It sounded like air.

"Maybe you're right."

"Course I am," she said, rising to clear the cup. "You'll figure it out. But only if you don't burn yourself out first."

I left the bakery with no destination but home. Just for today.

The next morning, the town's stillness had given way to speculation. Every customer at the store wanted to talk about Kansas. They spoke in hushed voices, like they were afraid he might still be listening.

Needing a break in the afternoon, I took a walk and found Gus hunched over Pete Olson's old fishing boat. Only, he wasn't fixing it—just holding a piece of sandpaper, staring at the hull like it might tell him what to do next. He didn't even notice me and Des until her tags jingled.

He flinched. "Geez, Tilly. You snuck up on me."

Up close, he looked terrible. Dark circles ringed his eyes, and a day's worth of stubble shadowed his jaw. He hadn't just had a rough weekend, he looked like he hadn't slept at all.

He set the sander down with hands that weren't quite steady. "What brings you down here?"

I cut straight to the point. "I need to talk about Kansas."

Gus swallowed hard. "Yeah. Terrible what happened."

"He left me a note," I said, watching his reaction closely. "Said he had information about my father."

Gus busied himself with the boat again, rubbing at a nonexistent spot on the hull. "Kansas was always scheming."

"The walking club ladies saw you three at the pub. Said Kansas and Frannie left in a hurry after you talked to them."

He let out a slow breath. "I may have mentioned that

Kansas didn't actually have the money to buy your store. Frannie didn't take it well."

"That's it?"

"Well, I might've been a bit... blunt about it." He scratched the back of his neck. "Had a few drinks in me."

Des trotted past with a stick, tail high. I turned back to Gus. "That doesn't explain why Kansas would write me a dramatic note claiming to know something about my father."

"Maybe he thought you'd bite if he dangled a story about Walter. Kansas didn't always think things through."

I couldn't argue with that. But something still felt off. Gus was too jittery, his answers too rehearsed.

"You sure that's all?"

His eyes met mine for the first time. "That's all I told him."

There was something in the way he said it: a wistfulness, almost a sadness. I tried a different angle. "Did Kansas have any allergies that you know of?"

The question caught him off guard. "Allergies?"

"Yes. Food allergies, maybe? Nuts? Medication?"

Gus stared at me, confusion replacing the nervousness for a moment. "He, uh—yeah, actually. Shellfish. Made a big deal of it when I splurged and ordered crab legs at the hotel restaurant one night. Said he couldn't even be near the stuff. Carried an EpiPen, though I never saw him use it."

A chill rippled through me. There hadn't been any seafood at the event—just perogies for the contest, and traditional social fare. Unless something had been deliberately contaminated.

"That night at the pub," I pressed, "after you told them about the money situation, did Kansas say anything about my father?"

Gus's hands stilled on the boat. "He... might have mentioned wanting to talk to you. Nothing specific." He picked up a rag and twisted it between his hands. "Listen, Tilly, I should get back to this."

I knew a dismissal when I heard one. "Sure. See you around, Gus."

As Des and I headed back toward downtown, I couldn't shake the feeling Gus had more to say. The shellfish allergy was a crucial piece of information, but his reaction told me there was more to the story. More about what Kansas knew, or thought he knew, about my father.

I was so tangled in my thoughts that when I turned onto Pine Street, I walked straight into Walter's fan club —or rather, they enveloped me like a well-coordinated fog.

"Oh, Tilly!" Nora exclaimed, clutching my arm with surprising strength for a woman in her seventies. Enid and Trish formed a half-circle around me, their walking poles angled like they meant business.

I couldn't help but notice the matching teal windbreakers with "Balsam Belles" stitched across the back in cheerful script. Looked like Enid had finally talked the others into their new moniker.

"Just awful about Kansas," Enid said, shaking her head so hard her tortoiseshell glasses slipped down her nose.

"So young," Nora added.

"He seemed in such good health," Trish finished, completing their three-part harmony of condolences.

I nodded politely, my thoughts still focused on my conversation with Gus.

"Tragic," I agreed, attempting to edge past them. "I really should—"

"You'll never believe what we heard," Enid cut in, her eyes gleaming with the particular excitement reserved for those possessing information others don't.

I sighed inwardly. Alien abduction? Secret twins? Time travellers? With these three, it was always a toss-up.

"What's that?" I asked, resigned.

They exchanged glances, a silent negotiation for story-telling rights. Nora won.

"Well," she began, lowering her voice to a dramatic whisper that was somehow louder than her normal speaking voice, "Enid heard from Delores at the insurance agent's that Frannie was asking about bereavement benefits and policy procedures this morning."

"Yup," Trish chimed in, unable to contain herself. "And Carol at the bank mentioned Frannie was in there asking about access to their accounts."

"She's making arrangements," Trish said.

I blinked, genuinely surprised. "Arrangements? Her husband just died!"

"It's fast," Enid agreed solemnly.

"It's very odd, if you ask me," Nora said, tapping her walking pole for emphasis. "Rushing around town at the first opportunity after losing her husband."

I hesitated, then asked, "Has she mentioned any plans for a service?"

The three women exchanged glances again.

"That's another peculiar thing," Enid said. "Frannie stopped by the church earlier. Betty was cleaning up after yesterday's service, and overheard Frannie talking to Reverend Nichols about the sanctuary being available Friday afternoon."

"Friday?" I couldn't hide my surprise. "That's only a few days away."

"Especially," Trish added pointedly, "since the poor man's body is still at the hospital and Dr. Marsh hasn't even finished his examination."

"And when I stopped by Mandy's for my morning

cinnamon bun," Nora added, "she said Frannie had already been in to ask about catering services for a 'small, private gathering' after the service."

The warmth suddenly drained out of the day. Frannie wasn't acting grief stricken. It sounded like someone cleaning house before slipping out the back door.

"That's not all," Trish said, lowering her voice. "My niece works at the clinic. Dr. Marsh told her Kansas definitely did not suffer a heart attack, like some were saying."

"What did he think it was?" I asked.

Trish glanced around before answering. "Some kind of allergic reaction, apparently. The final results won't be back for days, though."

Which could be plenty of time for Frannie to hold a memorial service, pack up their belongings, and be long gone before questions about the exact cause of death arose.

"There's more," Nora said, glancing around cautiously. "Len at the hardware store said Frannie phoned, asking about returning Kansas's new fishing gear—everything still in the packaging. Said they 'wouldn't be needing it anymore.'"

"And she had quite the collection of bags when she left the cleaners," Enid added. "Looked like she was picking up everything they'd dropped off since arriving in town."

I felt a rush of gratitude for these three women and their hawk-like surveillance of the town. They might couch everything in gossip, but their observations were sharp.

"I need to pay Frannie a visit," I said.

"Now?" Trish looked scandalized.

"If she's planning to leave town, I may not get another chance," I pointed out. "And I have some questions only she can answer."

The three women exchanged another set of meaningful glances.

"Well," Nora said slowly, "if you're going that way, you might want to know that Frannie's car was parked outside the bank a while ago."

"And when we saw Bertha," Enid added, "she said Frannie had been at the postal counter in your store, sending express packages. Address labels to somewhere in Texas, I believe."

I nodded, absorbing this information. "Thank you. I appreciate you sharing all this."

As they continued their patrol of Pine Street, I changed course toward the McBrides' lakeside cabin. I'd been so fixated on Kansas's role in my father's disappearance that I'd barely considered Frannie as anything other than his stylish appendage.

But maybe that had been a mistake. Maybe I'd been looking at the wrong person all along.

I needed to see Frannie before she disappeared with whatever secrets she—and Kansas—had been keeping.

CHAPTER TWELVE

Frannie's cabin looked different today—less charming, more temporary. The Mercedes parked in the gravel driveway had its back hatch open, revealing several designer suitcases neatly stacked inside. A "For Sale" sign had already appeared in the front window.

I paused at the front door, checking that Des was sitting calmly beside me. This time, I wasn't coming to play nice.

"Ready, girl?" I murmured to Des, who gave a soft whine in response.

Before I could knock, the door swung open. Frannie stood in the doorway, wrapped in an elegant black cardigan. Her eyes were hidden behind oversized sunglasses despite the overcast day.

"Tilly." Her voice was flat. Not hostile, not welcoming, just acknowledging my existence.

"Frannie," I returned, offering what I hoped was a sympathetic smile. "I'm so sorry about Kansas. I came to see if there's anything I can do."

She stepped back without expression. "Come in, if you like. I'm packing. I can't bear to stay here without Kansas."

Inside, the cabin looked like it had been erased—no pictures, no clutter, just suitcases and silence. A half-empty wine bottle sat on the counter beside a single glass.

Des sniffed the air, stiffened slightly, and pressed her side to mine like a warning.

"I heard you might be leaving soon," I said, trying to keep my tone neutral.

Frannie removed her sunglasses, revealing eyes that were red-rimmed but dry. "News travels fast in this town."

"It always has."

She busied herself aligning papers on the counter with deliberate care. "I need to take Kansas home. There's nothing for me here now."

Des paced behind me, nails clicking. I laid a calming hand on her back, but she didn't settle.

"I understand," I said, though I didn't. "Do you have family waiting for you back home?"

"Kansas was my family," she replied. "But I have friends. Support."

I gestured toward a chair. "Do you mind if I sit? I actually had a few questions."

Frannie didn't sit, just refilled her glass. "I'm not sure what I can help you with."

"The doctors at the hospital," I ventured carefully, "did they tell you what happened? Why Kansas collapsed?"

Frannie's shoulders stiffened. Des growled softly. I steadied her with my hand.

"They said it was his heart," Frannie replied. "These things happen."

That didn't track with the symptoms I'd witnessed, nor

with Trish's inside scoop from her niece at the clinic. I leaned in.

"Apparently he had a shellfish allergy... but you already knew that."

She blinked. "Yes, since childhood, but it's never been an issue. He was always careful."

Finally, I thought we were getting somewhere. "His symptoms looked like a severe allergic reaction. Are you sure nothing he ate could have triggered it?"

Her tone sharpened. "The doctors were quite clear it was heart failure."

I nodded, not wanting to push further. Frannie clearly wanted to avoid the topic of Kansas's allergies. "When are you planning to hold the service?"

Frannie reached for her wineglass. "Friday morning, small and private. Then I'm taking him home." She turned to face me directly. "I hope that's not why you're here, Tilly. To interrogate a grieving widow about funeral arrangements."

Des whined louder and wedged herself against my side, trembling.

"Of course not," I assured her. "But I need to ask—did Kansas ever talk about my father?"

Her expression flickered—something unreadable. "He was very invested in your father's store," she said slowly. "He mentioned Walter often."

Des circled behind my chair, her nails clicking against the wooden floor.

"But did he ever say anything specific? About his disappearance?"

Frannie took a deliberate sip before answering. "Kansas had his theories. He thought Devon Fontaine might have been involved."

That caught me off guard. "Devon? Why?"

"There was some sort of confrontation at a recent town council meeting. Walter openly opposed Devon's logging proposal, and apparently things got heated." She shrugged one elegant shoulder. "Kansas said Devon was furious. Called Walter an obstacle that needed to be 'removed permanently.'"

My pulse quickened. "Did Kansas report it?"

"He wasn't sure he'd heard it correctly. But later, when Walter disappeared..." She let the implication hang in the air. "Kansas felt guilty for not saying something sooner."

Des suddenly barked—a sharp, urgent sound that made both Frannie and me jump. I flinched.

"Des! Quiet," I commanded, but she continued pacing, her body tense. "I'm sorry about this. She's normally so well-behaved."

Frannie gave a tight smile. "It's fine. Animals can sense distress."

I stood, brushing off my knees. "I'm sorry, you were talking about Kansas feeling guilty. Did Kansas want to talk to me about that at the social?"

Frannie nodded, her eyes dropping to her glass. "He was worried. Said you might be poking into dangerous things."

"Did Kansas say anything else about Devon? Any proof he might have had?"

"I don't think so," Frannie said. "We didn't talk about it much. It upset him."

Devon had always seemed polished, corporate—calculated, but there was that gossip about his wife's death. And something else about Frannie's story rang true. Devon had motive. My father had opposed his logging plans fiercely.

Des chose that moment to lunge toward the kitchen counter, nose raised toward Frannie's papers that ended up scattered across the floor. I grabbed her collar, mortified by her behaviour.

"Des! Stop it!" I pulled her back, feeling my carefully constructed interview crumbling. "I'm so sorry, Frannie. I don't know what's gotten into her," I said, trying to pull the papers together.

"Don't worry about it. I've got it," Frannie said as she hurried over, gathering her papers and moving them out of reach.

I struggled to maintain my composure while forcing Des to sit beside me. "I should probably let you finish packing."

"Thank you for stopping by," Frannie said, walking me to the door. "I appreciate your concern."

I nodded, my thoughts churning as I headed down the steps with Des pulling eagerly at her leash. I'd barely reached the gravel path when a sleek, midnight-blue sedan rolled into the driveway, crunching to a halt beside Frannie's Mercedes.

Mayor John Bugle stepped out. He looked genuinely surprised to see me.

"Tilly," he said, his bushy eyebrows rising slightly. "I didn't expect to see you here."

"Just checking on Frannie," I explained, gesturing vaguely behind me. "Seeing if she needed anything."

"Same here," the mayor said, straightening his tie. "Awful business, what happened to Kansas."

I walked a few paces down the path, then paused. As I glanced back, I caught a glimpse through the cabin window: Frannie and the mayor, face to face. Her posture was rigid, her gestures sharp. No grief now—just business.

The mayor responded by closing the curtains with a swift tug.

Whatever was going on, it wasn't about funeral arrangements.

My earlier certainty evaporated. Frannie had redirected my suspicions toward Devon so smoothly, I'd almost missed what was happening. Now I doubted everything she'd told me—and my own judgment for believing her.

"Des, please," I muttered, struggling to keep her from lunging toward a passing squirrel. "Just behave for five more minutes."

Her performance at Frannie's had rattled me more than I wanted to admit. The well-trained, even-tempered dog she'd been up to now seemed like a fantasy compared to the restless animal pulling at her leash. Bringing her to these visits had been a mistake.

Willow Cabin appeared through the trees, its rustic exterior somehow less welcoming than before. I needed answers from Sean—real ones this time—but my confidence had taken a serious blow after my talk with Frannie.

Des suddenly stopped, ears perked toward the cabin. A muscle in her back twitched.

"What is it, girl?" I whispered, instantly alert to her change in demeanour.

Sean opened the door before we reached the porch, looking rumpled. His flannel shirt looked wrinkled as if he'd slept in it.

"Tilly," he said, voice flat, without energy. "And Des." His gaze drifted behind us, checking if I'd brought backup. "Didn't expect to see you."

"We need a real conversation, Sean."

Something in my tone must have registered, because he stepped back without question, holding the door wider.

"Coffee?" he offered.

"Already had three," I replied, stepping past him. "But thanks."

He gave a faint, distracted smile. "You're ahead of me—I

only just got back from the lake." He rubbed a hand over his face. "Was out early collecting samples."

Des hesitated at the threshold, which was so unlike her usual behaviour that I found myself urging her on.

"Come on, girl," I encouraged quietly. She entered reluctantly, staying unnaturally close to my side. Her nose twitched once, twice, nostrils flaring as she sniffed the air, then she lowered her head, giving a single uneasy *huff* near the doorway before pressing forward.

The cabin looked different. Sean's geology books were still stacked by the desk, rocks arranged in tidy rows, but now a half-packed backpack sat on the bed. What caught my attention, however, were the maps: several of them spread across the table, marked with different notations and elevation markers, with a compass and pencils scattered among them.

"Going somewhere?" I asked, nodding toward the bag.

Sean rubbed his jaw, stubble rasping against his palm. "Field work. Just for a few days. Maybe a week."

"Convenient timing." The words came out sharper than I'd intended.

His eyes narrowed slightly. "It's been planned for a while."

I let Des settle near the door while I moved toward the table. I wasn't here to get comfortable, but the maps had caught my interest.

"What's all this?" I asked, gesturing to the sprawled papers.

Sean hesitated, then gestured to the maps. "I'm planning a field expedition to the north ridge. Trying to reconcile these older surveys with the terrain I've been finding." He moved to the table. "The problem is, these maps were created decades apart using different methods. I need to find the most reliable route."

I studied the maps with genuine interest. "This ridge line follows a different path on each map."

Sean's eyebrows rose. "You know how to read topographical maps," he said, more like he was reminding himself of my experience rather than asking a question.

"Of course I do." I chuckled without looking up. "You learn to notice inconsistencies—they can be life or death in the field."

"Exactly," Sean said, his voice warming with professional interest. "I've been spending too much time second-guessing which path to take."

We stood side by side over the maps, the shared task creating a natural connection as we traced contour lines and compared coordinates. For a moment, we were just two people solving a problem together, and the tension between us eased.

"See this tributary?" I asked, pointing to a blue line snaking through the contours. "It's shown on both maps, but the newer one has it more accurately placed. I've hiked near there. The waterway definitely curves to the east like this one shows."

"That helps a lot," Sean said, looking genuinely relieved. "I was planning to use that as a landmark. You just saved me hours of unnecessary hiking."

"This route here," I traced a path with my finger, "follows the ridge and avoids that steep section entirely. Much easier terrain."

Sean marked the path with a pencil, nodding. "That makes much more sense than what I was planning." He glanced at me with what seemed like genuine appreciation. "Thanks, Tilly. You've got a good eye for this."

The brief collaboration had momentarily distracted me from my purpose, but as Sean straightened up from the maps, I remembered why I'd come. I took a deep breath.

"Sean, I need to talk to you about Kansas."

His expression shifted, the openness from our map discussion fading. "Yeah, I was there. Heart attack, right? Terrible thing."

"No," I said firmly. "It wasn't a heart attack."

That got his attention. His posture shifted, shoulders straightening further. "What do you mean?"

"It turns out that Kansas had a severe shellfish allergy, and his symptoms that night were consistent with anaphylaxis. But I don't remember seeing any food at the social that would trigger that kind of response."

"You think someone did it on purpose?" Sean asked carefully.

"I don't know yet. But it's strange, isn't it? A man in apparent good health suddenly has a fatal allergic reaction right when he was about to tell me something important." I watched his face for any reaction. "It feels connected somehow."

Sean pushed away from the maps, moving to the window. "That's a serious implication, Tilly."

"I know, but I have my suspicions."

"Why?" Sean asked, turning back to face me.

"Kansas had been acting strange since the night Gus apparently told him something at the bar. Then, at the social, he clearly wanted to tell me something important before he collapsed."

Des suddenly whined, pawing at the floor beside me.

"I just left Frannie's," I continued, ignoring Des's interruption. "She claims Devon threatened my father during a council meeting. Said Devon called him 'an obstacle that needed to be removed.'"

Sean turned back to me, brow furrowed. "And you believe her?"

I hesitated. "I did, at first. But something didn't add up. I saw her with Mayor Bugle after I left. She dropped the grieving widow act pretty quickly."

"So you're here because...?" Sean let the question hang.

Because everyone suddenly had something to hide—and maybe Sean did, too.

I met his eyes. "I want to know if you're hiding more than just your reality TV embarrassment."

A muscle twitched in Sean's jaw. "I told you why I reacted that way with your father."

"But you didn't tell me why you're really in Balsam Bay," I countered, moving back to the maps. "These aren't just for a book. You're mapping discrepancies in the official surveys." I tapped one of the sheets. "Your gear is too high-end for someone just writing a book. You can afford to rent this cabin for months, and I know it isn't cheap. You said you had a hard time getting work after Australia. Not really the picture of a man rolling in disposable cash."

Des suddenly barked. It shattered the quiet. She lunged toward the door, almost breaking free of my grip on her leash.

"Des! Stop it!" I pulled her back, mortified, as she continued to growl. "I'm so sorry. She's never like this."

Sean had jumped back, hands raised defensively. "Is she okay?"

"I don't know what's gotten into her today," I admitted, struggling to maintain control. "She's been acting strange since this morning."

Des quieted but remained tense.

"Maybe she senses your stress," Sean suggested, keeping his distance. "Dogs pick up on that."

I felt my face flush with embarrassment. First Frannie, now Sean. I couldn't even control my father's dog, let alone solve this increasingly complicated mystery.

"I'm sorry," I said again, fighting to keep my voice steady. "But I still need answers. Your specialty is in resource evaluation, those are high-end survey tools, and you're clearly well-funded despite claiming the Australia incident hurt your livelihood." I gestured toward the maps. "You're not just writing a book. You're surveying the area for someone."

Sean's eyes widened—not at the accusation, but at how much I'd pieced together.

"You've been doing your homework," he said, a note of respect in his voice.

"Callie found some of your published papers online. They're all about geological assessments for mining operations." I held his gaze. "So, who hired you to survey Balsam Bay?"

Sean hesitated, clearly weighing his options. Des growled again, a low rumble in her chest. I tightened my grip on her collar, feeling increasingly overwhelmed.

His eyes flicked to mine, then away. Not evasive—just uncertain. Like he was trying to figure out how much truth he could afford to give me. I could see the struggle on his face, and for the first time, I believed he wasn't trying to lie—he just didn't know what to say.

"Look," he finally said, "I am writing a book. That part's true. But yes, I'm also under contract with a resource company. That's as much as I can say. I signed an NDA."

"Who's paying for all this gear and cabin time?" I pressed. "The same people who might benefit from my father's disappearance?"

"It's not that simple, Tilly. I'm a geologist, not a corporate spy. I collect data—that's it."

"And who gets that data? Devon Fontaine?"

Sean's expression remained neutral. "Devon?" He looked momentarily confused. "I told you, I can't discuss my client."

Des growled again, a low rumble in her chest. I tightened my grip on her leash, feeling increasingly overwhelmed.

"That's convenient," I snapped, frustration seeping into my voice. "Everyone in this town has secrets they're conveniently unable to share."

"It's not illegal to work for someone, Tilly."

"No, but it's suspicious that you didn't mention it. You're cultivating this 'geologist-turned-author' image while secretly surveying the area for a mining company. Or is it lumber?" I took an accusatory step forward.

Des chose that moment to lunge again, this time breaking free of my grip. She charged at Sean, barking furiously, forcing him to scramble onto a chair to avoid her snapping jaws.

"Des! No!" I shouted, lunging for her leash. I managed to grab it, but not before she knocked over a stack of books and scattered a collection of rock samples across the floor.

Sean remained on the chair, eyes wide with alarm. "Tilly—"

"I'm so sorry," I gasped, yanking Des back with more force than necessary. My cheeks burned with humiliation. "I don't know what's wrong with her."

"Maybe she's picking up on something we're missing," Sean suggested carefully, stepping down once I had Des secured.

"Or maybe I'm just terrible at taking care of my father's dog," I said bitterly. I felt tears threatening and fought them back. This day was unraveling spectacularly.

"Look," Sean said, his voice softening as he kept a cautious distance. "I'm not hiding anything sinister. Here—" He crossed to his desk, pulled open a drawer, and extracted a flash drive. "Take this."

"What is it?"

"All my data. Soil samples, bedrock analysis. Everything

I've collected. My NDA only prevents me from naming my employer."

I stared at the drive, then at him, torn between suspicion and desperation for any information. "Why give me this now?"

"Because I didn't hurt your father, I didn't hurt Kansas, and I'm not out to destroy Balsam Bay." His expression was earnest. "And because it's important to me that you know that."

Des continued to strain against her leash, making it impossible to think clearly. Every ounce of confidence I'd had that morning had evaporated. I'd misread Frannie. I couldn't control Des, and Sean wasn't acting like the villain I'd made him out to be—because he wasn't one.

"I should go," I said finally, accepting the flash drive with my free hand. "I need to take Des back to Joe's and regroup. Clearly, I'm in over my head."

Sean nodded but looked disappointed. "Tilly, be careful. Whatever's happening here, it sounds like it's bigger than just Walter or Kansas."

"I know," I said, my voice barely above a whisper. "That's what scares me."

Outside, I stood for a long moment, trying to collect myself while Des whined. My father would have handled this better. The thought hit me with unexpected force. He would have kept Des calm, known which questions to ask to get to the bottom of things.

I shook myself and walked away. Decision made. If I couldn't even manage my father's dog, what made me think I could solve his disappearance?

It was time to take Des back to someone who actually knew what they were doing.

CHAPTER THIRTEEN

The kitchen timer buzzed for the third time, but I barely heard it. The kettle had boiled dry an hour ago, the forgotten mug beside me, still empty. Sunrise had long since passed, and the sky held all the markings of a perfect day, but inside, I remained fixed in place, lost in the fragments of my father's life spread across the kitchen table.

Des watched me from her spot by the window, head resting on her paws, eyes tracking my movements as I shifted papers from one pile to another. Every so often, she let out a soft sigh, as if to say, *Still nothing?*

I'd been at it for hours, going through the scraps from Dad's desk drawer again and again. The fragments were still just that—a puzzle with too many missing pieces: faded property maps, circled obituaries, highlighted sections of the town charter. Nothing fit. It was like trying to read a story with half the pages torn out. I could tell he'd been digging into something about the town's past—especially the mine—but I couldn't piece together what he'd found or why it had scared him enough to vanish.

If he had vanished. And wasn't in that canoe after all.

Jason knocked just after lunch, the sound of his knuckles against the door frame startlingly loud in the quiet house. Des didn't even bother to bark. She just stretched and went to greet him, as if to say *this one's allowed.*

Jason stepped inside, his RCMP face firmly in place. The careful mask he wore when he couldn't afford to be my brother.

"Got a minute?" he asked, settling his hat on the hook like he owned the place.

"That depends," I said, gathering the papers into a neat stack. "Is this a social call or professional business?"

""Bit of both." He took a seat at the table without waiting for an invitation.

"Callie's at the store with Bertha," I said, setting the kettle to boil. "Tea?"

"No. This won't take long."

That got my attention. I turned to face him. "What's up?"

"I spoke with Dr. Marsh about Kansas." He drummed his fingers on the table. "He's leaning toward anaphylaxis. Severe allergic reaction."

I felt a surge of vindication. "I knew it—"

"But," Jason cut in, holding up a hand, "there's no sign of foul play."

"Come on," I said, tossing the tea bags into the pot with more force than necessary. "That's not—"

"Tilly," he said, voice gentler now, "there were three dozen perogy entries. Cross-contamination happens. Hidden ingredients, shared trays. It's messy. It's not murder."

I crossed my arms. "He wanted to talk about Dad, then he died. That's not a coincidence."

Jason didn't argue. But he didn't agree, either. "It might

matter. But until I have something concrete—anything—I can't go around making accusations. Especially not when tensions are already so high."

"It's not a conspiracy when the dots connect," I said, sharper than I meant to.

Jason's expression softened. "Or maybe he just wanted to push you to sell the store, but things went sideways before he got the chance."

I moved to the window, turning my back to him. Des followed, brushing her muzzle lightly against my leg like a reminder.

"The mayor called me this morning," Jason continued. "Said you've been asking too many questions around town. That you're making people uncomfortable."

I whirled back to face him. "Since when is asking questions a crime?"

"It's not." Jason's voice remained steady. "But it can make people... defensive. Especially when those questions imply they might be involved in something illegal."

Maybe that was the point. Maybe someone wanted me loud and obvious—so I'd get pulled off the board before I asked the right questions.

He hesitated, then added, quieter now: "And if someone higher up catches wind that you haven't stepped back from this, it'll be my head on a platter. They'll think I'm feeding you intel, or not doing enough to contain it. I won't just lose trust. I could lose my job."

That stopped me cold.

Jason wasn't just offering gentle warnings. He was standing between me and the line I hadn't realized I'd already crossed.

"So that's it? Kansas drops dead and we all move on?"

Jason stood, straightening his belt. "Just cool it for a bit before this drags us both under. Focus on the store. On Callie." He put his hat back on. "Before you end up stirring up more trouble than you bargained for."

After he left, I sank back into my chair, Des nudging at my hand. The warmth of her fur against my fingers should have been comforting, but all I felt was a growing sense of defeat.

Everything I thought I knew about Kansas's death suddenly felt shaky. If it was just an allergic reaction—a terrible accident—then where did that leave me? Was I connecting dots that didn't actually form a picture, hunting for a mystery because I couldn't accept the simple, brutal truth that Dad had capsized his canoe and was gone?

Des whined softly, sensing my distress.

I looked down at her—at her patient brown eyes, her muddy paws from this morning's walk, the way she'd glued herself to my side after our visits to Frannie's and Sean's. She was another responsibility, pulling at my limited focus.

Des needed more attention than I could give right now with everything else going on. I wasn't cut out for this juggling act—solving Dad's disappearance, running his store, and properly caring for his dog all at once.

"Come on, girl," I said, grabbing her leash from the hook by the door. "Let's go for a drive."

Des's tail wagged tentatively as I clipped on her leash. She followed me to the car, jumping into the backseat with her usual enthusiasm.

As I drove the familiar road out of town toward Joe's place, I tried to frame what I was about to do as a practical choice, not a retreat. Joe had been the one to choose Des for Dad. He'd picked her out, helped with her training, known her longer than I had. Right now, with my attention split between digging for answers and the store, I couldn't provide the consistent focus she deserved.

Joe was outside when I pulled up, splitting logs with practiced swings of his axe. He paused when he saw my car, setting the axe handle against the chopping block as I parked.

"Tilly," he nodded, his eyes moving to Des in the backseat. "Everything alright?"

I got out, letting Des jump down beside me. "No," I admitted. "Not really."

Joe's weathered face showed no judgment, just quiet understanding as I explained—about Kansas's death, about Jason's visit, about Des's strange behaviour with Frannie and Sean.

"She deserves someone focused on her right now," I finished, hating how it sounded like an excuse. "Someone who isn't splitting their attention between a missing father and a dead man."

Joe was quiet for a long moment, looking at Des, who sat perfectly behaved at my side, showing none of the erratic behaviour I'd described.

I swallowed the lump forming in my throat. "Please, Joe. Just until I figure things out."

Joe nodded, not with agreement, but with resignation. "She'll be alright here." He reached down, gave her a slow scratch beneath one ear. "Won't you, girl?"

Des looked up at me with those intelligent brown eyes. No whining, no barking, no dramatic displays. Just that steady, unwavering gaze that reminded me so much of Dad during our rare disagreements. That same mixture of disappointment and patience, as if waiting for me to come to my senses.

"I should get back," I said abruptly, breaking eye contact with the dog. "Callie will be home from the store soon."

I handed Joe her leash, along with the bag of food and

supplies. "Thank you. I'll come back for her when... when I've sorted everything out."

Joe took the items with a nod, his weathered face unreadable. But there was something in his eyes—not judgment exactly, but a quiet assessment that made me want to look away.

"You know," he said finally, his gaze shifting to Des, "your dad used to say a dog chooses their person as much as a person chooses their dog."

"Dad didn't choose her for me," I pointed out, shoving my hands into my pockets to hide their slight tremor. "I was just the only family left to take her."

Joe shrugged. "Maybe. But Des didn't hesitate."

I swallowed hard, forcing myself to maintain the casual tone of someone making a practical decision, not abandoning the last living connection to their father. "She'll be happier here. With someone who knows what they're doing."

"If you say so, Tilly." Joe's voice held no sarcasm, just a simple acceptance that somehow felt worse than any argument.

As I drove away, I avoided looking in the rearview mirror. I didn't want to see Des watching me leave. The emptiness in the car matched the hollow feeling in my chest. I'd lost my direction with the search, and now I'd given up the one connection I still had to Dad.

Jason was right. I was running myself in circles and ignoring the things I could still hold on to.

***

The drive back felt longer than thirty minutes. The car's silence—normally a comfort after years of Callie's teenage music choices—settled around me like a rain-soaked sleeping bag.

Twice, I caught myself glancing toward the backseat, half-expecting to see Des's alert face in the rearview mirror. Twice, the emptiness hit me all over again.

"You did the right thing," I told myself aloud, the sound of my voice startling in the quiet car. But the words rang hollow, unconvincing even to my own ears.

By the time I pulled into the driveway, dark clouds had gathered overhead, promising the season's first real storm. Fitting weather for what felt increasingly like a day of loss on all fronts. I sat in the parked car for several minutes, watching the wind tug at the balsam firs in the yard—those tall evergreens that had given the town its name—before finally forcing myself to go inside.

The house welcomed me with silence. No jingling collar tags. No clicking nails on hardwood. No soft huffs of dog breath from the corner. I moved through the rooms like a stranger, suddenly aware of how quickly I'd come to expect Des's presence in a space that had been my father's alone for decades. Had I really only known the dog for a few weeks? It felt longer.

I opened the screen door to find Frannie standing on the porch. Her clothes were still impeccably coordinated, but she looked even more exhausted than yesterday, the careful makeup not quite concealing the deepening shadows under her eyes. She clutched a small handbag in white-knuckled hands.

"Tilly," she said, with a perfunctory smile. "I hope you don't mind me stopping by again so soon."

"Of course not," I replied, stepping back to let her in. "How are the preparations going?

"Everything's ready," she said with a sigh. "Though of course, the actual burial will have to wait until…" she trailed off, her hand making a vague gesture. "Well, you know how these things go." She glanced around the empty house. "But that's not why I'm here. After our conversation yesterday, I found something I think you should see."

I wasn't ready for company, but I wanted to hear what Frannie had to say. "Can I get you something? Tea? Water?"

She shook her head. "No, thank you. I won't stay long."

We sat at the kitchen table, the papers from my earlier investigation hastily pushed to one side. Frannie set her handbag on her lap, fingers drumming lightly on the clasp.

"I was going through Kansas's things after you left yesterday," she said, her voice perfectly controlled. "And I found some new information about Devon Fontaine."

Frannie reached into her handbag. "This is from Kansas's laptop."

She pulled out a small USB drive, holding it delicately between two fingers. "It has emails between Kansas and Devon. I didn't read everything, but I know what blackmail look like." She paused. "I thought about going to the police. But what would I say? 'My husband was acting twitchy and now he's dead'? They'd just chalk it up to grief. Or worse, think I was trying to stir something up."

I stared at the drive. Small, innocuous. And suddenly, the centre of everything.

"Devon approached Kansas without my knowledge," she said, gaining momentum now. "He offered to help finance Kansas's bid for your father's store—in exchange for access to parts of the property. Kansas didn't tell me at first. Just said the financing had come through, like it was no big deal. I didn't think to question it."

She rubbed her arm. "Then Kansas started acting differently. Edgy. Eventually, he told me about the deal with Devon. At first, he thought it was just business—nothing to worry about. But then the details started piling up—permits, projections, expansion plans. Talks of logging. More mining. That's when he realized how deep in he was. And he realized how deep in he was. But after your father disappeared, that's when he really got nervous."

I said nothing. Just watched her. Waited.

"The night before the social, he kept pacing. Said he wanted to do the right thing. That he'd made a mistake." Her eyes flicked to the drive. "I think he was planning to walk away from the deal. Maybe even tell you—go public with everything."

It was too perfect. Devon served up as the villain. Just enough detail to sound real—vague where it mattered most.

Her gaze met mine then—cool, unflinching. "I didn't marry Kansas for love. But I didn't plan on being a widow, either. If Devon had anything to do with that, I want to know."

"Is my father mentioned in these emails?" I asked, trying to find connections between the two men.

Frannie's eyes flickered with something. "Not directly," she said carefully. "But there was an email where Devon warned Kansas that your father might be an obstacle to their plans." She leaned forward slightly. "I think that's why Devon was so eager to have Kansas buy the store. He wanted someone more... cooperative than your father in control of that property."

"What kind of development plans?" I asked, not touching the drive yet.

"The kind that would make it easier to get permits for expanded logging operations. And eventually, mining." She tapped the USB drive. "Devon was very specific about the value of your father's property and its strategic location. Land surveys, projected timelines, even pressure points on council votes. Everything he needed to push it through was in there." She hesitated, then added, "If Walter really did get in Devon's way, and then Kansas did, too..." She didn't finish the thought, but the implication landed like a stone.

I stared at the USB drive, more suspicious of Frannie's intentions than I had been yesterday.

"Why bring this to me now?" I asked, still not touching the drive.

Frannie's eyes darted away, then back. "After Kansas... I don't know who's watching. Who's listening. I figured you'd know what to do with this—quietly."

I picked up the USB drive, weighing it in my palm. Whatever was on this tiny piece of plastic might help untangle the questions surrounding Dad's accident and Kansas's death.

"I'll look at it," I said. "But Frannie, if there's anything else you know—anything at all—now's the time to share it."

She stood abruptly. "That's all I have. I should go. The arrangements need attending to."

I walked her out, watching as she hurried down the path to her car.

Once she was gone, I closed the door and leaned against it. Something about her story had knocked me off-balance. I'd been chasing answers for days, and now Frannie just handed me everything I needed?

I sat at the kitchen table, staring at the plastic rectangle. Why would she give me evidence that tied her husband to a development scheme? Was I following a trail—or being led down one? Dad used to say the most dangerous trap was the one that looked like a shortcut.

I reached for my laptop. Then stopped. The emails could wait. I needed to clear my head—approach whatever was on it with caution, not desperation.

I tucked the drive into my pocket and turned to the kettle. Tea felt like the right thing. Dad's thing. Steadying.

But as the silence pressed in, I glanced toward the back

door, half-expecting Des to appear. She didn't bark or fuss—just stayed close. I'd given her up because I thought I couldn't manage both the mystery and the dog. Now, stirring honey into a mug I wasn't sure I even wanted, I felt the weight of everything I'd set aside. The mystery. The dog. Both slipping.

The phone's shrill ring cut through my thoughts. I crossed to the wall-mounted unit, grateful for the distraction from my spinning thoughts.

"Hello?"

"Tilly, it's Joe." His voice was tight with concern. "Des is gone."

My heart thudded hard against my ribs. "What?"

"I took her for a walk after you left. She was fine, but when I got back, I had to take a call. Must've left the gate unlatched. By the time I got off the phone, she was nowhere to be found."

"She couldn't have gone far," I said, already reaching for my keys. "Have you checked—"

"I've checked everywhere," Joe cut in. "She's not on my property. Called the nearest neighbours, too. Nothing."

I closed my eyes, a wave of guilt washing over me. "This is my fault. I shouldn't have—"

"Don't waste time on that now," Joe said firmly. "I'll keep looking here. You check in town, places she knows."

"I'll find her," I promised.

I slumped into a kitchen chair, staring at the emptiness surrounding me. The mug of tea steamed, forgotten. The USB drive dug into my thigh through my pocket, its importance suddenly diminished by Des's disappearance.

When I'd arrived in Balsam Bay, I'd been so confident. What if I'd been wrong about everything? What if there was no mystery to solve, just the brutal reality of accidents and consequences? What if my search for deeper meaning was just a way to avoid accepting that sometimes people just disappeared from your life?

I pressed the heels of my hands against my eyes, fighting back the stinging threat of tears. This wasn't the time for self-pity. Des was out there somewhere, probably trying to find her way back home. I needed to focus on finding her, not wallow in my failures.

CHAPTER FOURTEEN

I'd spent fruitless hours driving up and down the highway as the sun went down, calling Des's name, scanning the ditches and tree lines. Eventually, Callie called me home, worried about me driving around in the state I was in. She took the keys and tried to steer me toward bed, promising the whole town would be on the lookout for Des. But sleep was the last thing on my mind.

Word spread overnight. Mandy made late-night calls, quietly establishing an unofficial phone tree. Bertha insisted the best thing I could do was stay put. "She'll come back to the last place she felt safe," she'd said, like it was fact. And maybe it was. In wilderness survival, you're taught that if you're turned around, and the terrain stops making sense, you don't keep moving. You stay where you are and let the rescuers come to you.

So I waited—heart thudding like a beacon—praying Des would find her way home. Hoping she'd rescue me, like I was the one who was lost.

With Des out of reach, I turned my thoughts to the other thread unravelling in front of me.

"We're missing something. About Kansas," I said, my voice hollow in the quiet kitchen.

Callie looked up from her laptop, the blue light casting shadows across her face. "You can't blame yourself for Kansas's death."

"Can't I?" I pushed back from the table, the legs of my chair scraping against the floor. "I was so sure he was behind Dad's disappearance. I was watching him. And now he's dead—right in front of everyone—and I still don't know what happened to Dad."

I moved to the window, looking out at the darkness. The spot by the door where Des usually slept was empty, a quiet void I couldn't ignore.

"Joe will find her," Callie said softly, knowing exactly where my thoughts had wandered.

"I know." I rubbed at a smudge on the glass. "I just—I shouldn't have given her back."

"You were overwhelmed."

"I was scared," I corrected, turning to face my daughter. "Scared I couldn't handle another responsibility. Scared I'd mess up with her the way I've messed up trying to figure out what happened to Dad and Kansas."

Callie closed her laptop and leaned forward. "Then let's unmess it. We have evidence that suggests Grandpa might still be out there somewhere. Kansas knew something, and he died because of it. These are facts."

My lips twitched in what might have been the ghost of a smile. "Look at you, sounding like me."

"I learned from the best." Callie stood, stretching. "So what would the best teach me to do right now?"

I tapped my fingers against the window frame, falling into the familiar rhythm of decision-making I'd used throughout my career.

"We go back to the start," I said finally. "Fresh eyes. No assumptions."

"Everything we know." Callie nodded.

"Everything," I agreed, returning to the table with renewed purpose. "Let's lay it all out chronologically."

The kitchen transformed into a war room as we worked methodically through the night. It was easier to focus on timelines and theories than the ache of not knowing where Des was. I brewed fresh coffee while Callie cleared the table, spreading out maps of Balsam Bay, printed copies of Dad's notes, and names of the key players.

"Grandpa disappears. Canoe accident, but no body."

"We know he was researching the mine, and something spooked him." I continued, arranging index cards in a neat line.

"Then we have Gus, who wanted Dad's Canada Post contract. Besides acting shifty, the only involvement he had was driving Dad's truck back home from the launch site." I frowned. "But Gus acts nervous, not guilty."

"And there's Sean Patrick, who 'found' the canoe." Callie made air quotes. "He had an argument with Dad, and his story about being here to write a geology book doesn't add up."

I realized I'd hadn't told Callie what I'd learned about Sean's secret contract, nor had I checked the thumb drive of data he'd given me, so I quickly filled her in.

"He's right." Callie confirmed as she browsed the files. "Nothing unexpected. It lines up with what you said."

I filed Sean away—no longer a suspect, just a man with secrets that weren't mine to chase.

"So, Devon Fontaine, one of the mine reopening's staunchest supporters," I continued, placing a sticky note with Devon's name on the table. "Dad and Kansas were the most vocal council members opposing him."

"And the McBrides." Callie placed their names side by side. "Kansas kept pushing Dad to sell the store. Only it turns out Kansas didn't have the means to buy it."

I nodded, studying the patterns forming. "The walking club ladies overheard Gus telling Kansas and Frannie something shocking at the bar—that's when Frannie learned Kansas was broke."

"And now Kansas is dead." Callie touched the timeline. "Right when he seemed ready to tell you something."

Silence settled between us as we absorbed the reframed information.

"The USB drive," I said suddenly, straightening. "Frannie said it would help me understand why Devon would want Kansas silenced."

Callie raised an eyebrow. "Bit eager to point fingers elsewhere, isn't she?"

"Very." I retrieved my laptop from the living room, the power cable trailing behind me. "She said it contained emails between Kansas and Devon—proof they had a deal. Devon would help Kansas finance buying the store, and Kansas would support reopening the mine."

"Convenient evidence," Callie noted dryly.

"Especially the part where Kansas apparently got cold feet and was threatening to back out." I plugged in the USB drive. "According to Frannie, Devon would have done anything to keep Kansas on track."

Callie moved behind my chair, peering at the screen. "Emails look real enough."

The USB contained a folder labelled "Kansas-Devon" with

a dozen email exchanges. The conversations started professionally, grew friendly, and then turned tense in the last weeks. In the last email, Kansas threatened to "go public with everything" if Devon didn't back off.

"That puts Devon in a pretty bad light," Callie muttered.

"Let's see what else is here." I backed out to the main directory and sorted by date. "These emails are from the last six months, but there's a file created just yesterday?"

That familiar rush hit me—like stepping onto solid ground after searching blind. I switched to thumbnail view and scrolled slowly through the files.

"There," Callie pointed. "That's not an email."

At the bottom of the list was a PDF document, tucked between larger files. The filename was just a string of numbers. I clicked it open.

The document loaded—a bank transfer confirmation. Sender: Eighth Pine Management. Recipient: Francesca McBride. Amount: $250,000. Date: last Sunday... the day after Kansas died.

"Eighth Pine Management," I repeated slowly. "I'm sure I've heard that name before."

Callie was already typing on her phone. "Give me a second... Here. Chamber of Commerce donor list from last year's Winter Festival. Eighth Pine Management sponsored the ice sculpture contest. And guess who accepted the cheque on their behalf?"

Callie turned her phone so I could see the local newspaper photo. Devon Fontaine, smiling beside an ice carving of a wolf, holding an oversized cheque with the Eighth Pine logo.

"Devon's company paid Frannie two hundred and fifty thousand dollars the day after Kansas died," I said, my voice measured and quiet. The quiet that came before certainty.

"It's Devon," Callie said, breaking the silence. "It has to be.

He and Kansas had their arrangement, Kansas tried to back out, threatened to expose something—"

"And Devon silenced him," I finished, but my expression remained thoughtful. "Then paid Frannie to keep quiet about what she knew."

But something in my gut wasn't sitting right. It read like a confession—but maybe that was the point. I'd spent years following that feeling into wilderness searches, trusting it when logic and evidence seemed to lead elsewhere.

"What?" Callie asked, catching my hesitation.

"Nothing," I shook my head. "Just making sure we're thinking this through completely."

I saved a copy of the bank transfer to my laptop and backed up the entire USB to my cloud storage. Then I ejected the drive and tucked it into my pocket.

"What now?" Callie asked, the question hanging in the pre-dawn kitchen.

I glanced at the window, where the first hint of grey was lightening the eastern sky. The corner where Des should have been remained empty, a void more significant than I had been willing to admit.

"We're close," I said, almost to myself. "But I don't think we're seeing the complete picture yet."

"So, what's the next step?" Callie asked.

I hesitated. "I don't know. Not yet. But something's coming into focus—I just don't know what it is."

"We'll figure it out together," she said, steady as ever.

I gave a tired smile, touched by her loyalty but wary of what might be coming. "You've done more than enough, Callie. I don't want you getting pulled any deeper."

"Mom—"

"Please." My voice was soft, but the weight behind it was

unmistakable. "I've already lost Grandpa. I couldn't take it if something happened to you, too."

Callie didn't argue. Just stayed close, watching me with concern as I stared down at the timeline. Everything pointed somewhere. I just wasn't yet sure where.

Callie studied my face, recognizing the expression she'd seen a hundred times before—determination crystallized into something unbreakable.

"At least tell me what you're thinking," she said finally.

I gathered the timeline we'd created. It still felt too easy, too neat. Like a story someone wanted us to believe.

"It fits," I said slowly, "but maybe too well. I don't know if we're solving a mystery or stepping into one."

Callie watched me, quiet. "Then we keep going," she said. "We don't have to commit to anything yet."

I nodded, though unease curled at the edges of my thoughts. We had pieces. We had possibilities. But the truth didn't feel steady underfoot—not yet.

As I spoke, a sound came from the back door—a soft scratching, then a low whine that made both of us freeze. I moved first, crossing the kitchen in three quick strides and flinging the door open.

Des stood on the back step, mud-caked and exhausted, but with the unmistakable light of recognition in her eyes.

Des stood frozen in the doorway, her fur matted with mud and pine needles, her sides heaving from exertion. For one suspended moment, we simply stared at each other. Then Des took a tentative step forward, her tail giving a single uncertain wag.

"Oh my gosh," Callie whispered behind me.

I dropped to my knees. "Oh, my girl!."

The dam broke. Des lunged forward, crashing into me with such force that I nearly toppled backward. Her whole body quivered with exhaustion and relief, her cold nose buried against my neck.

"I'm sorry," I murmured into her fur. "I'm so sorry."

Des smelled of lake water and pine sap, of wild places and determination. I closed my eyes, the weight of the dog against my chest filling a void I'd been pretending wasn't there.

"She must have tracked you from Joe's," Callie said, wiping at her eyes.

Des finally pulled back, her tongue darting out to lick my chin before sitting properly, as if reporting for duty despite her dishevelment.

"She needs water," I said, my voice thick. "And food. And probably the world's longest bath."

Callie was already filling a bowl. "I've never seen an animal so filthy look so dignified."

It was true. Despite the mud and twigs, Des held herself with composure, watching me with eyes that seemed to say, *Of course I came back. Where else would I be?*

I ran my hand along Des's side, checking for injuries as she lapped noisily at the water Callie set down. Nothing seemed broken or bleeding, just the expected scrapes and scratches from moving through dense underbrush.

"She really is Grandpa's dog," Callie said with a smile. "Stubborn as all get-out."

The words struck me with unexpected force. Yes, Des was Dad's dog—the last living connection to my father. And like Dad, Des had refused to follow the expected path.

"I need to call Joe," I said, reaching for my phone. "Let him know she's safe."

"I'll text Mandy," Callie said. "She'll spread the word."

As I stepped into the living room to make the call, I heard Callie behind me.

"You ridiculous, wonderful dog," she murmured, her voice thick with relief. "I knew you'd be back."

I glanced back to see her hugging Des, face buried in the scruff behind one ear. Des melted into it like she was home.

I pressed the phone to my ear, relieved when Joe answered immediately despite the early hour.

"Joe, it's Tilly. Des is here."

"Thank goodness." Joe's relief was evident even through the crackling connection. "Is she alright?"

"Muddy, but seems fine. She must have followed our scent trail back to town."

"I'm not surprised," Joe said. "She's been restless since you drove away without her. Kept watching the road. I'm sorry I couldn't keep her contained."

"Don't apologize," I said, watching through the doorway as Callie wiped Des's paws with a towel. "I'm the one who should be sorry. I shouldn't have given up on her."

Joe was quiet for a moment. "She belongs with you, Tilly. Walter would have wanted that."

After ending the call, I returned to the kitchen where Callie had managed to clean the worst of the mud from Des's coat. The dog looked markedly improved, though still in need of a proper bath.

"Joe says she's been trying to escape since I dropped her off," I said, sitting at the table. Des moved to my side and stood close, solid as ever.

"She knew where she needed to be," Callie replied, washing her hands at the sink. "Now that Des is home and safe... what do we do about Devon?" Callie asked, quieter this time.

I glanced down at Des, whose steady presence anchored

me to the moment. "Not much we can do—not yet. A suspicious payment isn't proof of murder. And Devon's too careful. His company's got lawyers on speed dial."

Callie frowned. "Then what now?"

I ran my fingers through Des's fur. And then I said it out loud—something I hadn't been ready to claim until that moment. "We nudge him. Get him talking. People reveal things when they think they're winning."

"And how do we get him to think that?"

I looked over at Callie, the pieces sliding into place. "We give him what he wants. I tell him I'm ready to sell the store."

Her mouth dropped open. "You're—wait, what?"

"It's bait. He thinks I'm giving up—leaving Balsam Bay, leaving all this behind. I'll mention the USB, but just barely. Just enough to rattle him."

Des shifted beside me, as if sensing my resolve. She wasn't Dad's anymore. She was mine.

"You're not going alone," Callie said firmly.

I smiled faintly. "No. Not really." I scratched behind Des's ears. "But I won't do anything reckless. I'll meet him somewhere public—maybe the café. I'll tell Jason where I'm going."

"You still think Devon's guilty?"

I hesitated. "I don't know. The evidence points to him. But something about the way Frannie handed over that USB... it's too easy. Too neat."

Des shifted again, curling tighter against my leg. She didn't care about deception or distraction. She'd come back to the person who mattered. The rest was just noise.

"I still don't like it," Callie said.

"I know."

I looked at the USB one more time, then down at Des—steady, loyal, certain.

"But I think I've got what I need now," I said quietly.

Des looked up at the shift in my voice, her eyes alert and knowing. I ran a hand along her head—her presence no longer surprising, just right.

And with that, something in me clicked into place—a steadiness I hadn't felt since Dad disappeared.

Des had made it home.

Now it was my turn.

CHAPTER FIFTEEN

After Des's remarkable return, I couldn't bring myself to let her out of my sight. She'd crossed miles of wilderness to find me; the least I could do was keep her close.

I'd given her a proper bath, combing burrs and twigs from her coat while she sat with remarkable patience for a dog who'd just survived a wilderness trek. She still smelled faintly of lake water beneath the dog shampoo, but the mud was gone. What remained was a steady presence I hadn't expected —but one I found myself leaning on more than I'd realized. And I'd honoured that feeling by doing what was needed: slowing down, staying present, and not rushing headfirst into a decision I couldn't undo.

Still, I'd tossed and turned most of the night, my brain continuously circling back to that bank transfer. The evidence appeared incriminating, except it all felt just a bit too tidy. Like finding a confession already gift-wrapped.

It was early, and the store was still closed—just me and Des settling into her corner bed like we'd done this for years. I flipped on the lights and made my way to the coffeemaker.

The bell over the door jangled, making me jump. Gus stood there looking like he'd seen a ghost—shoulders hunched up, eyes darting around like a cornered rabbit checking the exits.

"We're not open yet," I called, kicking myself for not locking the door after carrying in the newspaper delivery.

"I know," Gus said, coming in anyway. His voice sounded like a rubber band stretched too tight. "Need to talk to you. Privately."

Something about him seemed off—the weird pasty look under his usually red face, the way he kept picking at a loose thread on his sleeve. Des perked up, her eyes locked on our visitor, but she stayed put. Smart dog.

"Coffee's fresh," I said, nodding toward the pot. My version of an olive branch.

Gus shook his head. "Can't stay long." Another glance over his shoulder through the window, like he half-expected the bogeyman to be lurking on the sidewalk.

I gave him a once-over, taking in the raccoon shadows under his eyes and the way his hands shook. "What's on your mind, Gus?"

He sucked in a breath like he was about to jump off a cliff. "It's about your dad."

My heart did a little tap dance. "What about him?"

"He's not dead."

Three words. Three tiny words that hit me like a freight train. My knees went wobbly, and suddenly the floor wasn't quite where I'd left it. Dad. Alive. My brain exploded in fifty directions—relief, shock, confusion, and yeah, a flash of straight-up anger.

Somehow I kept my poker face, though my heart was slamming so hard I figured Gus could probably see my shirt moving. I grabbed the counter edge to stay grounded, knuckles going bone-white.

"That's quite a statement," I managed, my voice way steadier than it had any right to be with the emotional hurricane whirling inside. I made myself focus on his trembling hands instead of the storm in my head.

"It's true," Gus croaked, his voice cracking like thin ice. "I staged the scene. The canoe, the damage—all of it." His Adam's apple bobbed up and down like it hurt. "Walter asked me to help him disappear."

I hung onto the counter's edge while the room did a slow spin around me. "Why would my father fake his own death?" Somehow my voice stayed level, even while my insides were doing somersaults.

Gus shot another look at the windows, checking the empty street. "He was being threatened. About his research into the mine." His voice dropped so low I nearly missed it. "I didn't do it to hurt him. I did it to keep him safe. And to protect others."

The coffeemaker chose that moment to gurgle and hiss, the cozy kitchen sound weirdly out of place in this upside-down moment. So Dad had been threatened. Threatened badly enough to ditch everything—the store, his whole life, his family? And here I'd been, metaphorically combing the lake for a body, when he'd left under his own power—just not by choice.

"So you helped him pull a disappearing act," I said, my brain slowly connecting dots that suddenly made a picture. All those weird bits that never fit—the stuff missing from the scene, the odd details. Des, not acting like a dog who'd lost someone forever, but like one who'd been told to stay put. She'd known all along. The little furry conspirator had known.

Gus nodded like he was carrying the weight of the world. "It all happened really fast. After I told him, Walter and I came up with a plan to make it look like he was dead. He needed my help to stage an accident. Something people would buy." He hesitated, then rubbed his right hand with his thumb.

After I told him. I caught the phrasing a second too late.

"I cut myself hauling the gear—left blood on one of the paddles. Couldn't leave it there, not with my DNA on it. So I took it home."

My stomach twisted. I remembered his bandaged hand when we first arrived in town. I just hadn't known what I was looking at. And that explained the missing paddle.

"Where is he now?"

"I don't know. Honest to God. We set everything up in less than a day. That night, a black SUV rolled up and took him. Last I saw, it was heading out of town." Gus dragged a hand through his thinning hair, leaving a streak of sweat at his temples. "Haven't heard a peep since."

Des had gotten up to move against me. That warm, solid weight kept me from floating away as my entire world flipped upside down.

"I took that photo of Walter getting into the SUV. Kept it in case I needed proof he left alive," he added, answering the question I hadn't asked. "I sent it to anonymously to Callie's blog after the town hall. Hoped it'd bring you some comfort. Didn't think it'd just light a fire under you."

So that's where the photo came from, I thought. "Why spill this now?" I asked, sounding way calmer than I had any right to.

"Because I'm leaving Balsam Bay. I don't know when I'll be back."

"That sure sounds like something a guilty person would do."

Gus looked at me. It wasn't guilt looking at me, it was fear.

"My family ordered me to get rid of Walter," he said flatly. "They said if I didn't handle him, they'd 'take care' of Jason and you instead." His voice cracked. "That's why I helped your dad disappear instead. I couldn't... I couldn't do what they asked."

My stomach dropped. I'd known the Bugles all my life, grown up with Gus, seen his father cutting ribbons and shaking hands. Never once had I imagined there was something so evil beneath that polished surface.

"The Bugles aren't who you think they are, Tilly." Gus's face had gone ashen. "That's why I'm leaving town. They told me to lay low until everything blows over, but what they really mean is they're furious I didn't follow orders. I helped Walter instead, and now..." He swallowed hard. "Let's just say I know what my father and the rest of them do to people who don't fall in line."

I studied his face, seeing the raw fear there. For the first time, I was seeing beyond the Bugle family's public facade—not just the influential pillars of the community everyone respected, but something much darker.

Gus's shoulders dropped like someone had cut the strings. "I screwed up, Tilly. It's all my fault. Got plastered at *The Rusty Lantern*. Kansas and Frannie were there, and I let my stupid mouth run about Walter not being dead." His throat worked as he swallowed. "Kansas just laughed it off—thought I was just another drunk talking garbage. But Frannie... she didn't crack a smile."

His eyes dropped to stare at his hands. "And now Kansas is dead. Because of my big mouth that night. I can't..." his voice broke like glass.

The image snapped into focus like the shutter of a camera —Kansas trying to tell me something at the social before he keeled over. That too-perfect timing of the USB drive showing up. The weird money transfer that practically screamed "look here!"

"What you're saying—" I started.

"I'm saying watch your back," Gus cut in, his voice tight with urgency.

"Why stick your neck out telling me this?" I asked. "If your family finds out..."

"I can't have you and Jason still wondering if your dad's alive or..." He stopped himself from saying it. "And Jason's RCMP. I couldn't dump this on him. He'd have to file reports, make it all official."

I nodded, starting to understand just how impossible his position was. "Thank you."

Once he was gone, I just crumpled down next to Des, the tough-girl act I'd put on for Gus's sake, finally cracking wide open. The empty store gave me permission to feel everything I'd been bottling up. My breathing went ragged and choppy as relief and complete disbelief duked it out inside me.

"He's alive," I whispered, as the waterworks finally broke through and spilled down my face. I buried my nose in Des's fur, letting myself have this one moment where the walls came down. My whole body was lit up—relief and fury sparking off each other.

I'd doubted my gut, second-guessed every memory, and lost sleep over what I might've missed or done differently. And the whole time, Dad had been out there somewhere, probably going crazy wondering if we were okay.

Des made this soft whining sound and nudged my hand with her cold nose, giving me that look that practically screamed, *Told you so, dummy.* Those eyes, with that steady look, stared into mine, and suddenly I just knew she'd been in on it the whole time. That explained her peculiar habit of checking the windows each morning and evening like she was expecting a delivery, the way she'd gather Dad's slippers and place them neatly by his chair every night before bed. What everyone mistook for a grieving dog's confusion was actually a furry lookout. As Bertha had muttered just the other day, 'That dog's not mourning—she's on sentry duty.' I'd laughed it off then, but Bertha had always been unnervingly perceptive.

I swiped at my eyes with my sleeve and pulled in a deep breath. "Well, girl," I said, my voice wobbling a bit, "guess we've got our work cut out for us."

"He's alive?" Callie echoed, her voice barely a breath in our kitchen. "Grandpa's alive, and Gus helped him pull a vanishing act?"

"That's Gus's story," I said, flipping on the kettle for tea. I'd locked up the store early, needing some quiet to wrap my head around Gus's bombshell and fill Callie in. "And yeah, I buy it. Nothing else makes sense with how Gus has been acting—or all those weird things that never added up at the scene."

Callie was quiet for a moment, then reached for her laptop. "Wait—hang on. I think I found something the other day without realizing what I was looking at."

I crossed the kitchen as she opened a bookmarked blog post.

"This local photographer posted a sunrise series—he hikes up near the ridge trail above the boat launch to shoot landscapes. I saved it because the colours were gorgeous."

She clicked through the images until she stopped on a wide shot of the shoreline below.

"There," she said, pointing. "That's Grandpa's truck. Parked near the launch. Timestamp says 5:18 a.m. The day he disappeared."

I leaned in. "That's definitely it. Not an unusual time if Dad wanted to get some early morning fishing in."

Callie nodded. "But here's what caught my eye."

She clicked to the next photo. At first glance, it looked like more trees and morning mist—until you spotted the figure coming out of the trail.

Ball cap. Broad shoulders. One paddle in his hand.

"That looks like Gus," Callie said. "Didn't think much of it until today."

My breath caught. "He said he took the other paddle with him after he cut his hand. Didn't want to leave evidence behind."

Callie nodded. "So there he is. Hiking back from staging the scene, just like he said."

We both just sat there as it sank in—Dad was alive. Des gave a little whine under the table and flopped down across my feet like a sandbag.

"Mom?" Callie's voice pulled me back. "You okay?"

"Yeah," I said softly. "It's just... a lot."

Callie gave me space for a few breaths. "But wait," she said slowly, her tone shifting as she worked it through. "If Kansas heard the truth from drunk Gus... and Frannie was there, too..."

"And then Kansas dropped dead right after trying to talk to me at the social," I said. "It fits a little too well, don't you think?"

Callie nodded grimly. "And now this?" She tapped the screen. "This backs up Gus's version. And the digital files Frannie gave you—"

"—feel like a misdirection," I said.

"But that money transfer—"

"Yeah, Eighth Pine Management is Devon's company." I reached into my pocket and placed the USB drive on the table. It sat there like a loaded mousetrap. "Every piece of this feels calculated. The timing, the evidence, even the way it was delivered. Like someone wants us to stop digging right here."

Callie sat back, arms folded. "So someone overheard Gus spill the truth. Put two and two together. And then—"

"Silenced Kansas before he could say anything more," I finished. "And left us a trail leading to someone else."

Callie was already pulling out her phone. "We need to tell Uncle Jason—"

"No." I stopped her hand. "Not yet."

"Mom, we've got Gus's confession. We've got the photos. The USB. Why wait?"

I looked down at Des, who gazed up at me with those same clear, unwavering eyes. She didn't chase ghosts—she followed trails. And she always knew when to wait.

"Because it's not enough," I said. "Not to make it stick. We need more than motive and guesses. We need something real."

I weighed my options.

"Frannie's hosting that memorial for Kansas tomorrow," I said slowly. "Everyone will be there. Anyone trying to cover their tracks will be on edge."

Callie frowned. "So we just... watch?"

"We listen," I said. "There's always a crack. A flinch. A look."

Des sighed and snuggled in beside me.

"I don't need a confession," I murmured. "Just a moment."

Callie met my gaze, her nod slow and deliberate.

I leaned back, already picturing the folding chairs, the uneasy faces. Frannie's tears and Devon's donations. Two stories too polished to be true.

CHAPTER SIXTEEN

The morning of Frannie's memorial service for Kansas dawned grey and soggy. The kind of day where the heaviness in the air matched my mood. Clouds pressed low against the trees, and the mist hadn't so much lifted as given up entirely and turned to drizzle. The whole town felt water-logged, like we were all waiting for something to break—sky, or silence, or both.

I stood at Dad's kitchen window, watching droplets race each other down the glass. Behind me, Des sprawled across the tile floor, tracking my every move with her eyes. She didn't get up. Just watched, steady and calm. Her presence was weighty in the room, steadying. A warm contrast to the chill pressing in from outside.

The USB drive sat on the counter next to a chipped mug. Small. Unassuming. In another life, it might have held tax files or family photos. Now it was the closest thing I had to a bomb.

I hadn't slept much. Gus's revelation yesterday had cracked everything wide open—and knocked the wind out of me. Dad was alive. He'd staged his disappearance with Gus's help after receiving threats. Someone had killed Kansas to keep the truth buried. And now I had a file pointing straight at Devon.

At least, I hoped it pointed at Devon. If this didn't pan out —if the documents were doctored or Devon managed to explain them away—I wasn't sure where that would leave us.

"You look like you've been chewing on rocks all night," Callie said, padding into the kitchen in her pyjamas and thick socks.

"Just going over the plan again." I turned from the window. "You clear on what to do if I'm not back by six?"

Callie's mouth tightened, her expression shifting from sleepy to alert in seconds. "Call Uncle Jason. Tell him everything."

"Everything," I confirmed, grabbing the kettle. "Every bit Gus gave us."

"I still don't understand why we can't just go to him now," she said, sliding into a chair at the table. "With Gus's confession about Grandpa—"

"Because Gus is gone," I said, sharper than I meant to. I took a breath and softened it. "Probably halfway to nowhere by now. And all we have is circumstantial evidence and a USB drive we can't prove wasn't tampered with."

Callie nodded, but her brows didn't smooth out. "You're really going to confront Devon?"

"I need to look him in the eye," I said, pouring hot water into two mugs. "We need something concrete. Something that can't be explained away or swept under a rug by powerful influences."

I handed her a mug. She wrapped both hands around it, the steam curling up toward her face.

I headed upstairs to change, giving myself ten minutes to

pull it together. Practical clothes: dark jeans, my navy blazer, a white blouse that could pass as crisp even when I felt anything but. No jewellery, no makeup, no fuss. I wasn't dressing for impact. I was dressing to vanish into the crowd, to be the woman no one noticed.

By the time I came back down, Callie had her laptop open and the news page loaded.

"I'll be monitoring the memorial livestream," she said, all business. "The church started doing it during the pandemic. If anything looks off, I'll text you."

"That's my girl," I said, giving her shoulder a squeeze. "Remember—"

"No heroics, I know." She looked up from the screen. "Just come home in one piece, okay?"

"Count on it," I promised.

I whistled softly for Des. She rose immediately, ears alert, posture ready, like she knew we were heading into something more serious than a walk.

I moved toward the door, but paused with my hand on the knob. Something about the weight of the moment—Des beside me, Callie watching from the table, the USB waiting on the counter—made me still.

Des sat next to me, calm and patient. She looked up, eyes meeting mine with that same unreadable, grounding focus she always had. She was waiting for me to lead. Trusting me. And suddenly I wasn't sure I deserved it.

Not after what happened with Lucy. Not after the choice I made.

And just like that, I was back there. Back in Victoria. Back in the woods.

It had been raining then, too.

Lucy had been my partner for six years. Jet-black coat, eyes sharp as broken glass, a mind that worked faster than most humans I knew. She'd lived for the job, for the chase, for the partnership. She'd trusted me absolutely.

And I'd let her down.

There was a hiker—young, unprepared, the kind of over-confident outdoorsman who didn't check weather reports or pack a first aid kit. He'd gone missing in a stretch of tangled backcountry, and we were called in late in the day, a storm rolling in from the west.

Lucy picked up a scent fast. She was certain—her body language told me that much. But the path she wanted to follow was steep, partially flooded, and thick with debris. The other team members were concerned. I was concerned. As the field team lead, I made a judgment call.

We redirected the search.

By the time I admitted Lucy had been right, by the time we got back to her original track, it was too late. We found the young hiker curled against a boulder, barely shielded from the wind. He was already gone.

Lucy never looked at me the same after that. Still loyal. Still obedient. But the spark? That quiet confidence in my judgment? It wasn't there anymore. And neither was mine in myself.

I left the team a few weeks later.

Even now, the guilt hadn't softened with time. It sat heavy in my chest, a scar that hadn't quite healed.

Des let out a soft huff and nudged my leg. I blinked, returning to the present.

She was so much like Lucy—and yet, not. She hadn't been trained for this, hadn't grown up in a regimented world of drills and disaster. But she had that same knowing in her eyes. That instinct.

And she'd chosen me.

Somehow, despite everything I'd broken and buried, this dog had wormed her way in and decided I was hers.

I crouched down and rubbed behind her ears. "You're not my second chance, girl," I murmured. "You're something new. And I won't screw it up this time."

Des nudged my palm, gentle and sure, and just for a second, the knot in my chest loosened.

I stood again, steadier now. "Let's go," I said.

Des stepped out first, into the mist and the quiet.

And I followed.

The memorial service was held in the small chapel at Balsam Bay United Church, a modest brick building with stained glass windows that cast patches of muted colour across the pews. The place was about half-full, with mostly familiar faces from around town. I settled near the back, Des tucking herself under the pew with a quiet sigh, out of the way but ever alert.

Des went pretty much everywhere with me now. After her wilderness trek, people stopped asking questions—this was Balsam Bay, after all. If your dog was well-behaved and smarter than most folks, doors tended to open.

Frannie sat in the front row, a vision of restrained grief in a tasteful black dress, her shoulders curved just enough to suggest sorrow without being theatrical. The casket was closed, draped with a simple arrangement of white lilies. The Belles occupied a pew near the middle, all three wearing identical navy hats with small veils that made them look like a Greek chorus.

Devon sat three rows from the front, beside Mayor Bugle. I watched him throughout the service, noting how he frequently checked his watch, how his attention drifted during the pastor's generic eulogy about Kansas's "entrepreneurial spirit" and "community dedication."

The service was mercifully brief. No one seemed eager to share personal stories, and Frannie's brief words were polished to a shine, empty of any genuine emotion. As people began filing toward the reception in the church basement, I noticed Frannie quietly slip out a side door rather than joining the gathering. Interesting.

I waited for my opportunity, keeping my eyes on Devon as he exchanged a few brief words with the pastor. When he headed for the main exit instead of downstairs to the reception, I made my move, timing my approach carefully to catch him just as he reached the church steps.

"Devon, could I have a word?"

He turned, surprise flickering briefly across his face before settling into polite neutrality. "Tilly. Of course." He gestured toward a small garden path to the side of the church. "Shall we?"

I nodded, Des keeping pace beside me as we walked toward a stone bench beneath a weeping birch. Devon's posture remained relaxed, but I caught his eyes flicking toward Des with mild curiosity.

"I was sorry to hear about your dog going missing," he said, sitting down. "Glad to see she found her way home."

News travels fast in small towns. I kept my expression neutral. "She's quite resourceful."

"Much like her owner, I suspect." His smile didn't quite reach his eyes. "What can I help you with? I doubt this is a social call."

I pulled the USB drive from my pocket. "I recently came into possession of some interesting information." I kept my voice casual, like we were discussing the weather. "A bank transfer from Eighth Pine Management to Francesca McBride.

Two hundred and fifty thousand dollars, the day after Kansas died."

The shift was subtle, but unmistakable. Devon's shoulders stiffened, his expression freezing for a fraction of a second before he recovered.

"That's quite specific," he said carefully.

"It's quite interesting," I countered, watching his face. "Especially since Eighth Pine Management is your shell company."

Devon's eyes narrowed. "You've been busy."

"Let's just say I've been motivated."

He was quiet for a moment, studying me with newfound calculation. When he spoke again, his voice had dropped an octave.

"Where did you get this information?"

"Does it matter?" I kept my gaze steady on his face, cataloguing every micro-expression. "What matters is why you paid Kansas's widow a quarter million dollars right after he died of a suspicious allergic reaction."

Devon stood abruptly, pacing a few steps away before turning back to face me. Des stayed perfectly still, watching him with alert eyes.

"This is absurd," he said, but there was no real heat to his protest. "You're implying—"

"I'm not implying anything," I cut in. "I'm asking a straightforward question about a documented financial transaction."

He stared at me for a long moment, then let out a sharp laugh. "You think I killed Kansas McBride? Or had him killed? That's what this is about?"

I didn't answer, just waited.

Devon ran a hand through his hair, the gesture reading as

frustration, not calculation. "Yes, I sent money to Frannie. As a gift, if you must know."

"A gift," I repeated flatly.

"An investment opportunity," he clarified. "Kansas and I had discussed the possibility of him purchasing your father's store. After his passing, I offered Frannie the capital to pursue that option if she was interested. A show of goodwill for a recent widow with uncertain finances."

The explanation sounded rehearsed, yet his indignation seemed authentic. My certainty wavered.

"That's quite generous for someone you barely knew," I pressed.

"Business is business," Devon said with a shrug. "The store property has strategic value for future development. I wouldn't let an opportunity slip away because of an unfortunate death."

"And you always conduct business through shell companies?"

His eyes hardened. "I've been in this industry long enough to know that discretion has its advantages." He leaned in. "Where did you get that USB drive?"

"Frannie gave it to me," I said, watching his reaction carefully. "A few days ago. She thought I should know about your arrangement with Kansas."

Something flashed in Devon's eyes—genuine surprise mixed with what looked like dawning comprehension.

"Did she now?" he said softly, almost to himself. Without another word, he straightened, checking his watch with sudden urgency. "If you'll excuse me, I need to attend to something."

He walked away with purpose, pulling out his phone as he strode toward the parking lot.

I gave him a thirty-second head start, then whistled softly to Des. "Let's go, girl."

Des and I followed at a distance, hanging back near the hedgerows that lined the church parking lot. Devon climbed into his black Range Rover, the engine roaring to life. I slipped into my vehicle and waited until he pulled onto the main road before following.

My phone buzzed with a text from Callie. *Where are you? Frannie skipped the reception, just noticed Devon's gone, too.*

I quickly tapped back. *Following Devon. I think we're headed toward Frannie's cabin. Tell you later.*

"This feels like we're in a movie," I muttered to Des, who sat alert in the passenger seat, her ears perked forward. "Just with worse casting and no dramatic soundtrack."

Devon's SUV turned onto Lakeside Drive—heading straight for Frannie's cabin. He must have noticed she didn't stick around for the reception. I kept my distance, pulling over by the public boat launch, when I saw him park in the driveway. Through the trees, I watched him march up the front steps and pound on the door with enough force to rattle the frame.

I hesitated for half a second. This wasn't legal surveillance, but then again, neither was paying off someone after a suspicious death.

"Come on," I whispered to Des, clipping on her leash. "Nice and quiet."

We moved through the trees, sticking to the soft pine-needle ground that muffled our footsteps. Years of wilderness tracking came back to me as we approached the cabin from the side, using the natural contours of the land for cover. I could just make out Devon's raised voice through the partly open window facing the lake.

"What were you thinking?" Devon demanded. "Giving her that drive? Have you lost your mind?"

Frannie's reply was muffled, but her tone was defensive.

"I don't care what excuse you've concocted," Devon continued. "You've compromised everything! She told me about the bank transfer, Frannie. You think that won't raise questions?"

A cold weight settled in my stomach. Des stood at my side, solid and steady, a low rumble building in her chest that I quickly hushed with a hand on her muzzle.

"I did what I had to do," Frannie's voice came clearer now. "She was sniffing too near the truth." A pause. "It was supposed to redirect her attention. I didn't realize that file was on there."

"Well, it was." Devon's tone was ice. "And now she thinks I had Kansas killed."

"You knew what you were getting into." Frannie's voice had a calculated edge I hadn't heard before. "No one twisted your arm."

Des growled again, soft but insistent. This time I didn't stop her. Something about Frannie's voice had changed—the grieving widow persona dropping away to reveal something harder beneath.

"This isn't what we agreed to," Devon said, his voice lower now, more controlled. "The arrangement was clear. You handle your end, I handle mine."

"Adapt, Devon. That's what survivors do," Frannie replied coolly.

I strained to hear more, but their voices dropped to an urgent murmur. I inched closer, conscious of every twig and leaf underfoot. Des stayed at my heel, her body tense.

"...should've told me," Devon's voice drifted out, clearer again.

"I'm not the one who insisted on using that stupid shell company!" Frannie snapped. "If it had been cash, like I suggested—"

"This has nothing to do with me," Devon cut in. "You're the one who—"

Frannie suddenly appeared at the window, and I froze, pressing myself against the cabin wall, heart hammering. Des went still beside me, but her hackles were fully raised.

"Someone's out there," Frannie said sharply, and I heard footsteps moving toward the door.

Time to go. I tugged Des back, retreating swiftly through the trees the way we'd come. We'd barely made it halfway to the car when I heard the cabin door slam open.

"Tilly Lafleur?" Frannie's voice called out. "I know that's you!"

I kept moving, picking up the pace, Des trotting obediently at my side. We reached the car and climbed in just as Devon's vehicle roared to life. I ducked down, watching through the trees as he pulled away, driving back toward town with enough speed to kick up gravel.

I waited another two minutes before starting my engine, turning away from the cabins and taking the long way back to town. My heart was still racing, but my thoughts had already jumped ahead—unpacking what I'd heard, reshuffling every assumption like loose gravel underfoot.

Devon hadn't denied sending the money. But his reaction to Frannie putting the USB drive in my hands wasn't the calculation of a mastermind. It was the fury of someone whose plans had been derailed. And Frannie... Frannie had been steering me toward Devon all along, carefully crafting a narrative that put him at the centre of everything.

"You're the one who..." Devon had started to say before Frannie cut him off. The one who what?

The one who killed Kansas?

I glanced at Des, who gazed back with those steady brown eyes.

"I think we've been looking at this all wrong, girl," I murmured. Des tilted her head, listening. "Devon's involved, but he's not calling the shots. He's being manipulated just like I was."

Des gave a small whine of agreement. Or maybe she was just responding to my voice. Either way, I took it as solidarity.

The pieces were shifting, rearranging themselves in my head. I'd been so sure Devon was behind everything—the mine reopening, Dad's disappearance, Kansas's death. But I'd been wrong about Dad. And maybe I was wrong about the rest, too. What if he was just another player on the board? What if someone else had been moving the pieces all along?

I steered my car toward the general store, still processing what I'd overheard. My plan to confront Devon had backfired spectacularly—or succeeded beyond my expectations, depending on how you looked at it. Either way, I'd unwittingly set something in motion that couldn't be undone.

As I pulled up the driveway at Dad's house, my phone buzzed with another text from Callie. *Reception's winding down. Everyone asking where Frannie went. Everything ok?*

I stared at the screen for a long moment before replying. *Yes. I'll be in soon.*

And that was the understatement of the year. I'd been so focused on catching Devon, I hadn't noticed I was the one being baited.

Frannie had handed me that USB like it was a lifeline—but it was a leash.

What secret was so dangerous, she'd risk everything to keep it buried?

I leaned my forehead against the steering wheel, frustration washing over me. One step forward, two steps back. The investigation had felt so clear after Gus's revelation, but now I was adrift again, questioning everything.

Des nudged my arm with her nose, her warm presence grounding me.

"You're right," I said, straightening up. "No use wallowing."

I needed to regroup, to follow where this new information led. Because one thing was clearer than ever: Frannie McBride hadn't been swept up in the current.

She was steering the boat.

CHAPTER SEVENTEEN

I'd been pacing for nearly an hour before I finally sat down and let the USB drive glare at me from across the table. The conversation between Devon and Frannie had kept me up half the night, replaying in my head like a song with missing lyrics. "You're the one who…" Devon had started to say, before Frannie cut him off. The one who what? The answer was there —I could feel it—but just out of reach.

Des lay at my feet, chin on her paws, one ear perpetually cocked toward the door as if expecting a familiar footfall at any moment. Whenever the floorboards creaked, her eyes would dart hopefully toward the entrance before settling back on me with that knowing look. Callie had already left for the store, taking over my shift with Bertha for the morning so I could sort through the tangled web my investigation had become.

I'd told Callie everything—the confrontation with Devon, following him to Frannie's cabin, the argument I'd overheard. She'd taken it all in, her journalist's mind connecting dots faster than I could voice them.

"So Frannie's been playing us," she'd said. "But if Devon isn't behind everything, where does he fit in?"

That was the question that had kept me awake, turning in slow circles with no answer in sight. Devon was clearly involved—but not in control. His reaction to the USB hadn't been cold or calculated. It had been messy. Furious. Not the kind of fury that comes from being caught, but from being blindsided.

Frannie had cast him as the villain, and I'd bought it. Every bit of it.

I rubbed my eyes, feeling the grit of too little sleep. The pattern was there. I just couldn't see it yet.

My phone buzzed with a text from Jason. *Got something. Mandy's at 10?*

I texted back a quick confirmation, then pushed back from the table. Whatever Jason had found, it might be the piece I was missing, or at least a new angle to consider.

"Come on, Des," I said, grabbing my jacket. "Let's go see what the official channels have dug up."

Des followed me to the door, her nails clicking against the hardwood in a comforting rhythm. After her epic journey home through the woods, she had been sticking to me like a furry shadow. I couldn't say I minded.

Mandy's bakery was busy when we arrived, the morning rush still in full swing. The Balsam Belles occupied their usual table by the window, huddled over steaming mugs and speaking in the urgent half-whispers that meant fresh gossip was being dissected. The rich aromas filled the air, momentarily lifting my spirits.

"There she is!" Mandy called over the counter when she spotted me. "Your usual? I just pulled fresh cranberry scones from the oven."

"Sounds perfect," I said, settling at a small table near the back where Des could tuck underneath without blocking the walkway. "Jason will join me in a bit."

Mandy nodded, already moving to prepare my order. "Everyone's talking about the memorial," she said, glancing around before lowering her voice. "Pretty sparse crowd, if you ask me. And Frannie didn't seem broken up about it."

"No," I agreed, "she didn't."

"Devon looked like he'd rather be anywhere else," Mandy continued, setting down my coffee. "Kept checking his watch the whole time, according to Nora. Though who can blame anyone, really? Reverend Nichols has a gift for making twenty minutes feel like two hours."

I smiled despite myself. "Thanks, Mandy."

She gave me a warm pat on the shoulder before heading back to the counter, leaving me to nurse my coffee and watch the door. Jason arrived fifteen minutes later, his uniform crisp, even though the circles under his eyes suggested he'd had about as much sleep as I had.

"Morning," he said, sliding into the chair across from me. "Thanks for meeting."

Des shifted under the table to accommodate Jason's long legs, giving his ankle a friendly nudge with her nose.

"What've you got?" I asked, keeping my voice low.

Jason glanced around before leaning in. "We found something at Gus's place when we did a wellness check after hearing he might have left town." He paused as Mandy appeared with his usual black coffee and a fresh cinnamon bun. Once she'd moved away, he continued, "A bloodied canoe paddle partially burned in his backyard fire pit. It's a match to Dad's missing second paddle."

My pulse kicked up. So Jason had found it. The secret was unraveling, one piece at a time. "Are you serious?"

"Dead serious. And the blood's been confirmed as Gus's—not Dad's."

I struggled to keep my expression neutral, mind racing.

"So, what are you thinking?" I asked carefully, not wanting to reveal what I knew.

Jason took a sip of his coffee. "Honestly? It's not looking good, Tills. Gus has disappeared, Kansas is dead after a public argument with Gus, and now we find a bloodied paddle that matches the one missing from Dad's canoe."

I knew that Gus had helped Dad disappear rather than harmed him—but I couldn't say that without revealing Gus's confession. And without Gus to confirm it, my word alone wouldn't be enough. Not to mention the risk to Jason's job if I went public with accusations I couldn't prove.

"Wait," I said, focusing on the thread I could pull. "You think Gus killed Kansas? That makes no sense. Why would he?"

"Maybe Kansas found out something about Dad's accident. Maybe Gus panicked." Jason's voice was calm, measured—the voice he used when delivering bad news. "We're still putting it together, but the timing is suspicious."

I wanted to grab him by the shoulders and shake the truth into him—that Dad was alive, that Gus had helped him escape, that Frannie has something to do with Kansas's death. But without proof, I'd sound like I was grasping at straws.

"What about the shellfish angle? Kansas died from anaphylaxis, right? Has Dr. Marsh confirmed it was shellfish?"

Jason nodded. "Preliminary tox screen showed traces of crustacean proteins in his system." He hesitated. "With Gus suddenly gone, it's looking less like an accident."

"And you think that someone was Gus?"

"I think we need to find Gus and ask him some hard questions."

A wave of frustration rose in my chest. This was all going sideways. The police were focusing on Gus—the one person who'd actually told me the truth—while Frannie continued her grieving widow act unchallenged.

"So that's it? Case closed? Gus did it all and ran?"

Jason's expression softened. "I know you want more, Tilly. But sometimes the simple answer is the right one."

"Even when it doesn't make sense?" I countered. "Gus is a lot of things, but a killer? Come on, Jason."

"People surprise you." He hesitated, then added more gently, "I know you've been looking for connections, some bigger conspiracy. But maybe it really is what it looks like. Dad had an accident. Kansas died from anaphylaxis because Gus panicked after telling him something he shouldn't have. It's tragic, but it happens."

I heard what he wasn't saying: the case was closing, the answers weren't changing, and my continued digging was becoming a problem. The patronizing undercurrent made my teeth clench.

"You two need a top-up," Mandy interjected, appearing with a fresh pot of coffee. "Did you hear Frannie's leaving town tomorrow? Now that Kansas's body's been released, she's taking him back to Dallas for burial."

Jason nodded. "She mentioned that at the station this morning. Came in to finalize some paperwork."

My pulse quickened. "Tomorrow?"

Mandy shrugged. "I guess there's nothing keeping her here anymore."

"Except for a police investigation into her husband's suspicious death," I pointed out.

An awkward silence fell over the table. Jason shot me a warning look, while Mandy's expression shifted to something uncomfortably close to pity.

"Dr. Marsh had ruled it an accidental death because of anaphylaxis," Jason said quietly. "The investigation part is mostly wrapped up, pending Gus being found for questioning."

"And you don't find the timing suspicious? Kansas dies right when he's about to tell me something important, and a week later, his widow's skipping town?"

Mandy and Jason exchanged a glance that made my stomach twist. The look people give when they're worried someone's going off the deep end.

"Tilly," Jason began, his voice taking on that patient tone I hated, "I understand this has been hard with Dad missing, and then Kansas. It's a lot."

The bell over the bakery door cut him off. Frannie walked in, elegant even in casual clothes, her hair pulled back in a simple ponytail that somehow made her look younger, more vulnerable. The conversation in the café dimmed momentarily as people took note of her presence, then resumed with the forced normalcy that follows celebrities or tragedies.

Frannie noticed me immediately. Her steps faltered briefly before she straightened and approached our table, a sad smile firmly in place.

"Tilly, Jason," she greeted us, her voice perfectly modulated to convey gentle grief. "So nice to see familiar faces before I leave."

Jason stood, offering a respectful nod. "Ms. McBride. How are you holding up?"

"As well as expected," she replied, the practiced line delivered with just the right touch of weariness. "The arrangements are nearly complete. We'll be on the road by tomorrow afternoon." She turned to me, her eyes carefully melancholy. "I wanted to thank you both for everything. The town has been so supportive during this difficult time."

I managed a tight nod, not trusting myself to speak. Des had gone rigid beneath the table, her body pressed against my legs as if trying to anchor me.

"You're welcome," Jason said, filling the silence. "Have a safe trip back."

She turned, preparing to leave, but paused mid-step.

The front door opened, and in walked Mayor Bugle, composed as ever.

He didn't say a word to Frannie. Their eyes met—just for a second—but it was enough to shift something. Her mouth tightened. She adjusted the strap of her purse like she was steadying herself.

Frannie hesitated, then turned more fully toward me. "Tilly, I was wondering if you might have time for a walk later? Down by the lake? I've always found it so peaceful there." She glanced around, lowering her voice. "I'd like to talk to you privately before I go."

Warning bells clanged in my head. After what I'd overheard at her cabin, Frannie wanting to get me alone set off every internal alarm I had. But refusing would look suspicious, especially with Jason watching.

"Sure," I said, forcing a smile. "Around two?"

"Perfect. I'll meet you at the public beach access." Frannie's answering smile never quite reached her eyes. "Now, if you'll excuse me, I need to pick up some pastries for the road."

As she moved toward the counter, the Balsam Belles intercepted her, enfolding her in a trio of sympathetic clucks and murmurs. I watched as Enid patted her arm, Nora offered a handkerchief, and Trish said something that made Frannie duck her head in gracious acknowledgment.

It was the perfect performance. And everyone bought it.

"You see?" Jason said quietly. "She's just trying to find closure."

I bit back the retort that threatened to spill out. Around us, conversations had resumed their normal cadence. Mandy was back behind the counter, filling orders with her usual cheerful efficiency. Life in Balsam Bay was already settling back into its routine, the brief disruptions of Walter's disappearance and Kansas's death already being absorbed into local lore.

And here I sat, certain that a murderer was about to walk free, while everyone else was ready to move on.

"I should get going," I said, pushing back from the table. "Things to do before my walk with Frannie."

Jason caught my wrist as I stood. "Tilly, I know that look. Whatever you're planning—"

"I'm not planning anything," I lied, gently extracting my arm. "Just being neighbourly before she leaves town."

His expression said he didn't believe me for a second. "Don't go stirring things up for no reason. I could lose my job if the higher-ups think I'm giving you information or not reining you in."

"When have I ever done that?" I asked with forced lightness.

The look he gave me could have dried wet paint. "Do you want the list alphabetically or chronologically?"

I managed a small smile, grateful for the momentary break in tension. "I'll behave. Scout's honour."

Des followed at my heel as I headed for the door, her body language still tense. Outside, the late morning sun had broken through the clouds, casting long shadows across the sidewalk. I stood for a moment, letting the warmth soak into my skin as I considered my options.

Frannie wanted to meet me alone, by the lake. The question was: why? To confess? To threaten? To eliminate another loose end?

I glanced down at Des. "What do you think, girl? Should we go fishing for the truth?"

Des's tail gave a single, determined wag.

Whatever Frannie had planned, I'd be ready.

The beach was bustling when I arrived. Near me were a couple of families laying out picnic blankets and an elderly man throwing sticks for his retriever at the water's edge. I checked my watch: just before two. I'd arrived early deliberately, wanting time to scan the area and get my bearings before Frannie showed.

Des trotted ahead, nose to the ground, investigating every interesting scent along the shoreline. The beach was mostly pebbles here, with occasional patches of sand. Rocky outcroppings created small tide pools where children sometimes hunted for interesting stones and tiny fish. Perfect for a private conversation away from prying ears, but also isolated enough to be concerning.

Just to be safe, I'd sent Callie my location and planned meeting, with strict instructions to call Jason if she didn't hear from me by three.

I spotted Frannie making her way down from her cabin to the beach path right at two o'clock, her cream-coloured windbreaker catching the sunlight. She moved with calculated grace, the picture of understated elegance. No one would look at her and think "murderer." But that was rather the point, wasn't it?

"I'm glad you came," she said as she reached me, her voice pitched to just the right level of subdued warmth. "I didn't want to leave things unfinished."

"Of course," I replied, keeping my tone neutral. "What's on your mind?"

Frannie glanced at Des, who had returned to my side, watching the newcomer with alert eyes. "I thought we could walk while we chat."

I nodded, and we set off along the shoreline, Des ranging ahead and then circling back, always keeping us in sight.

The beach was coming alive around us. What had seemed like a quiet afternoon was transforming into something busier as more locals arrived, claiming their favourite spots. A family with teenagers was setting up a volleyball net. Two older couples unpacked a lavish picnic spread. A frisbee game had started near the water's edge.

"I wanted to clear the air," Frannie began after we'd walked in silence for a minute. "About yesterday."

"Which part?" I asked mildly. "The memorial, or the argument with Devon I overheard at your cabin?"

To her credit, she didn't flinch. "So you did follow him. I thought as much." She sighed, a small, calculated sound.

A frisbee landed nearby, followed closely by a sun-bleached teen who froze mid-apology when he saw Frannie.

"Mrs. McBride! I'm really sorry about Mr. McBride. He was always cool to me when I worked at the marina."

Frannie's smile turned gently mournful, her voice softened by just the right amount of sorrow. "That's very kind, Josh. Thank you."

He nodded awkwardly and jogged back to his friends. Frannie resumed walking as if the interruption hadn't happened.

"I shouldn't have given you that USB drive with the emails and payment information," she continued. "I was trying to protect myself."

"From Devon?"

"In a way," she said, her gaze fixed on the horizon. "Devon and Kansas had their arrangement about buying your father's store. When Kansas died, Devon expected me to step in and maintain the deal."

"Even though you never agreed to follow through with Kansas's plans," I filled in.

"Exactly." Her expression remained carefully controlled. "The two hundred and fifty thousand dollars was supposed to be the first payment. I thought if I walked away after Kansas died, that would be the end of it." She gave a tight, brittle smile. "Turns out, some deals are harder to escape than others."

The voices of the beachgoers rose and fell around us, creating a strange soundtrack to our conversation. A child squealed in delight somewhere behind us. A radio played soft rock from the volleyball area. Laughter drifted from the picnicking couples.

"You were suggesting Devon might have killed your husband," I said, not bothering to soften my words. "The USB, the transfer details... you quite deliberately pointed me in that direction."

"Wouldn't you?" A hint of steel entered her voice. "If you were in my position?"

Before I could answer, a phone rang—not mine. Frannie pulled hers from her pocket, glanced at the screen, and silenced it with a swift motion.

"Devon," she said by way of explanation, her lips thinning. "He's been calling every hour since yesterday."

"Persistent."

"He's desperate," she corrected. "And desperate people are dangerous."

Her phone buzzed again, a second later, as if to prove her point. This time, she didn't look at the screen—just clenched it tight in her hand.

Something changed in her posture. Her spine straightened, her tone sharpened.

We reached a spot where the beach narrowed, forcing us to walk single file past a rocky outcropping. As the passage widened again, Frannie glanced behind us, ensuring we hadn't been followed.

"I've been planning to start over in Dallas," she said abruptly, changing tack. "I have family there. Support." She turned to me, something unreadable behind her sympathetic expression. "But I need to ask you..."

"Oh?"

"Your father's store. Are you planning to keep it? Or would you consider selling?"

And there it was—the real reason for this beachside chat. Not closure, not clearing the air. She still wanted the store.

"I'm still deciding," I said carefully. "It's complicated."

"I understand. But if you did decide to sell, I'd like first consideration."

We emerged onto a wider stretch of beach again, but this section felt more exposed. Families dotted the shoreline, children splashing at the water's edge despite the cool temperature. The earlier sense of privacy had evaporated. Every few yards, someone would glance our way, whisper to their companion, or offer a sympathetic nod to Frannie.

"Thought you were starting fresh back home?" I asked, keeping my voice low.

Frannie hesitated. Just for a second.

"Some investments transcend personal tragedy," she said smoothly. "Kansas saw the store as the start of a new life for us. I'd like to honour that, in a way."

I almost laughed at the absurdity of it. Here was the woman who I was increasingly certain had killed her husband, calmly discussing business arrangements while we strolled along the beach, surrounded by people who saw only a grieving widow. The sheer audacity was breathtaking.

"I'll keep that in mind," I said, keeping an eye out for Des, who had disappeared from view. "But for now, I'm focused on understanding what happened to my father. And your husband."

Frannie's steps slowed. "I thought the police had determined those were unrelated incidents."

"That's what they say."

"I believe Kansas's death was a tragic accident," she said, her voice louder now, clearly meant to be overheard by anyone passing by. "As for your father, I'm sorry, Tilly. I truly am. But sometimes we need to accept when people are gone."

She checked her watch, a deliberate gesture. "I should get back. So much to do."

"Of course," I replied, matching her public tone. "Safe travels."

She took a step away, then paused, leaning in closer. "I hope you find what you're chasing, Tilly," she murmured, her voice pitched for my ears alone. "Whatever that is."

The undercurrent of condescension made my jaw clench. She thought she had me figured out—the grieving daughter clutching at conspiracy theories because she couldn't accept her father's death. It was a perfect cover; no one ever looks too closely at a pitiful figure.

Frannie turned away, threading through the beachgoers with practiced grace, acknowledging sympathetic nods with appropriate humility. I watched her retreating, wondering if I'd ever see her again after tomorrow.

A short-statured man in an official-looking windbreaker approached me, clipboard in hand. "Excuse me, miss. Just doing a quick beach survey about facilities. Do you have a moment?"

"Actually—" I began, but stopped as Des emerged from behind a rocky outcropping, trotting toward me with purpose. She stopped directly in my path, dropped something from her mouth, and looked up at me expectantly.

I crouched down, peering at the small object on the sand. It was a shrimp tail—pink, fresh, and distinctly out of place on a lakeside beach.

"What in the world?" I murmured, reaching for it.

Something made me glance up toward the beach access path. Frannie stood frozen halfway up the wooden steps that led to her cabin, watching. Our eyes met across the distance. Even from here, I could see the flash of panic before she turned and hurried away.

"Sorry," I said to the confused survey-taker. "I need to check something."

I followed Des back to the rocky outcropping, away from the crowded main beach and into a small, sheltered area largely hidden from view. Des pawed at a spot near the water's edge, where the incoming wavelets had just begun to lap.

I knelt down, pushing aside some small stones and loose sand. And there they were—five more shrimp tails, pieces of shell, and a couple of shrimp heads—partially buried but unmistakable. Fresh. Recent. Deliberately hidden.

The beach behind me hummed with activity—voices, laughter, music—all of it oblivious to what we'd just found.

My pulse quickened. This wasn't just litter. It was proof.

I collected the shrimp tails, securing them in a small plastic bag I kept in my pocket for Des's beach treasures. With shaking hands, I pulled out my phone and took several pictures of the spot where I'd found them, capturing the distinct rocky formation in the background to pinpoint the location.

"You clever girl," I whispered, running my hand over Des's warm head. "You knew all along, didn't you?"

A soft sound escaped her throat. She'd known something was wrong with Frannie from the beginning and had tried to tell me with her uncharacteristic behaviour. I just hadn't been listening properly.

I stood, heart pounding. The shrimp tails weren't just a clue—they shattered the lie Frannie was still trying to sell. The grieving widow. The reluctant buyer. The clean escape.

She was wrong.

"Come on, girl," I said to Des, my voice steady despite the adrenaline coursing through me. "We've got work to do."

As we walked back toward the parking lot, the shrimp tails safely tucked away in my pocket, I felt a calm determination settle over me. Frannie had one more night in Balsam Bay. One more night to tidy her narrative before slipping out of reach.

She thought she'd staged the perfect exit.

But she hadn't counted on Des.

And she had no idea who she was dealing with.

CHAPTER EIGHTEEN

The late afternoon sun streamed through the dusty windows of Dad's office at the back of the store, painting honeyed stripes across his cluttered desk.I'd tidied the space as best I could, though most of it had never been messy—just layered with quiet routines. His half-finished crossword puzzle sat aligned with his favourite pen, next to a coaster bearing a perfectly circular coffee ring, like even his chaos had boundaries.

Des stretched out beneath the desk, chin resting on her paws in a posture of relaxed alertness. Every few minutes, her ears would twitch at the sounds drifting down the hallway, where Callie and Bertha were wrapping up the day's business.

"You know this plan is completely bonkers, right?" Callie had said earlier, arranging Dad's ancient leather guest chairs at what she called "optimal confrontation angles."

"Completely," I'd agreed, watching her fuss with the seating. "But sometimes bonkers is the only option left on the menu."

"Just promise me you'll be careful," she'd said, the worry in her eyes making her look so much like me I had to glance away.

"I've got Des," I'd reminded her, scratching behind the dog's ears. "Best backup in Manitoba."

Now I checked my watch: *4:55 p.m.* Right on cue, a sharp chime cut through the quiet. Des's head lifted, ears perked forward like tiny satellite dishes. I straightened my shoulders and tried to embody what Callie called my "competent wilderness woman" vibe, which apparently involved excellent posture and slightly narrowed eyes.

Bertha's measured tones filtered down the hall, followed by the clipped cadence of Frannie's reply—and a deeper voice I hadn't expected. *Hmm. Reinforcements, was it?* I hadn't counted on that, but maybe it would work in our favour.

A light tap on the door preceded Frannie's entrance. She glided in wearing a dove-grey pantsuit—more boardroom than Balsam Bay. Behind her loomed Devon Fontaine, trying his best to appear casual but failing miserably.

"Hope you don't mind that I brought Devon along," Frannie said, her voice dipped in just enough sweetness to rot a tooth. "I thought another perspective might be helpful for our discussion."

"I'm just here for moral support," Devon added, though the tight lines around his eyes suggested a different story entirely.

"The more the merrier," I replied, gesturing toward the waiting chairs. "Please, have a seat."

Des abandoned her post under the desk and padded over to sit beside me, her warm presence against my leg steadying my nerves like a furry anchor.

"I appreciate you taking time to meet," I began, leaning back in Dad's chair, which creaked in the same reassuring way it had when I was twelve, "especially pushing back your departure by a day to do it. If you're serious about running the store, I'm willing to talk."

Frannie crossed her legs at the ankle, one expensive shoe dangling just so. "I'm very serious," she replied, the words coming a beat too quickly. "Kansas always saw potential in this place. I'd like to carry forward with his vision."

Devon nodded vigorously beside her, like one of those dashboard bobbleheads hitting a pothole. "Frannie's been giving it a lot of thought."

I leaned forward, resting my elbows on Dad's desk. "I have to say, I'm curious about the timing," I said, carefully casual. "I thought you were eager to return to the States. To be close to your friends."

"Plans change," Frannie replied without missing a beat, as smooth as lake water on a windless day. "I thought about everything that's happened recently, and I realized how much this community means to me." Her expression softened into something practiced but convincing. "Kansas loved it here. I think staying would honour his memory."

Devon jumped in like he'd been waiting for his cue. "She's really committed to making a fresh start."

Frannie had never given anyone the impression that she enjoyed being in Balsam Bay, so this was coming out of left field. "Is that right?" I kept my tone conversational. "I misjudged you. I was always under the impression that you missed the big city life and everything it has to offer."

Frannie gave a small, confident smile. "And I'm ready for a change of pace. The slower rhythm here is... comforting."

It was a good answer. Too good, really—polished smooth as a river stone. Everything about her responses felt calibrated, adjusted to eliminate any rough edges that might catch on my questions.

Des's ears flicked toward Frannie, the canine equivalent of raising an eyebrow.

"Let's talk about the practical aspects," I suggested, picking up a pencil and twirling it between my fingers. "Running this store isn't just about turning a profit. It's about knowing that Mrs. Kowalski doesn't get out much anymore and needs someone to run her mail to her house twice a week, and that the Henderson boys will try to buy fireworks whether it's Victoria Day or not."

"I understand that completely," Frannie assured me, her gaze flicking over the office without really taking anything in. "Kansas had such plans for modernizing while preserving the store's... charm." She hesitated over the last word like she'd just found it in a foreign language dictionary. "I intend to honour that balance."

Devon nodded so enthusiastically, I half-expected his head to detach. "Frannie has a real eye for potential."

I resisted the urge to roll my eyes. "The Canada Post counter would remain your responsibility," I noted, tapping the pencil against the desk. "Especially now that Gus isn't here to challenge the contract." I looked to see if that had any effect on either of them, but neither batted an eye. "That means being here seven in the morning, even when it's minus thirty and your fancy car won't start."

"I'm not afraid of hard work," Frannie said with what sounded like genuine conviction. "Or winter challenges."

As she rattled off her plans for the store—plans that sounded suspiciously like they'd been drafted on Devon's letterhead—I found myself momentarily disoriented. She was good. Really good. The answers flowed naturally, with just enough personal detail to seem authentic. If I didn't know better, I might actually believe she wanted to stay in Balsam

Bay and sell fishing tackle to cranky retirees and too-excited tourists.

Had I got it all wrong? Was I seeing murder and conspiracy where there was just grief and opportunity?

Des shifted against my leg, her warm weight a silent reminder. No. I hadn't imagined the shrimp tails at the beach, or Frannie's reaction to them. I hadn't imagined her panicked conversation with Devon at the cabin. I'd been right about Kansas's death. I was right about this.

"You mentioned buying, not leasing," I said, keeping my tone light as a summer breeze. "I assume you're using Devon's generous gift to finance the purchase?"

A microscopic hesitation, there and gone so quickly, I might have missed it if I hadn't been watching for it. "Yes, Devon's been tremendously helpful with the details," Frannie said, her smile a fraction too wide.

Devon cleared his throat like he'd swallowed a moth. "As we already discussed at the memorial," Devon said, settling back in the chair like a man confident in his version of events, "I'd already committed those funds to Frannie to pursue purchasing the store. It was meant to be an investment opportunity after her loss." He smiled, too quickly. "Just trying to help."

Another practiced answer, but this time with a clear tell. Whatever the real arrangement was, Devon wasn't entirely comfortable with it. Interesting that he was still sticking to that story, even now.

"I see," I said, letting silence stretch for a beat longer than was comfortable. "And what about Kansas's businesses back in the States? Last I heard, most of them had shut down or filed for bankruptcy. That wouldn't impact this purchase, would it?"

Frannie's smile tightened at the corners. "That's all being sorted through the estate," she said, clipping each word neatly.

"Kansas had plans for rebuilding. That's partially why he was so interested in starting fresh here with the store." Her fingers tapped once on the armrest. "The financing for this purchase is completely separate from those... situations."

I nodded, making a show of consideration. "I don't doubt your commitment, Frannie. But running this store means being part of this community in ways I'm not sure you've considered."

"I'm a fast learner," Frannie countered, a hint of impatience finally cracking her polished veneer.

My phone buzzed in my pocket. I glanced down discreetly to see a text from Callie. *It's up*.

"Excuse me one moment," I said, pulling out my phone. I opened the expected link Callie had sent, skimming the newest blog entry on her *Temporary Town Life* blog. The headline stood out in bold: *Mystery at Balsam Bay: RCMP Sources Confirm Seafood Allergy in Death of Kansas McBride.*

I began reading portions aloud, watching Frannie's face. *"Investigators are exploring whether a delivery of specialty shellfish may have been involved, possibly ordered through a unique cold-chain courier. Sources say the shrimp may soon be identified..."* I looked up. "Did you know about this?"

Devon's brow furrowed in genuine confusion. "What's this about shrimp?"

But Frannie wasn't looking at either of us. Her expression had gone still, like a pond suddenly freezing over, as the blood drained from her face.

"I—" she began, then stopped, rising abruptly from her chair. "I just remembered—I have some paperwork from the lawyer in my car. Give me one second—"

"Frannie—wait," I called, but she was already moving, crossing the office with the determined stride of someone who's just spotted a washroom after three hours on the highway.

Devon half-rose from his chair. "Frannie? What's going on?"

But she was already down the hall and out the main door. Devon looked from me to the doorway, bewilderment written across his face.

"I don't understand," he began, but I was already on my feet, Des alert and moving beside me.

"She's running," I said, already moving.

Devon blinked like I'd started speaking in Morse code. "What? Why would she—"

But I was already down the hallway and into the front of the store. Through the front window, I caught a glimpse of Frannie's grey pantsuit as she sprinted not toward her vehicle in the parking lot, but toward the wooded path beside the store that led to the lake.

"Mom?" Callie appeared from behind the counter, concern etched across her face. "What just happened?"

"She's running," I repeated, moving toward the door. "We can't let her get away."

Des had already caught the scent, her nose working the air as she pushed ahead of me. Behind us, Bertha called out something that sounded suspiciously like, "Show her who's boss, Matilda!"

"Get Jason!" I called over my shoulder as Callie followed us out. "Tell him it's Frannie—she's heading into the woods!"

And then Des and I were moving, tracking a killer across terrain I knew better than she ever could.

The trail forked about two hundred metres behind the store—one branch continuing toward the lake, the other curving up toward the bluffs. Frannie's footprints were clear in the soft earth, heading uphill. Des confirmed it, nose down and tail straight, her entire body focused on the task at hand.

Callie caught up just as we reached the fork, her phone clutched in her hand like it might try to escape. "Jason's on his way," she panted. "What do we do now?"

I pointed toward the right fork. "You stay here. If she doubles back, I need someone watching."

"But—"

"No arguments," I said firmly. "We don't know what she's capable of when cornered. And someone needs to direct Jason when he arrives."

Callie hesitated, then nodded reluctantly.

Des and I were moving again, following the ascending trail into the trees. The path quickly narrowed, becoming wilder with each step. Pine needles carpeted the ground beneath towering balsams, their canopy filtering the late afternoon sunlight into dappled patches. The familiar scent of pine and damp earth centred me, reminding me of countless hikes with Dad in these same woods.

I slipped into search and rescue mode almost without conscious thought—assessing the trail, looking for signs of recent passage. A broken spiderweb across a narrow section told me someone had passed within the last half hour. Fresh scrapes in the moss where someone had slipped confirmed we were on the right track.

"Good girl," I murmured to Des as she paused to check a crushed patch of leaves before continuing onward. She might not have had Lucy's years of formal SAR training, but her instincts were spot-on.

The trail narrowed further as we climbed, the bluff's

edge visible through the trees on our left. A snag of grey fabric on a branch made me smile—Frannie's designer suit was about to get a lot more "distressed" than its creator had intended.

"She doesn't know this land," I muttered to Des, who flicked an ear in my direction. "She's cutting west—trying to get to the road."

But the road was farther than Frannie realized, with difficult terrain between here and there. Her panic had led her to choose the worst possible escape route—something any local would have known to avoid.

We rounded a bend—and stopped cold.

Frannie McBride stood frozen on a narrow section of path, one misstep from a sharp drop into the rocks below. The bluff hemmed her in on one side, a wall of tangled underbrush on the other. Her dove-grey pantsuit was streaked with dirt, her sleek updo collapsing into windblown wisps. She clutched a branch for balance, chest rising and falling in shallow, frantic breaths.

Our eyes locked. One second. Two.

Then she bolted.

Not toward the cliff—but back down the trail, straight at me.

"Frannie, don't—" I barely got the words out.

She shoved past, wild-eyed, aiming to sprint back the way we'd come. Des was faster.

One sharp bark split the silence. Then a blur of motion—Des launching like a goalie diving for a playoff puck, cutting Frannie off mid-stride. Her solid weight collided with Frannie's legs, and the woman went down hard with a strangled cry, skidding into the underbrush.

She flailed, stunned, but Des was already on her—no growl, no teeth, just a firm, immovable sit across Frannie's thighs like a four-legged boulder. Her ears twitched forward, eyes locked on mine.

I exhaled, my own heart slamming against my ribs.

"Good girl," I breathed, stepping closer. "Stay."

Des didn't budge. Frannie did—a little. Just enough to test her limbs and realize she wasn't going anywhere.

"I wouldn't," I said, crouching beside her. "She may look cuddly, but she's had quite the week." I flicked a pine needle from my sleeve. "And so have I."

Frannie stilled. Her breath came in shaky bursts. Her polished facade had cracked wide open.

And this time, there was no fixing it. Frannie's carefully constructed facade had finally, completely crumbled. Her mascara formed raccoon circles beneath eyes wide with panic, and her composure had vanished faster than a box of donuts at Jason's station.

"You don't understand," she hissed, anger spilling out faster than she could stop it. "This wasn't my life. I didn't sign up to rot in the woods while Kansas chased some backwoods fantasy and dragged me down with him."

I waited, not interrupting. Sometimes silence draws out more than questions ever could.

Frannie's hands trembled against the forest floor, designer manicure now rimmed with dirt. "I needed a way out." Her voice tightened, raw with frustration. "He made promises he couldn't keep, dragged us here on a fantasy, then left me to play the dutiful wife while everything crumbled."

Des shifted her weight slightly, a low rumble in her throat as she sensed the cold calculation beneath Frannie's distress.

"The shrimp at the social," I said quietly.

Frannie didn't deny it. Her chin lifted slightly, a flicker of defiance crossing her face. No remorse, just the irritation of someone caught in an inconvenient situation.

I didn't press for more details. The full confession could wait for Jason and the formal interview. For now, it was enough to have confirmation of what I'd suspected all along.

Jason appeared around the bend, looking improbably neat in his RCMP uniform despite the hike up. He slowed when he saw Des holding Frannie at what could only be described as paw-point.

"Tilly?" he asked, confusion and concern flickering across his face.

"She confessed," I said simply, gesturing toward Frannie.

Jason looked from me to Frannie, then back again. His brow furrowed. "She confessed?"

Frannie didn't speak. She just sat there, mascara smudged, dirt-streaked, breathing hard.

Jason exhaled slowly, rubbing the back of his neck like he was pushing the truth into place. "You were right," he said at last. "About all of it."

A small, sad satisfaction settled in my chest—not triumph, but a kind of confirmation that my instincts hadn't failed me.

Jason stepped forward, helping Frannie to her feet with professional courtesy. She didn't resist as he read her rights, her energy seeming to have drained away entirely.

"Let's get her back to the store," Jason said, his tone neutral now. "We'll get her statement, then transport her officially."

Frannie didn't fight it. The panic had worn off, leaving behind a hollow resignation.

I hung back for a moment, letting them get ahead before following. My pulse was still high, but something heavier settled beneath it. The truth had landed—but it didn't bring the satisfaction I expected. It just made everything quieter.

Des remained at my side, watching me with those intelligent eyes.

"Good girl," I said, crouching to ruffle the fur around her

neck. "Though I think you enjoyed that takedown a little too much. Your inner linebacker is showing."

Her tail swept a slow, satisfied arc through the fallen pine needles. This steady, loyal creature had known all along—had tried to warn me at Frannie's cabin and Sean's place. She'd seen what I missed.

"I'm sorry I didn't listen sooner," I told her, feeling the soft warmth of her fur beneath my fingers. "I promise to pay better attention next time you think someone's sketchy."

Des made a small, contented sound that clearly translated to *I told you so*, then turned to follow Jason and Frannie down the trail.

We caught up just as the trees thinned at the edge of the woods. Callie was waiting at the fork, relief washing over her face when she spotted us.

"Look at you," she said, falling into step beside me. "All that's missing is a deerstalker hat and a pipe."

"Wrong detective. Wrong continent," I replied with a smile.

We emerged from the trees to find several RCMP vehicles parked behind the store, lights flashing in the gathering dusk. Bertha stood arms akimbo in the doorway, her expression suggesting she'd known all along that something like this would happen. The Balsam Belles had materialized as if by magic, already passing judgment in hushed tones.

Devon was talking animatedly with one of the officers, his gestures growing more agitated by the second. When he spotted our little procession, he fell abruptly silent, disbelief written across his face.

"Well, that's a look you don't see often on Devon Fontaine," Callie murmured. "Genuine surprise."

As Jason guided Frannie into the store, I scanned the small crowd that had gathered, drawn by the sirens and flashing lights. Nora and Enid were already speed-dialling everyone in their contacts, while Trish took what she probably thought were subtle photos with her phone.

"Got to hand it to small towns," Callie said. "No need for press releases when you've got the Belles on the job."

I smiled, but the victory felt bittersweet. Dad was still out there somewhere, alive but hidden, not knowing that we'd uncovered the truth at last.

"We'll find him," Callie said softly, reading my mind with uncanny accuracy. "Once the dust settles, we'll find Grandpa."

I nodded, allowing myself to believe it. The most difficult trail I'd ever navigated had led me here, to this moment of clarity. Finding Dad—bringing him home safely—that would be the next journey, but not one I'd face alone.

Des stood close, anchoring us both. My father's dog. My dog now, too.

"Come on," I said to both of them. "I think we've earned ourselves a pizza and whatever passes for wine in this town."

"And ice cream for the hero," Callie added, looking down at Des, whose tail immediately picked up speed at the magic word.

I smiled, then nodded toward the trailhead. "But first, let's see how Jason's planning to handle our would-be store owner."

CHAPTER NINETEEN

"Let's get one thing straight," Jason said, pacing the length of Dad's cramped office. "This isn't formal. But before I drive anyone to the station, I need answers."

He shot me a look—equal parts exasperation and reluctant respect.

Frannie sat in Dad's squeaky guest chair, pine needles clinging to her designer pantsuit, her perfect hair now frizzed like she'd stuck her finger in a socket. The forest chase had ruined her polished image. Good.

"I've already explained," she said, brushing dirt from her sleeve. "I was upset and needed air. Tilly misunderstood."

"Misunderstood?" I couldn't help but snort. "You bolted out of here like your designer pants were on fire the minute I mentioned shrimp and Kansas's allergies."

Des sprawled under the desk at my feet, looking deceptively lazy, though I noticed her eyes never left Frannie. Smart dog.

Callie leaned against the filing cabinet, arms folded, watching everything with the intense focus of someone mentally taking notes for later. The look on her face reminded me so much of myself at her age that I almost smiled despite the tension crackling through the room.

"Innocent people don't generally sprint into the woods when asked about seafood," I added, spinning Dad's ancient swivel chair so I could face Frannie directly.

Jason pinched the bridge of his nose. "Tilly, maybe you should explain what evidence actually led to…" he waved vaguely toward the window where flashing police lights still painted the parking lot in red and blue, "all this."

"Gladly." I grabbed my notebook from the desk, flipping past scribbled observations and half-formed questions.

"Kansas died of anaphylaxis at the social," I began. "He had a known seafood allergy, and the autopsy confirmed it was triggered that night."

"A tragic accident," Frannie said softly—managing to look both sad and impatient.

"Except it wasn't," I said. "You made sure shellfish contaminated his food. Specifically, the perogies."

"You don't know what you're talking about!" she snapped, the mask cracking.

I pulled out a small plastic bag from the desk drawer, holding it up for Jason to see. "Des found these buried in the sand at the beach after my chat with Frannie yesterday. Shrimp tails. Fresh ones."

Jason took the bag, examining the pink remains with a frown. "Where did you find these?"

"At the beach. Small cove near the stairs by Frannie's cabin. Partially buried, like someone wanted to hide them." I gave Frannie a pointed look. "Someone who panicked when my dog started digging."

"This proves nothing," Frannie said with a dismissive wave. "People have picnics."

"People don't bury seafood remains at freshwater beaches," I shot back. "And they don't look like they're about to faint when a dog uncovers them."

Frannie's smile tightened at the corners. "You think you're so clever? You have no idea what it's like to lose everything and still put on a smile."

"Then let's talk about that package you picked up the day before the social. Parker signed for it—marked 'perishable,' with dry ice warnings. Odd timing."

"I receive packages all the time."

"Not like this. Not right before you suddenly entered the perogy contest. Mandy told Callie how surprised she was—said you weren't a fan of the local cuisine."

Frannie shifted in her seat, her composure slipping just a fraction. "I was trying to take part in community events. Kansas wanted me to make an effort."

"Remember Mabel's grandson, Richard, at the social?" I asked. "He grabbed a plate of perogies, but tossed them after one bite—said they tasted funny. Everyone figured he was just being picky."

Frannie's expression didn't change, but her fingers tightened on the armrest.

"Only now it makes sense," I said. "He grabbed one of your perogies—meant for Kansas—but spat it out. Guess shrimp didn't sit right with him... or Kansas."

"That's... conjecture," Frannie said, but her voice had lost some of its conviction.

"Is it?" I challenged. "Everything lines up too perfectly: the seafood package delivery, your sudden interest in making perogies, Richard's reaction to the taste, and Kansas's fatal allergic reaction."

Frannie waved me off. "You can't prove anything."

"Actually, we can," Jason said from the doorway. "The

shipping company keeps records of what's inside packages marked 'perishable.' Food safety regulations."

I flipped to another page in my notebook. "The timing is what gets me. The morning of the social, Kansas left me a note saying he had important information about my father. Information he never got to share because he collapsed before we could talk."

"Coincidences happen," Frannie said, but her voice had cooled about ten degrees.

"True. But then there's the USB drive you so helpfully gave me." I held up the small device. "The one with emails between Devon and Kansas, and—most damning—proof of a quarter-million dollar transfer from Eighth Pine Management to your personal account the day after Kansas died."

Over by the door, Devon made a strangled noise. "I've already explained that was for the store investment—"

"Yeah, that's what you claimed," I interrupted. "But when I confronted you about it at the memorial, you weren't just surprised—you were furious with Frannie for giving me the evidence."

"I was concerned about appearances," Devon protested weakly.

"You were panicking," I corrected. "I overheard your argument at Frannie's cabin afterward. 'You've compromised everything,' you said. Not angry about the payment—angry she'd revealed it."

Jason's eyebrows shot up to his hairline. "You were eavesdropping!"

"Research," I said without missing a beat. "And it showed something interesting. Devon isn't calling the shots here. He's just the money guy."

Frannie's perfectly manicured nails drummed once against

the armrest. "You've got a real flair for melodrama, but you don't have actual proof."

"Let's talk motive, then," I said, leaning forward. "Kansas was broke. His businesses back home had tanked. He couldn't actually afford to buy this store."

"That was our business—until he made it my burden."

"Which Gus Bugle announced to the entire bar that night at *The Rusty Lantern*," I continued. "The night you stormed out, realizing your husband wasn't the meal ticket you'd signed up for."

Two spots of colour appeared on Frannie's cheeks. "You have no idea what my marriage was like."

"You're right about that," I admitted. "But I know what happened just before that. Kansas heard something important from Gus about my father. He was going to tell me at the social. And suddenly—*poof!*—Kansas is dead from his seafood allergy, and you get a huge cash injection right after."

Jason stepped closer. "What exactly did Gus tell Kansas?"

I met my brother's eyes. "Gus came to me right here in this store and confessed that Dad is alive. The Bugles were pressuring Gus to 'handle Walter,' but instead, he helped Dad fake his death and disappear. That's what Kansas found out, and what he wanted to tell me."

Jason's jaw literally dropped. "You knew this and didn't report it?"

"I was gathering evidence," I said, not backing down. "And I was worried whoever silenced Kansas might come after Gus next—which they did. Gus left town after his family found out he'd been talking. And you found his blood on Dad's missing canoe paddle."

"That doesn't mean I had anything to do with it," Frannie interjected, her voice rising slightly.

"No? Then explain your sudden change of plans," I challenged. "First, you're heartbroken and need to leave town immediately. Then after Kansas dies, you decide to stay and run a general store in a town you've been openly contemptuous of. Why the switch?"

"I told you, I was honouring—"

"Kansas's memory, sure," I cut her off. "But that doesn't explain your rehearsed answers about running the store, or your fight with Devon over payments, or why you bolted like a spooked rabbit when I mentioned shrimp."

Frannie's composure finally started seriously cracking. "This is a witch hunt! You have nothing concrete—just wild speculation and coincidences!"

"Really?" I flipped through my notebook. "We have shrimp tails that will match the proteins found in Kansas's system. We have the package delivery. We have your sudden interest in making perogies. We have the quarter-million-dollar payment. We have your panic and flight when confronted." I snapped my notebook shut. "And we have your confession to me on the bluff about Kansas 'not being the man you married' and 'needing a way out.'"

The room went so quiet you could've heard a mouse sneeze. Even Des seemed to hold her breath, her warm weight against my leg the only sign she was still there.

"You poisoned your husband's food with shellfish," I said, my voice steady. "You did it right before he could tell me the truth about my father."

Callie shifted, her eyes narrowing. "That explains Des."

Jason looked over. "How so?"

"She reacted at the social—when Kansas collapsed," I said, following the thread. "I didn't catch it at the time, but Des sniffed him and wouldn't leave his side. She was picking up on the shrimp."

Callie nodded. "You told me she went weird at Frannie's, too."

"She did. Knocked a stack of papers off the kitchen counter —one of them was the recipe Frannie used for the perogies. Des went straight for it, nose working like it was laced with peanut butter."

Jason raised an eyebrow. "And Sean's place?"

"He'd been collecting samples down by the lake that morning," I said. "The same spot where Frannie dumped the shrimp shells. Des wasn't reacting to the people—she was tracking the scent. The same scent that was on Kansas's body."

I reached down and scratched behind Des's ears. "She's been onto the truth this whole time. I just didn't know how to hear her."

"That's not... I didn't..." Frannie's perfect facade finally crumbled for real.

"The question is why," I pressed. "What made killing Kansas worth it? It wasn't just his money problems—there was something bigger at stake."

Frannie's eyes darted to Devon, who was sweating like he'd just run a marathon in a wool suit.

Devon's not the answer," I said. "He's just the bagman. Someone else pulled the strings—the same someone who wanted my father gone, and believed he was, until Frannie opened her mouth."

The silence stretched between us like taffy. I waited, watching Frannie's internal struggle play across her face. Des shifted slightly, her ears pricked forward like satellite dishes.

Finally, Frannie's shoulders sagged. When she spoke, her voice had lost its warmth, revealing something hard underneath.

"Kansas was a loser," she said flatly. "A failure playing businessman in a backwater town. I married him for security, and he lost everything." Her eyes, when they met mine, were as cold as lake ice in January. "So I traded him in for a better offer."

"From the Bugles," I said.

Frannie's laugh was sharp enough to cut glass. "Of course from the Bugles. They've been running this town for generations. When Gus started blabbing at the bar that night, I saw my chance."

"You went to them," Jason said, his voice tight with controlled anger.

"Directly to them," Frannie confirmed. "They made me an offer. 'Handle Kansas, and you'll be taken care of,' they said. He was becoming a problem—he'd developed a conscience. Said it wasn't right for you to think your father was dead. Believed reopening the mine would devastate the town. He had to be stopped."

"So you killed him," I said simply.

Frannie shrugged like we were discussing a change in dinner plans. "I knew it would work. He was always so careful about his allergy. All his life, avoiding shellfish. One dose was all it took." Her face hardened. "It was quick. More than he deserved."

"And the money?" Jason asked.

"A down payment," Frannie said, her voice flat. "For services rendered. After Kansas died, I thought I'd be done. But the Bugles had other ideas." She gave a cold little laugh. "Apparently, I'd passed the test. And they don't like to waste a good asset. The store became my cover story—a way to stick around and keep tabs on things."

"With Devon as your business partner," I added.

"Devon just follows orders," Frannie said dismissively. "He has no idea what the money was really for. The Bugles compartmentalize their operations."

Devon looked like he might be sick. "Frannie, what have you done?" he croaked.

She ignored him completely, her eyes fixed on me with cold curiosity. "You know, you're smarter than they said. They figured you'd be too busy grieving daddy to notice what was right under your nose."

"They underestimated me," I said simply.

"Clearly." Her smile was all teeth, no warmth. "But it doesn't matter. You can't touch them. Not really."

"Maybe not today," I agreed. "But this is just the beginning."

Jason stepped forward, face grim. "Francesca McBride, you're under arrest for the murder of Kansas McBride." He called in Constable Singh. "We'll continue this conversation at the station."

As Singh led Frannie away, Devon tried to follow, babbling about his innocence, but Jason stopped him with a raised hand. "Mr. Fontaine, we'll need a statement from you, but you're not being charged at this time."

Devon sagged with visible relief.

After both Frannie and Devon were escorted out, the room felt suddenly empty, though no less tense.

"That's enough for an arrest," Jason confirmed, tucking away his notes. "With her confession and what we've got, she's not walking free."

Callie finally moved from her spot by the filing cabinet, letting out a whistle. "Holy cheese balls," she murmured. "That was crazy."

"It's not over," I said. "The Bugles are still out there. Dad's still in hiding."

"One battle at a time," Jason said, his voice gentler now. "You did good, Tills."

I nodded, the victory feeling hollow—like winning a hand

of cards only to realize you're still down in chips for the night. Something clicked in my mind as I replayed Frannie's confession.

"The private conversations I observed between Frannie and Mayor Bugle after the social... they weren't just casual check-ins, were they? He was keeping tabs on her progress. The Bugles aren't just some nebulous family influence—the mayor's directly involved."

Jason's expression tightened. "That's a serious accusation."

"One we can't prove. Yet." I sighed. "But it fits."

"Come on," Jason said, heading for the door. "Let's get some air."

The RCMP cruiser idled quietly out front, its lights now dimmed to a steady pulse. Whatever crowd had gathered earlier had mostly drifted off, satisfied—for now—with the evening's drama. A few lingered near the edge of the lot, murmuring theories, but even the Balsam Belles had packed up for the night.

Jason and I stepped outside, grateful for the cooler air. Des moved in lockstep beside me.

"She really named the Bugles," Jason said, voice low.

"Directly," I nodded. "But it's still just her word."

He rubbed his face, suddenly looking older. "That's how they work—layers of insulation between themselves and the dirty work. Makes them hard to touch." He glanced toward the cruiser, where Frannie sat staring out the window. "Devon will be questioned, but I doubt he knows much."

"He thought he was in the loop," I said. "But he was two steps behind the whole time."

Jason gave a tired sigh. "Still, we got Frannie. The shrimp tails, the delivery, her confession—it's solid."

"For Kansas's murder," I said, the words landing hard. "Not for what happened to Dad."

Jason's expression softened. "One fight at a time. This is still a win. Not the whole truth, but a big piece."

I watched as officers took statements from wide-eyed locals. Bertha stood in the doorway like she'd just witnessed both the rapture and an alien landing—shocked, but vindicated.

"So the Bugles just... walk?" I asked, heat creeping into my voice. "Even though they're behind all of it?"

"For now," Jason said. "On paper, they're clean. And Frannie's not exactly a reliable witness. But I'll be watching them. Closely."

"That's not justice."

"It's a start." He rested a hand on my shoulder. "And if Walter's really alive, that changes everything. We just need to find him."

"Before the Bugles do," I said, that worry finally cracking through. "Gus is already gone. Dad could be next."

Jason shook his head. "They don't know we know. Frannie didn't have time to warn them. As far as they're concerned, she got caught for killing her husband—a personal crime with a clear motive. That's it."

Des leaned against me. I reached down, rubbed the spot she liked just behind her jaw, drawing calm from her quiet presence.

"What about Gus?" I asked, glancing toward Devon, still being interviewed—not arrested—under the glow of another cruiser's lights.

"He's not in trouble," Jason said. "Frannie's confession

cleared him of Kansas's murder. And he tried to help Dad—even if his methods were... unconventional."

"He made a mistake," I said softly. "But he tried to fix it. That took guts."

Jason nodded. "He's gone for now. Probably safer that way. I'll let you know if he turns up."

I hesitated. "So what now? Do we build a case against the Bugles?"

"Carefully. Methodically. We find Gus if we can. And Walter." He paused. "But Tilly... be careful. You've stirred up a hornet's nest. And the Bugles don't forget."

"You think they'll come after me?"

"I think they don't like loose ends," he said grimly. "And right now, you're the biggest one in Balsam Bay."

Callie approached, her expression equal parts triumph and exhaustion. "Uncle Jason, they want to know if you're heading to the station now or later."

"Now," he said, straightening. "They'll need me for the formal interview." He turned to me. "We'll talk tomorrow. Until then, keep your head down."

"Not exactly my specialty."

He almost smiled. "I've noticed." Then, serious again: "But try."

As Jason headed for his cruiser, Callie slipped her arm through mine. "So—takeout and ice cream?"

"Yes, please," I breathed. "Extra pepperoni, extra pineapple?"

"Obviously. Though I still think pineapple on pizza is borderline criminal."

"More for me and Des, then," I said, managing a smile.

We watched the last police car pull away, leaving the lot strangely quiet. The remaining onlookers began to disperse, though I knew today's drama would echo through the town for weeks.

"It's weird," Callie said as we crossed the gravel. "Feels like this should be over. But it's not."

"Because it isn't," I murmured.

Des trotted beside us, alert but calm—the dog who'd found crucial evidence, chased Frannie without hesitation, and seemed to know, instinctively, who could be trusted.

"Dad's out there," I said, gazing up at the first stars appearing in the deepening blue. "Somewhere."

"We'll find him," Callie said with quiet certainty. "Now that we know, we'll find him."

I nodded, choosing—for once—to believe it. If Des could navigate miles of wilderness to come home, we could find Walter. He wasn't just missing anymore.

He was waiting.

As we climbed the porch steps, I felt it: a flicker of resolution, a quiet sense of forward motion. One mystery down, another unfolding. The Bugles were still out there. But so were we.

And we weren't done yet.

CHAPTER TWENTY

The evening crowd had finally trickled out of McKay's General Store, leaving behind the summery scent of sunscreen, mosquito repellant, and the faint tang of blue raspberry from a half-melted slushy Callie found abandoned behind the postcards. I flipped the sign to *Closed* and stretched, my shoulders protesting after a day spent restocking shelves and ringing up purchases.

July had brought a sticky heat to Balsam Bay, turning late evenings into hazy golden hours that invited porch-sitting and cold drinks. Through the windows, I watched tourists amble down Main Street, ice cream cones in hand, enjoying the midweek quiet.

Des lay sprawled behind the counter, one eye cracked to monitor my movements. Above her, Callie's hand-painted sign swung gently in the breeze from the oscillating fan: *Des on duty. Biscuit bribes accepted.*

"Think that's the end of our post-arrest tourist rush?" Callie called from the back office, where she'd been updating her blog for the past hour. *Temporary Town Life* had gained a loyal following since "The Great Shrimp Caper"—as the locals had dubbed it.

"Not a chance," I said, counting the till. "Mrs. Peterson told me there's a tour bus from Winnipeg coming tomorrow. Apparently, we're the latest stop on the *Small Town Mysteries* tour."

It had been more than a week since Frannie's dramatic forest chase and confession. A week of finding a rhythm that felt surprisingly right—like slipping into a jacket you didn't know you'd missed until it fit just so.

The mail drop box by the front counter held the usual stack of letters and a few small packages—locals knew I sorted it after hours. Margaret Peterson had returned an opened can of tomatoes she bought yesterday—claimed they were too tinny —and left a jar of homemade blueberry jam for the trouble. I'd set it aside for breakfast.

The store was changing—subtly, steadily—becoming less Walter's and more ours. Callie's rearranged shelving—"Grandpa's system defies all logic, Mom"—actually made sense now. Even the house felt different. That bright orange accent wall I'd painted in the kitchen no longer felt like sacrilege.

I secured the day's take in Dad's old safe. "Don't forget Mr. Gregoire's coming first thing for his special-order fishing flies."

"Already pulled and bagged," Callie replied, joining me up front. "And I reminded Mrs. Walchuk her favourite maple candies are in."

I smiled. Somewhere between being dragged to this "backwater town" and chasing a murderer through the woods, my city-girl daughter had become a competent shopkeeper's assistant. She still griped about the Wi-Fi and lack of 24-hour anything, but there was a new ease in her movements.

We were staying. The realization had crept in quietly, like roots settling into familiar soil. The condo in Victoria still existed—but as a backup plan, not a destination. This was home now. The place where answers might still be found. Where Des had tracked me through miles of bush. Where the mystery of my father's disappearance still waited.

The familiar door bell rang overhead.

"We're closed—" I began, then stopped.

Sean Patrick stood in the doorway, backpack slung over one shoulder, boots caked with summer mud. Windblown hair, sun-kissed face—he looked like he'd just walked in from the bush and hadn't bothered with a shower.

"Bad timing?" he asked, raising an eyebrow.

"Depends what you're selling," I said, grinning. "Coffee? Beer? Geological insights?"

"Just catching up," he said, stepping inside. "Got back from the field. Figured I'd see if anything happened while I was gone."

Des lifted her head and huffed at him—no growl, just acknowledgment. Progress, considering she'd nearly taken off his pant leg during our last encounter.

"If anything happened?" I poured a mug. "Well, let's see. Caught a murderer, chased her through the woods, watched her confess." I slid the coffee across the counter. "So, no. Nothing major."

Sean blinked. "You're kidding."

"She's not," Callie said, hopping onto the counter. "You missed everything."

"Her? Do you mean Frannie?" he asked, stunned. "I thought Devon—"

"Join the club," I said, leaning on the counter. "That was the plan—get us chasing Devon while she skipped town."

I gave him the condensed version—Frannie's retreat, Des's heroic tackle, the confession. Sean listened, the line between his brows deepening.

"She really killed Kansas?" he asked.

"Shellfish allergy. She triggered it at the social," I said. "Confessed after we caught her trying to bolt."

"But why?"

I shrugged, deliberately vague. "Let's just say the marriage didn't turn out quite as profitable as she hoped. And when things fell apart, she had other people whispering in her ear." I wasn't about to share what we really knew about who Frannie was working for. That information stayed strictly between Jason, Callie, and me.

Sean set his mug down carefully. "I'm sorry I wasn't here."

"Would you have helped?" I asked, not unkindly. "You're working for someone with an interest in the mine. How would I know where you stand?"

He nodded, accepting the hit. "My contract's legitimate—geological surveying. Nothing shady." He ran a hand through his hair, leaving it even more dishevelled.

"I know. Your data checked out. Callie had a geologist friend verify it." I let his surprise hang. "What? You didn't think we'd check?"

"Smart move," he conceded. Then more quietly, "Are we okay?"

I studied him—earnest eyes, muddy boots, callused hands wrapped around his mug. "Closer than before. But I've got my eye on you, rock licker."

His mouth twitched. Des, apparently satisfied with whatever inspection she'd been conducting, padded over and nudged his hand.

"Well, look at that," I said. "The crime-fighting mutt approves."

"Crime-fighting mutt?" Sean echoed.

"Des has about fifty nicknames," Callie said. "The Perogy Protector. Shellfish Sheriff. Nancy Drool."

"People come in just to meet her," I added. "Some kid asked for her paw print yesterday."

A knock on the door interrupted us. Bertha stood outside, arms full of what looked like a coffee cake. I hurried to let her in.

"Sign says 'Closed,'" she remarked as she bustled in.

"So I've been told," I said.

She plunked the cake on the counter. "Mrs. Kowalski's daughter-in-law had her baby this morning. Eight pounds, six ounces. They're calling her Matilda."

"They're not naming her after me," I protested. "Margaret's grandmother was Matilda."

"Uh-huh," Bertha said, clearly unconvinced. She gave Des a fond pat as she passed.

"Thought she might be missing her bacon ends," she added, pulling a paper-wrapped bundle from her pocket. Des's tail thumped in response. "Walter always gave her a treat after closing."

"Keep that up and she'll follow you home," I warned.

"Not a chance. That dog knew where she belonged the minute you showed up," Bertha said. "Nearly tore Joe's fence down trying to get back to you."

The truth of it settled in warmly. Des picked her person. I just took a while to catch up.

"How's business?" Bertha asked, giving the store a once-over.

It was the first time I'd seen Bertha in a few days—she'd finally taken a long-overdue mini vacation and left me and Callie to run the store solo. Somehow, we'd managed not to burn the place down.

"Better than expected," I admitted. "We've had tourists coming in just to see where Frannie was caught."

"Ridiculous," Bertha muttered, adjusting a canned goods

display. "They're calling this place 'The Perogy Peril Place' down at the café."

"I prefer 'Shrimpgate General,'" Callie said. "Has a better ring."

The bell chimed again.

"Sorry to barge in," Enid called, followed by Nora and Trish —each carrying a giant zucchini. The Balsam Belles had arrived.

"Garden overflow," Enid explained, laying her squash on the counter. "Consider it a thank-you for livening up the town."

"Not bad for your first case," Trish added. "Though you could've called us. We power-walk three miles every morning. We'd have cut Frannie off at the ravine."

I pictured them in visors and walking poles, forming a geriatric roadblock. "Next time," I promised.

"Oh, there will be," Enid said ominously. "This town's got more secrets than pine needles."

"Starting with Devon," Trish said in a dramatic whisper. "Off on a 'business trip.' Left yesterday with enough luggage for a month."

"Convenient," Nora added, eyebrows raised.

The bell chimed once more. Mandy breezed in with a tray of experimental pastries and a grin.

"Evening, all! Testing recipes. Who's hungry?"

The store shifted, filling with voices and laughter, the scent of coffee and cinnamon wrapping around us. For a moment, it felt exactly like what Dad had envisioned this place to be.

"This is survival food," Mandy said, pressing something into my hands that looked like a muffin collided with a cinnamon bun. "Perfect for getting through Balsam Bay winters."

I took a bite—cinnamon, apple, and something I couldn't name—just as the door opened again.

Jason stepped in, still in uniform but with a looseness in his shoulders I hadn't seen in weeks. He nodded to the group, made his way to me, and leaned in.

"Got a minute?"

I nodded and led him to the back of the store. Des followed, silent and watchful.

"Frannie's confession is holding up," he said. "She's naming names, but without proof..."

"The Bugles are still untouchable," I finished.

"For now," he agreed. "Devon's not being charged—nothing concrete to tie him to anything."

"He's just away on business," I said. "According to Manitoba's finest intel network." I nodded toward the Belles.

Jason smirked. Then his voice dropped. "I did some quiet digging and found Gus. He's safe—staying with a cousin in Thunder Bay. Wanted to say thank you."

Relief washed through me. I'd been worrying more than I wanted to admit. Standing up to family like the Bugles took guts.

"And Dad?"

Jason's face softened. "We'll find him. Together."

I nodded. Walter McKay was alive. Hiding—but alive. And we were on the right track.

"I never thought I'd say this," I said quietly, "but I'm staying. Not just to find Dad. I'm staying in Balsam Bay."

Jason smiled. "Figured as much when you painted the kitchen."

"It was just one wall!"

"It was burnt orange. That's a commitment colour."

I couldn't argue.

We returned to the front, where talk had turned to the

upcoming Aurora Nights. The Walchuks were already prepping for the stargazing event that would draw crowds from across the province.

As the last guests trickled out, a quiet joy settled in. Yes, Walter was still missing, and the Bugles were still a threat, but it didn't feel quite as heavy anymore.

The cabin door shut behind us with a satisfying thunk as Callie, Jason, and I piled into the SUV after dinner at Joe's place. The evening had been pleasant—simple food, comfortable conversation about Des's tracking abilities and Joe's hopes for his new litter of husky pups.

"I'll never understand how city folks survive without fresh-baked bread," Joe had said, breaking us off thick slices still warm from the oven. "Nothing like making it yourself, though Mandy's comes close. That woman has magic in her fingertips."

The drive back to town was quiet, each of us lost in our own thoughts. Jason had shared a few vague updates on the Frannie case—formal charges, bail hearings, the works. Des dozed in the back seat, exhausted from playing with Joe's dogs.

As we pulled into the driveway, something made Des stir. Her head came up sharply, ears pricked forward, nose working the air through the cracked window.

"What is it, girl?" I asked, immediately alert.

Jason's hand moved instinctively toward his hip where his service weapon would normally be, though he was off duty now. "Stay in the car," he said, his voice shifting to professional mode.

"Not likely," I replied, already halfway out the door.

Des sprang from the back seat the moment I opened the

door, but instead of barking or growling, she approached the darkened house with focused intensity. Her behaviour wasn't alarmed—more purposeful.

"Someone's been here," I said, noticing subtle signs that would be invisible to anyone who hadn't spent years tracking through wilderness—a slight depression in the soft earth by the porch steps, a branch on the lilac bush bent at an unnatural angle.

Jason nodded, face grim in the moonlight. We approached the silent house with cautious steps. Des waited at the door, not barking, but alert in a way that made the hair on my neck stand up.

Jason inserted the key with practiced ease, pushing the door open slowly. The house beyond lay in darkness, quiet and still. Nothing seemed disturbed at first glance—no overturned furniture, no rifled drawers. Just our home, as we'd left it hours ago.

Except.

In the dim glow of moonlight filtering through the windows, something sat on the kitchen table. Something that hadn't been there when we left.

Jason flicked on the lights.

A single rock—smooth, river-worn granite with bands of quartz cutting through it like frozen lightning—sat perfectly centred on the wooden tabletop. Beneath it, anchored by the stone's weight, lay a folded piece of paper.

My heart stuttered, then raced. I knew that rock. Seen it a thousand times. Dad had carried it in his pocket for as long as I could remember. He called it his "thinking stone," claiming the act of rolling it between his fingers helped clarify complex problems.

Jason crossed to the table in three quick strides, examining the area but not touching anything. "No signs of forced entry," he said, professional mask firmly in place. But I could see the muscle jumping in his jaw, the slight tremble in his normally steady hands.

He recognized the rock, too.

"It's okay," I said softly. "It's him."

Des, oddly calm now, settled onto her haunches beside me, tail sweeping the floor in slow, deliberate strokes.

I approached the table slowly, reverently, as if approaching an altar. With careful fingers, I slid the paper out from under the rock, unfolding it with a breath held tight in my lungs.

The handwriting was unmistakable—neat, precise capitals that slanted slightly to the right, just as they had on every shopping list and birthday card he'd ever written.

My girls—

I didn't mean for this to land on your shoulders, but I'm not sorry to have you home.

Des has good instincts—use them.

Take care of each other and stay alert.

You have all my love. I hope that will be enough.

See you when the shadows lift.

No signature. None needed.

I passed the note to Jason, whose hand trembled visibly as he took it. He read it quickly, then turned away, one hand rising to cover his eyes. When he spoke, his voice was rough with emotion.

"He was here. In this house."

Callie stepped forward, reaching for the note. "Can I?"

I nodded, watching as she traced her fingers over the capitals, the same way I had. Des shifted closer to her, pressing against her leg as if sensing her need for comfort.

"He knows we caught Frannie," Callie said. "But he's still not safe, is he?"

I shook my head. "Frannie was just the hired help. The real threat is still out there."

"Wait," Callie said, looking at me. "If Grandpa was in danger for what he found out... doesn't that mean you could be, too?"

I met her eyes. "Not yet," I said. "Grandpa uncovered something. I'm still sorting through the pieces."

Callie didn't look convinced, but she didn't push.

Jason regained his composure, his voice steadier now. "Then we keep our eyes open. And we don't make it easy for anyone watching."

I nodded. "Dad will reveal himself when it's safe. We have to trust him." I reached out, and let my hand drift over Des's head, the gesture automatic. "And lucky for us, we've got an inside tracker now."

Later, after Jason had left and Callie had finally gone to bed, I stood at the kitchen window, gazing out at the silhouette of pine trees etched against the night sky. The rock sat heavy in my pocket, a talisman against uncertainty.

Kansas had wanted the store for income. Devon wanted the land that came with it. Frannie, as always, wanted control. But Walter? He'd stumbled onto something bigger—and now we were all standing in its shadow.

It wasn't a gold mine under the floorboards. Just too many people with plans—and too few willing to share them.

Somewhere out there, beyond the reach of porch lights and street lamps, my father was watching. Waiting. Finding ways to let us know he was okay, even as danger kept him in the shadows.

Des padded up beside me and let out a low sigh, her gaze

steady on the night beyond the glass. Together, we looked out at the darkness—not with fear, but with determination.

"Never thought I'd be the one tracking down answers instead of missing hikers," I said, running my fingers through her fur. "But I guess we all end up exactly where we're supposed to be."

Des huffed softly, and I smiled. The Bugles were still out there. The full truth remained just beyond our grasp. But we'd solved one mystery, and the next was already unfolding.

As I turned from the window, the familiar weight of Dad's river stone warm in my pocket, I realized I was ready—for the next question, the next secret—for this town of fir trees and stories that refused to stay quiet.

I was home. And someday soon, Dad would be, too.

You've reached the end of *Death at Balsam Bay*.
Some questions have been answered. Others are just beginning.
Tilly has uncovered a truth she never expected—
and keeping that secret might be the hardest thing she's ever done.
But in Balsam Bay, secrets don't stay buried for long.
And with the return of the northern lights,
what's been set in motion is only the beginning.

Continue the story now in
Death at Aurora Point
Book Two in the Tilly Lafleur Mysteries.

Visit MaisieGraves.com for details.

STAY IN THE LOOP

Want more Balsam Bay?

Join my newsletter for new book updates, behind-the-scenes notes, and the occasional appearance from Des.

New subscribers also receive a free short mystery set in Balsam Bay.

Sign up at: MaisieGraves.com/newsletter.

No spam. No noise. Just thoughtful mysteries and good company.

THANKS FOR READING

Thank you for spending time with Tilly, Callie, and Des in Balsam Bay.

If you enjoyed the story, I'd be grateful if you left a review. Even a few words make a difference and help other readers find the series.

There's more to uncover in Balsam Bay—and the story isn't over yet.

ALSO BY MAISIE GRAVES

Tilly Lafleur Mysteries

Death at Balsam Bay

Death at Aurora Point

Death at Diamond Hill

Death at Melvin House

Short Stories from Balsam Bay

Whispers in the Snow

The Disappearing Scarecrow

Snow on the Airwaves

Discover all of Maisie's books and formats at

MaisieGraves.com/books

ABOUT THE AUTHOR

Maisie Graves writes small-town cozy mysteries with real stakes and buried secrets.

Her Tilly Lafleur series follows an amateur sleuth as each case pulls her deeper into a town she thought she knew.

Maisie lives in Canada and is always working on the next mystery.

maisiegraves.com

facebook.com/maisiegravesauthor

instagram.com/maisiegravesauthor

goodreads.com/maisiegravesauthor

bookbub.com/authors/maisie-graves